"Alaska is the perfect setting for a protagonist looking to hide out and start over—while encountering some werewolves along the way. . . . The hero and heroine have wonderful and believable instant chemistry and it's fun to see them learn about each other beyond their powerful attraction."

—*RT Book Reviews* (4½ stars, Top Pick)

"Exciting, hysterical, sexy . . . No one writes paranormal romance with as much sarcasm and charm as Molly."

—*Harlequin Junkie* (5 stars)

THE ART OF SEDUCING A NAKED WEREWOLF

"Harper's gift for character building and crafting a smart, exciting story is showcased well."

—*RT Book Reviews* (4 stars)

"The characters are appealing and the plot is intriguingly original."

—*Single Titles*

HOW TO FLIRT WITH A NAKED WEREWOLF

"Mo's wisecracking, hilarious voice makes this novel such a pleasure to read."

—*New York Times* bestselling author Eloisa James

"A light, fun, easy read, perfect for lazy days."

—*New York Journal of Books*

D0179985

Books by Molly Harper

In the land of Half-Moon Hollow

The Dangers of Dating a Rebound Vampire
I'm Dreaming of an Undead Christmas
A Witch's Handbook of Kisses and Curses
"Undead Sublet" in *The Undead in My Bed*
The Care and Feeding of Stray Vampires
Driving Mr. Dead
Nice Girls Don't Bite Their Neighbors
Nice Girls Don't Live Forever
Nice Girls Don't Date Dead Men
Nice Girls Don't Have Fangs

The Naked Werewolf Series

How to Run with a Naked Werewolf
The Art of Seducing a Naked Werewolf
How to Flirt with a Naked Werewolf

The Bluegrass Series

Snow Falling on Bluegrass
Rhythm and Bluegrass
My Bluegrass Baby

Also

Better Homes and Hauntings
And One Last Thing . . .

Available from Pocket Books

Praise for the Half-Moon Hollow novels

A WITCH'S HANDBOOK OF KISSES AND CURSES

"Harper serves up plenty of hilarity . . . [in] this return to the hysterical world of Jane and crew."

—*Publishers Weekly*

"Clever wit and heart. . . . Fans of the series and readers new to Half-Moon Hollow will enjoy the fun and frivolity." —*RT Book Reviews* (4½ stars, Top Pick)

"A fun, sexy, fast-paced story." —*Fresh Fiction*

THE CARE AND FEEDING OF STRAY VAMPIRES

"A perfect combination of smarts and entertainment with a dash of romance."

—*RT Book Reviews* (4½ stars, Top Pick)

"Filled with clever humor, snark, silliness, and endearing protagonists." —*Booklist*

NICE GIRLS DON'T BITE THEIR NEIGHBORS

"Terrific. . . . The stellar supporting characters, laugh-out-loud moments, and outrageous plot twists will leave readers absolutely satisfied."

—*Publishers Weekly* (starred review)

"Molly Harper is the queen of side-splitting quips. . . . Hilariously original with imaginative adventures and one-of-a-kind characters." —*Single Titles*

The Dangers Of Dating A Rebound Vampire

MOLLY HARPER

Pocket Books
New York London Toronto Sydney New Delhi

Pocket Books
An Imprint of Simon & Schuster, Inc.
1230 Avenue of the Americas
New York, NY 10020

This book is a work of fiction. Any references to historical events, real people, or real places are used fictitiously. Other names, characters, places, and events are products of the author's imagination, and any resemblance to actual events or places or persons, living or dead, is entirely coincidental.

Copyright © 2015 by Molly Harper White

All rights reserved, including the right to reproduce this book or portions thereof in any form whatsoever. For information, address Pocket Books Subsidiary Rights Department, 1230 Avenue of the Americas, New York, NY 10020.

First Pocket Books paperback edition April 2015

POCKET and colophon are registered trademarks of Simon & Schuster, Inc.

For information about special discounts for bulk purchases, please contact Simon & Schuster Special Sales at 1-866-506-1949 or business@simonandschuster.com.

The Simon & Schuster Speakers Bureau can bring authors to your live event. For more information or to book an event, contact the Simon & Schuster Speakers Bureau at 1-866-248-3049 or visit our website at www.simonspeakers.com.

Interior design by Leydiana Rodríguez
Cover photograph by Gene Mollica

Manufactured in the United States of America

10 9 8 7 6 5 4 3 2 1

ISBN 978-1-4767-0601-6
ISBN 978-1-4767-0604-7 (ebook)

For Leah, Jaye, Nicole, Heather, and Mom

Acknowledgments

As always, it takes a cast of talented people to get my book from desktop to page. A big thank-you, as always, to my agent, Stephany Evans, and my editor, Abby Zidle, who are not afraid of letting me put my characters in ridiculous and dangerous positions. Thank you to Jennifer Fusco and Melanie Meadors at Market or Die Author Services, who never shy away from proofing late-night blog posts.

To Leah Hodge, Heather Osborn, Nicole Peeler, and Jaye Wells: you are the best bad influences a girl could ever ask for. Mom, thanks for keeping us all in line and well fed. To Jeanette Battista, my work wife: thank you for all the times you have read nonsensical snippets of information and helped me turn them into chapters. I am so lucky to have my evil snark twin for a critique partner. To Eli Knight: thank you for making my fight scenes better and teaching me every incorrect Sun Tzu quote I know.

Thank you to my family for everything you do to keep me on track. And thank you, as always, to my husband, David, for the inspiration.

1

You never get a second chance to make a first exsanguination.

—*The Office After Dark: A Guide to Maintaining a Safe, Productive Vampire Workplace*

The sensible beige pantsuit was mocking me.

It was hanging there, in my closet, all tailored and boring. And beige. *Yes, wear me to work, and let all of your new coworkers know that you have no personality!* it jeered at me. *Look at you, all nervous and twitchy. Why don't you just stay home and work for the Apple store, you big baby?*

"That is one judgmental pantsuit." I flopped back onto my bed and stared at the ceiling. I deserved this job. I was qualified for it. I'd gone through a particularly difficult test of my intelligence and ingenuity to get it. So why was I so nervous about my first day?

"Because you are Queen of All Neurotics," I grumbled, scrubbing my hand over my face. "Long may you reign."

Honestly, I was nervous because this job—programming an internal search engine of vampires' living descendants for the World Council for the Equal Treatment of the Undead—meant something. Because if I played my cards right, this would be the only first day of work I would ever go through. The Council was known for offering increasingly attractive perks and salaries to hold on to competent human employees, resulting in lifelong appointments. Then again, if I played my cards *wrong*, this could be my last-ever first day of work, because I would be dead.

OK, if I continued this line of thinking, what would the final outcome be? Not taking the job with the Council. And then I tried to picture my sister Iris's face if I told her that I'd decided not to take the job after all. First there would be elation, and then relief, and then would come the "I told you so's." I really hated the "I told you so's," which were sometimes accompanied by interpretive dance.

Even after having months to adjust, Iris was "displeased" about my employment, which was like saying PETA was displeased by the popularity of TripleMeat Whataburgers. Iris wanted me to work in some respectable office, where my coworkers wouldn't pose an immediate threat to my person. It was nice to know she cared about my safety, but seriously, she was getting on my nerves.

"Right. Spiting your sister is an excellent personal motivator. Let's go." I launched myself out of bed, slipped into the suit, and pinned my hair into a responsible-looking chignon. I was thankful, at least, that I didn't have to deal with Iris's hair. It wasn't that her dark curly hair wasn't beautiful, because it totally was, especially now that she had all that vampire-makeover mojo on her side and looked like a sexy undead Snow White—if Snow White was remotely sexy or tousled, which was tough to pull off in that Disney headband. The point was, I could barely handle my own heavy dark hair. I couldn't imagine throwing crazy curlicues into the mix.

Iris and I also shared our mother's cornflower-blue eyes and delicate features, though I'd inherited Dad's height. It really irritated Iris when her "little sister" propped her elbow on top of Iris's head. Which meant I did it every chance I got.

Yawning, I picked up my equally practical beige pumps and checked my purse for the third time that afternoon. I'd stayed up all night, then slept through the morning, in an attempt to adjust my schedule to my new hours, working from two p.m. until two a.m. This was considered the early-bird shift for vampires, and it was going to be an adjustment for my very human body clock. But at least I would see more of my recently vampirized sister and her equally undead husband.

The house, as expected, was pitch-black, thanks to the heavy-duty sunshades my brother-in-law had installed to protect him and Iris from sun exposure. Carefully, I clicked a button at the end of the hall and waited for the circular "tap lights" to illuminate the stairs.

I turned the corner into the kitchen and punched

in my personal security code. Before I could use my "clearance" to open the downstairs windows, I felt a sudden strike at my neck, the sensation of hands closing around my shoulders. I gasped as my unseen assailant yanked me back against his chest, hissing in my ear. I curled my fingers around the offending hands and dropped into "base," the stable fighting stance taught to me by the jiujitsu instructor Cal had insisted I train with for the past five months. Spreading my arms wide to loosen his grip, I thrust my hips back, knocking him off-balance. I stopped my face-to-floor descent with my palms, cupped both hands around his foot, and yanked—*hard*. The force of my pull was enough to send him toppling back on his ass.

I sprang up and flicked on the lights to see my beloved brother-in-law sprawled on the floor with a big, stupid grin on his face.

"Cletus Calix!" I yelled, giving him one last kick to the ribs before climbing onto one of the breakfast bar stools. "What is wrong with you?"

"I just wanted to get your blood going with a pre-work reflex test," he said, pushing to his feet. "Well done, you. Your reaction times are much faster."

I grunted and threw a banana at his dark head; of course, he caught it, because he has superhuman response times. Totally unfair. Cal had thrown these little tests at me nearly every day since I'd come home for the summer. Always at a different time, always with a different mode of attack. The fact that Cal had probably downed a half-dozen espressos just so he could get up at this hour was somehow very sweet and super-irritating all at the same time. I understood that he wanted proof that I could defend myself if necessary and that the insane amount of time and money he'd spent on my martial-arts education wasn't wasted. But seriously, I just wanted to make coffee without someone putting me in a choke hold.

"One of these days, Cal, you're going to sneak up on me, and I'm going to stab you with something wooden and pointy. It's not an idle threat. You've stocked my bag with a scary array of antivampire technology. If Ophelia ever decides to search me, I'll probably be fired based on the threat my change purse poses to the secretarial pool."

"Which means my evil plan will finally come to fruition." Cal snorted. He had lots of reservations about my working for the Council, so he'd devoted the past semester to preparing me for working around vampires. Brazilian jiujitsu classes, crossbow lessons, small-blade combat training. The good news was that I was no longer afraid of walking through the campus parking garage at night. The bad news was that most of the people in my advanced programming classes were now afraid of me, because they spotted my knifework gear in my shoulder bag that one time.

"And if you manage to stab me, Gigi, I will deserve whatever pointy revenge you inflict."

"You're so weird." I sighed, catching my reflection in the glass microwave panel. "Now I'm going to have to go fix my hair again."

"It's not that bad," Cal protested. I dashed into the powder room off the kitchen and ran a comb through my mussed hair. Cal leaned his long, rangy form against the doorway, watching me fuss. "Iris would get up and wish you luck, but she hasn't worked up to daylight waking hours quite yet. It's more of an advanced vampire trick."

"There's also the small matter of Iris not wanting me to work at the Council office," I said, leveling him with a frank smile. "It's OK, Cal, you don't have to sugarcoat it for me. I know I'm making Iris unhappy."

"I don't know what you're talking about," he said breezily, following me back into the kitchen.

"Aren't you kind of old for blithe denial? Like several thousand years too old?" I asked, ducking when he attempted to ruffle my hair.

"Keep it up, and I won't give you this delicious lunch I packed for you," Cal said, digging into the fridge and pulling a small blue canvas bag from the top shelf. I opened it to find that Cal had made me a California roll and nigiri with his own two little vampire hands. I'd developed a taste for sushi at school, and there were no quality Japanese restaurants in the Hollow. So Iris and Cal had watched YouTube videos to figure out how to make it for me, if only to save me from truck-stop sashimi. This might seem like a minor gesture until one considered that to vampires, human food smelled like the wrong end of a petting zoo. "You're the only human I know whose comfort food involves raw fish and rice."

"Vampires living in blood-bag-shaped houses shouldn't throw stones," I told him. "And this is very sweet. I sort of love you, Cal." I kissed his cheek, something that had taken him years to accept without flinching or making faces.

"You completely love me. Now, have a good first day at work. Play nice with your coworkers, but don't hesitate to use your silver spray. If you get into trouble, there's an extra stake sewn into the bottom lining of your purse. Call us before you drive home so we can wait up for you."

"Your employment advice is not like other people's employment advice."

Ophelia didn't deign to visit us on our first day. My fellow recruits and I talked exclusively to Amelia Gibson, the stern vampire head of HR, while sequestered—I mean seated—in the windowless conference room decorated in various shades of gray. In fact, almost everything in the newly renovated Council office was gray: gray walls, gray carpets, gray cement block, and gray laminate office furniture. Cold, impersonal, efficient, it wasn't exactly home away from home.

While the grim-looking security guards processed our security-pass photos, we had to sit through the upsetting orientation videos. Most of them involved strategies for not provoking our vampire coworkers into biting us. Since I was pretty familiar with these tips—including "Lunch Break Hazards: Say Good-bye to Garlic and Tuna Salad" and "Empty Toner Cartridges:

Replace Them or Die"—I spent my time studying my coworkers.

Jordan Lancaster was sweet-faced and might have looked like the girl next door, if not for the full ROY G BIV spectrum of streaks in her hair, the heavy navy-blue eyeliner, and the double nose ring. She'd chosen to wear a My Little Pony T-shirt declaring her allegiance to Rainbow Dash, dark-wash jeans, and high-top sneakers. I knew she looked unprofessional. I knew she was reinforcing the stereotype that computer geeks were poorly socialized kids with weird hair and unfortunate wardrobe choices. Ms. Gibson had looked directly at Jordan when she mentioned reviewing the dress code. But I couldn't help but feel just a little bit envious of her while I sat there, tugging at my uncomfortable pantsuit.

Also, I was considering stealing those violet Converse high-tops.

Marty McCullough was a tall, slender guy with piercing dark eyes and a pale, pleasant face. He wore a plaid work shirt and chinos and seemed just a bit too relaxed around the vampires, as if he thought they were too civilized to hurt him. I hoped he would figure out how wrong he was without my having to use the first-aid kit too many times.

Aaron Chen slept through the orientation, but no one could tell for the first hour or so, because his outdated and overgrown Justin Bieber haircut covered his eyes. And when Ms. Gibson woke him up, he didn't even say he was sorry. I think I was looking forward to working with him most of all.

It was sort of a mixed bag for me when it came to vampires and trust issues. I mean, Ophelia was a four-hundred-plus-year-old vampire who looked like a teenager and schemed like a Bond villain. So I was going to avoid any situation that would lead to sitting in her office near a hidden trapdoor. And sure, I'd been duped and supernaturally hypnotized by a vampire sent by a local supervillain to date me under false pretenses. But thanks to the hypnosis, I'd blanked out most of the unpleasant parts and only remembered dreamy scenes of teen vampire romance.

It was interesting to me that none of the programmers was older than mid-twenties. The oldest of us, Marty, looked to be about twenty-three or twenty-four. Then again, working at the Council office full-time, we would be exposed to many of the vampire world's secrets and machinations. We would have access to their leaders. We would figure out how they managed to save enough money to survive for centuries. That was a considerable liability, as far as the vampires were concerned. Maybe responsible adults in their thirties didn't work for vampires because they were too worried about the families they could leave behind.

And while there were a few vampires out there who could do the work, the Council didn't hire them. The rumor was that the Council members didn't trust their own kind enough to handle the genealogical information. Long-standing feuds between vampires could escalate swiftly if one knew where to find the living great-great-grandchildren of one's archenemy. So the coding was farmed out to us nonsuperpowered humans who had been through a rigorous, highly intimidating vetting process. The theory was that properly intimidated humans wouldn't use their access to secret vampire records to track down (or assist other vampires in tracking down) other humans to hurt them.

Also, by hiring human undergrads, they could employ us at a far lower pay grade than someone who could claim he had helped Charles Babbage perfect his idea of complex machines completing mathematical functions back in 1812. Two hundred years of work experience was a human resources nightmare.

When my coworkers and their wardrobes were no longer entertaining, my mind wandered to the mystery vampire I'd "met" over Christmas break. The "met" is in quotation marks because I hadn't actually introduced myself. Because, well, he hardly stood still long enough for me to see him, much less speak to him. At first, I thought he was a ghost. I'd barely been able to make out his facial features the first few times I saw him. And when Mr. Barely Visible finally became Fully Visible (and ho boy, was the visual nice), he'd surprised the ever-loving hell out of me by swooping in, kissing me like something out of a Nicholas Sparks movie, and then disappearing, literally.

That was one of the few things pre–Coming Out TV and movies got right about vampires. The undead were stealthy and sneaky and could pop in and out of view in the blink of an eye, which they usually did when a human was in mid-sentence, which, in my opinion, was super-rude.

The tragedy was that the hot mystery vampire had completely and cruelly dropped off the face of the earth after giving me the most world-altering kiss I'd ever experienced. It had been months since the Kiss, the meeting of mouths that rocked my world, shifted my paradigm, viva'd my revolution. And despite excessive lip-glossing for months, just in case I ran into him, I hadn't seen so much as a shadow. I was starting to think I'd imagined the whole thing, which would be completely plausible, considering my emotional turmoil over dumping my perfectly nice, all-too-human boyfriend, Ben.

I had too much bad vampire dating baggage to believe in magic and "meant to be" connections with the undead. There was no such thing as Love at First Bite. Passion, sure. Lust, sure. Strong feelings of impending nakedness, OK. But not love. Still, the kiss convinced me that I'd done the right thing in dumping that perfectly nice boyfriend. Because passion could be underrated. And if I was capable of feeling that much world-tilting passion for someone who might not exist, then clearly, my platonic, not-terribly-exciting relationship with Ben wasn't meeting my needs.

It was also possible that I was a deeply troubled hypocrite.

Up close, my vampire was center-of-the-solar-system hot. He looked like every hero in those Jane Austen movies that Iris's friends liked so much, golden hair that sort of curled around his face, eyes so light brown they appeared gold, high cheekbones, long straight nose, chiseled jawline, and a mouth that looked just smirky enough to say some really filthy things when persuaded. When I imagined meeting him again, he was always wearing a waistcoat and lounging around a stable full of fluffy, inviting piles of hay.

And that was a big part of why I didn't tell Iris about this, because that was the sort of thing for which she would mock me mercilessly.

Of course, I didn't know whether I would ever meet him again. Considering his five-month absence, I guessed not. Why had he even been in the Hollow? He seemed awfully "Continental" for Kentucky, though that really wasn't an indicator anymore, as our little burg seemed to be a magnet for vampires of all origins. Take Miranda Puckett's boyfriend, Collin, for example—tall, smooth, and British. I was pretty sure Collin *was* an extra in one of those Jane Austen movies Iris's friends liked so much.

Why had my vampire chosen me to pseudo-stalk? It would have been one thing if I'd only seen him the one time at the Christmas tree farm, but he seemed to follow me on several occasions. Had he known my schedule, or was he just that good at guessing where I'd show up? Maybe that was his special vampiric gift: he had a GPS. A Gigi Positioning System. (That sounded wrong but fun.)

Seeing my new (gray) office, the windowless workroom I would be sharing with my three teammates, made me feel as if I was right back in my "cozy" dorm room on campus. Four modular desks were stuck in four corners, abutted by four shelving units. I supposed the vampires considered it "private" since we would be working with our backs to one another.

Still, this was where the perks of working for vampires became stunningly clear: years of observing human weaknesses gave them enough information to know just how to lure us in. Each of our desks was flanked by a mini-fridge prestocked with sodas and juices we'd listed on our postinterview preference lists. A veritable buffet of geek fuel—Twizzlers, Doritos, ramen noodles, obscure gummy candy—would be refreshed "as needed." Our work desktops were custom-built from the fastest processors and computers available—as in "available on planet Earth," not available at our local Computer Barn. And each of our chairs represented the very latest in ergonomically supportive, butt-cradling comfort.

On the far wall, I spotted a console for the lavish Orange Door entertainment system, complete with digital jukebox touch board and four wireless headsets. We would be able to design personalized playlists from all of the songs available, well, anywhere and have them piped into our headphones while we worked—all of the mind fuel, none of the neighbor annoyance.

We had entered Nerdvana.

I noted that none of these little "gifts" from our employers would distract us from our work. We didn't get the Ping-Pong tables or kegerators of the early dot-com-boom legends. All of our perks were meant to fuel productivity through the night. I might have resented the overt manipulation, but I did love free music downloads, so I would take the benefits package without complaint.

The final touch, I supposed, was the enormous aquarium in the corner, filled with graceful, gliding tropical fish. Ms. Gibson explained that the fish tank was supposed to "accommodate the human need for color and light stimulation without the dangers of a window." I didn't think she intended to make us sound like cats in need of a flashlight to chase, so I let it go. The tank was pretty soothing, after all.

Despite these very nice toys, we wouldn't yet be receiving the leases for our company cars or anything from the "grand prize showcase" detailing our clothing allowance, full benefits, and a salary that would keep me in sushi and extra memory drives for years to come. First, we had to pass a probationary period. It was pretty sensible, really, when you considered the driving record of the average college student. It would probably be *more* sensible to give us a much longer probationary period, but we were only going to be working with the Council for a few months before we headed back to school.

Of course, the probationary period was sort of twofold. Some of us would work freelance for the Council during the school year if we proved ourselves to be competent, trustworthy, and non-vampire-provoking. We would be able to keep the cars, the salaries, and the other perks and then slide right into full-time post-graduation employment. Sure, it would add some angst to my spring semester, but the dental plan would be worth it.

Beyond the perks, the job was a challenge. It was a huge mystery waiting to be unraveled, and (thanks to a mid-semester switch in majors to computer science) I was one of a very few people who had the skills to do the thread pulling. And once the search engine was established, there would be other opportunities to work on the vampires' secret projects. Who knew what I would see, what I could learn, where they would send me? This was the beginning of an exciting adult life in which I could establish myself as something besides Iris Scanlon's baby sister.

We were dismissed early, but barely so, after signing a mountain of releases, waivers, and nondisclosure agreements. Most of the paperwork involved agreeing that our estates didn't have the right to sue the Council, no matter what happened. We also signed a single document in which we had to check "yes" or "no" regarding whether we wanted to be turned should we be injured on the job beyond the treatment capabilities of modern medicine. I was surprised to be the only one who actually mulled over this signature. Aaron, Marty, and Jordan all immediately checked "yes." Then again, I doubted whether those three had any actual vampires in their families. They'd never seen the postturning adjustment problems, the struggle with bloodthirst, the horrible burned-popcorn smell that lingered after vampires came into contact with sunlight. Most people thought it was all nighttime glamour and leather coats.

With a rather redundant warning not to discuss our nondisclosure agreement with our families, Amelia sent us home. At least, she sent Aaron, Marty, and Jordan home. She asked me to stay a few minutes because Ophelia had some papers she needed to send to Iris's business, Beeline. I stood outside Ophelia's office waiting for at least ten minutes, trying not to take it personally that I wasn't invited inside to wait or that when she finally handed the papers out to me, she just shoved an envelope through the doorway without actually showing her face.

"Thank you," I said, as pleasantly as I could, as Ophelia snatched her hand back and slammed the door.

"Generous compensation and a clothing allowance," I reminded myself as I walked out of the employee exit, rummaging around in my purse version of the Bag of Holding. "A 401(k) and a dental plan."

My keys were, as usual, at the very bottom of my bag. The parking lot was empty, but at least the humans had designated parking right under the lone streetlight. It was the vampire version of handicapped parking. I would take time to be offended by that once I was safely ensconced in my locked car.

I glanced around the empty lot, once and then again, while my heels made a quick *clip-clop* across the pavement. Just as I passed an unoccupied SUV, two strong hands closed around my shoulders.

I froze. I couldn't move, time stopped, and all I could think was *I'm going to die. Iris is going to deserve such an "I told you so."*

My feet flopped uselessly two inches above the ground as he—at least, I thought it was a he—dragged me toward the SUV. Given the fact that I was a little more than six feet tall, the guy had to be huge.

Fighting back the initial panic, I hoped somewhere in the back of my mind that this was another one of Cal's tests. I had to stay calm. This was just like getting thrown around the mat by my instructor, Jason. I just had to assess what needed to be done and go through the steps. I threw an elbow back but missed his ribs as his grip on my arms tightened. I wrapped my leg around his, hoping to make it harder for him to walk if he planned to carry me off. I threw my head back, hoping to connect with the bridge of his nose. But I missed there, too.

My heart raced. There was no way this could be Cal. My brother-in-law would have cackled like a loon if he'd evaded a head butt. Which meant this was real. Crap. I *was* going to die.

"Please," my assailant whispered, in a tone far gentler than one would expect from a guy who was attacking me in a parking lot. "You will stop now."

Nope, definitely not Cal.

"I don't want to hurt you." I relaxed only slightly against him as the calm thrum of that faintly accented voice settled in my chest. "Who are you?"

I whipped my head back toward him. "What?"

But instead of answering, he carefully turned me around to face him, setting my feet on the ground. And there he was, standing in front of me. Mr. Barely Visible. Mr. Probably Imaginary. Golden-brown eyes, high cheekbones, long straight nose, chiseled jawline, and a smirky mouth, the same features that had haunted me for the last five months. And I'd been right before: he was freaking huge, even taller than Cal, at least six-three or six-four.

"You!" I exclaimed.

The corner of that beautiful mouth lifted in a sort of mocking salute. "Me."

My mouth dropped open, and I growled. "You."

"Yes, me," he said again, stepping closer and leaning in so his body pressed mine against the SUV. His golden hair reflected an icy sheen in the sickly blue streetlights. "And who are you?"

I should have hit him. I should have pulled my fist back and slugged him for following me, for the five months of uncertainty, for the current invasion of personal space. But I couldn't, because, well, Iris had always insisted that violence wasn't the way to solve interpersonal problems. And because he probably would have moved too quickly for me to hit him. And because he smelled really good—like amber and wood smoke—and his mouth was hovering a breath away from mine . . . and reasons.

I'm sure there were lots of reasons, but I couldn't remember any more of them, because his mouth closed over mine and pulled me into a kiss so magically freaking delicious that I forgot to breathe. The man actually stole my breath. I curled my fingers around his shirt, yanking him closer as my lips moved desperately against his soft, cool mouth. Eventually, the lack of oxygen made my knees sag. I might have dropped back, smacking my head against the SUV, but he caught me, cradling my head in his hands as if it was some fragile treasure.

He pulled away, staring down at me, the beginning of a grin blossoming under the bluish light. But the smile faded, and the warmth in those eyes gave way, as a glacial fog slid over his pupils. It was as if they had no color at all. His face went slack and emotionless as his hand wrapped around my chin.

"What's wrong?" I asked, but his grip tightened hard around my jaw. I thought I felt the bone buckle as he whipped me around, crushing my back against his chest. I pinched the panic button on my keyless remote. In the distance, I could hear my car alarm wail.

The heretofore silent primal part of my brain that was supposed to warn me when I was being sized up as prey started bleating, *Mistake! Mistake!* And I was reminded that the reason vampires were so mysterious and dangerous was that they were capable of serious violence.

My primal brain was pretty late to the game.

"Stop it, right now!" I squirmed against his chest, pushing the cage of his arms to put some space between us.

Not a word. Not one facial twitch. No response, except pressing me tightly against his chest and wrapping his and around my throat, making it almost impossible for me to breathe. But he still didn't say anything, which was completely weird. Vampires were notoriously chatty during violence. And he wasn't biting me, which was even weirder.

My new boyfriend was either a manipulative mugger or a remedial vampire. I wasn't sure which was the better option.

I struggled, wiggling my arm loose, and reached for the ugly agate brooch on my lapel. With the press of a button, a cloud of colloidal silver spray mushroomed around my head. It was harmless to me, but as this guy was a vampire and therefore allergic to silver in all its forms, it stung enough to make him loosen his grip as he coughed and spluttered against my neck.

"I don't want to hurt you," I told him through gritted teeth. "But I will."

Bold words from the girl in the rumpled pantsuit.

Still twitching and retching, he loosened his hold enough that I could reach into my purse and grab the hairbrush strapped into a special compartment. The ordinary-looking purple plastic brush was another one of Cal's security contraptions. I squeezed the bristles until a silver stake popped out of the handle, and I rammed the point into my assailant's thigh. It wouldn't kill him, but he certainly wouldn't be chasing after me anytime soon.

"Augh!" he cried, letting go of my arms entirely and dropping me to the pavement like a sack of potatoes.

Cal would be thrilled to know his security equipment was effective.

My knees almost buckled from the landing, but I planted my feet. It was a good choice, considering that all of his weight pitched forward onto my back and bent me in half. The hands gripped at my hair, keeping my head down. I reached back, searching for the brush. I pulled it from his leg with a sizzling hiss, like angry bacon. No bacon should be angry.

I had raised it to stab the other leg when he suddenly shoved me aside. With one last, regretful look, he took off at vampire speed down the asphalt, disappearing from sight.

"Yeah, you better run." I panted, bending at the waist so I could prop myself on my knees and catch my breath. But the slick material of my suit gave way under my sweat-soaked palms, and my hands slid right off. I pitched forward and, unable to catch myself, toppled face-first onto the pavement.

Ouch.

Vampires have a very strong startle response. Try to stay calm. Imagine you're working with a nervous cat strapped to a stick of old dynamite.

—*The Office After Dark: A Guide to Maintaining a Safe, Productive Vampire Workplace*

He ran.

I sat there, completely bewildered, clutching my hairbrush just in case Blond-and-Gone came back. I couldn't believe that after five months of fantasizing about my mystery vampire, he'd just run off. That is, after kissing me and jumping me in a parking lot, and not in the fun way.

What the hell just happened?

"Gigi!" I heard a familiar voice yell from behind the cars. "Gigi, where are you?"

"Here!" I shouted.

Dick Cheney—the vampire, not the former vice president—materialized in front of me, nearly sliding under the SUV, he'd been running so fast. "I've got her." Dick spoke into the cell phone pressed to his ear. "She seems to be OK. I'll call in a few minutes."

I was dazed enough that I didn't move out of his way as he hung up the phone and scooted closer.

"Gigi," he whispered, ever so gently lifting my chin so he could inspect the pavement scrapes on my cheek. "What happened?"

Tall and rangy, with mischievous seawater eyes and dirty-blond hair, Dick Cheney represented an unlikely blend of fierce loyalty and pure sketchiness. He filled the "unreliable but adorable uncle" role in my life, while his lovely wife, Andrea, was my grown-up fashion icon. Dick had taken pains to become more legitimate over the years under Andrea's positive influence. He'd stopped wearing quite so many inappropriate T-shirts and invested in a number of *legal* businesses, but deep down, he would always be the guy you called when you needed the number for a topless housekeeping service.

"What are you doing here?" I asked, stretching my jaw to check for breaks.

"The panic button on your key sends an alarm to Cal's cell phone," he said, almost sheepishly. "And I might have been waiting a block away so I could follow you on the drive home. Because Cal asked me to, not because I'm creepy or anything. When your alarm went off, he called me and told me to get my butt down here on the double."

I rolled my eyes, but the movement made me dizzy,

so I just glared at him. "You, sir, are enabling a heli-copter vampire."

"Cal's just concerned for you!" he exclaimed, ges-turing to my face. "And rightly so. What happened to you?"

"A vampire attacked me, the deceitful bastard."

Dick frowned. "Deceitful?"

"Never mind."

"Did you recognize the vampire who attacked you?"

"No," I wheezed, the weird, unsure tone of my voice undone by the pain provoked when Dick pressed his thumbs against my jaw. Technically, it was true. I didn't recognize him. I had no clue who he was. That didn't stop my feelings from being hurt. Jerk. "He just came up behind me and grabbed me."

Dick tilted my face away from him so he could search my neck for wounds. "But he didn't bite you."

"He didn't even try," I told him. "Which I thought was weird. But he might not have had time. I un-leashed the full complement of antivampire Cal-tech on him."

"Really?" He beamed at me.

I laughed and realized I must have split my lip when my face smacked the ground. Hissing, I pressed my hand over it.

Dick took out a pocket-sized first-aid kit and dabbed at my mouth with an antiseptic wipe. At my raised eye-brow, he explained, "When you work with Jane Jame-son, you learn to be prepared for anything."

I recalled Jane's supernatural origin story, which involved being mistaken for a deer, shot by a drunk hunter, and turned into a vampire. "Fair enough."

He pulled me to my feet and tried to pick me up.

"I am not four years old," I told him. "I will walk. Now, where the hell are my shoes?"

His lips quirked into a fond little smile, reminding me of why I'd entertained a brief but intense schoolgirl crush on Dick for the first few months after my sister was adopted into his social circle. Buried deep underneath the many layers of sketchiness, he was sweet vampire nougat. "Come on, baby doll, let's get you home."

As we searched the parking lot for my far-flung pumps, I gave Dick a detailed report on how I had used the silver spray brooch and the brush stake. My only regret was that I didn't have a chance with the purse-sized flamethrower, because I was in the mood for toasting my mystery vampire like a hot blond Pop-Tart. Dick was thrilled that Cal's sick little toys had served their purpose and promised to help Cal find me even better tricks for next time. I had a feeling his less reputable connections would be involved somehow.

I filed the appropriate report with Ophelia, who, again, made me wait outside her office while she spoke to Dick. And given the yelling I could hear from Dick, I was sort of glad to be on this particular side of the door. Dick was not impressed with the security offered to the Council's human employees, and he was making his displeasure as an undead citizen known at vocal decibels I didn't know existed. This didn't seem to faze Ophelia in the least, as she tossed Dick out of her office without a word of apology to me.

After informing me that my unflappable boss expected me at my desk at the beginning of my shift the next day—assault was no excuse for tardiness—Dick insisted on leaving his El Camino at the Council office and driving my car home. I would have argued with him, but the adrenaline was slowly draining out of my system, and I felt as if I'd been hit by a truck.

"Is there any sort of bribe I can offer that would allow you to handle this quietly, in a way that will not result in my sister completely freaking out?"

"Well, that is going to be a problem," Dick said, as we pulled into the driveway to find a half-dozen cars parked in front of our house. I recognized Miranda Puckett's special black vampire-transport SUV and Gabriel Nightengale's sensible blue sedan.

I turned in my seat, glaring at Dick. "What did you do?"

"I may have made a few phone calls on the way to get you."

"You sent up the Bat Signal?" I cried. "Before you even knew what was wrong with me?"

"Somebody had to keep Iris contained!" he exclaimed. "She gets the same alarms from your key fob. I knew it would take that many vampires to hold her down."

I closed my eyes, shaking my head. "This . . . this is not going to go well."

Dick patted my arm sympathetically. "No, it is not."

• • •

I fixed my face as best I could in the makeup mirror and straightened my clothes. There was nothing to be done about the scrape on my cheek, but everything else I could cover with powder. The moment the car engine shut off, Cal and Iris swept out of the house in a blur of movement. Iris got to me first, lifting me off the ground in a bear hug. "Gigi!"

"Human!" I wheezed, as Iris squeezed the breath from my lungs and sobbed into my tattered jacket. Cal wrapped his arms around us both, resting his head against my bruised cheek. Over his shoulder, I saw Jane Jameson-Nightengale step out onto the porch with her tall, dark, and fangsome husband, Gabriel, and her childe, Jamie, who also happened to be my best friend. They stood on the porch, and while they weren't related, it was amazing that they all wore matching expressions of concern.

Also, I still couldn't breathe.

"Oxygen!" I wheezed against Iris's grip. Shrugging loose, I asked, "OK, who's ready for a thorough discussion of boundaries?"

"Sorry! I'm sorry." She sniffed, dropping me gently to my feet. "I just got so scared when the alarm went off, and Jamie and Jane had to pin me to the ceiling. And I bit Gabriel's arm—I'm really sorry about that, Gabriel!" she called back over her shoulder.

"It's all right," he said, rubbing absently at his torn sleeve. "It's better than what Jane would have done."

I looked at Jane, who just nodded, because she knew he was right.

Jamie took Iris's release of my person as an open invitation to jump in and sweep me off my feet, too. As sunny and blond as a teen vampire could be, Jamie was exactly as he had been when we were classmates at Half-Moon Hollow High. Goofy, open, and affectionate, like a Labrador puppy with fangs.

"You gave us a scare, kid," he muttered into my hair.

"I'm fine," I insisted. "You should see the other guy. Hey, what's this?" My hand snagged an envelope that was sticking out of Jamie's back pocket. At this point, I welcomed the distraction and snatched it up for a closer look. "So what's in the envelope?" I asked Jamie, waving the paper at him. "If you haven't noticed, I am in desperate need of a subject change."

"My schedule!" he said, presenting the paperwork with a flourish. "My adjustment counselor at UK sent it in today's mail!"

I squealed with more excitement than you'd expect over a college class schedule and hopped up and down, hugging Jamie's neck. After spending two semesters proving that he could function in a community-college classroom without devouring his classmates, Jamie was joining me at the University of Kentucky that September.

While I was thrilled about Jamie's secondary education, Ophelia was not happy. She couldn't move three hundred miles to campus with her boyfriend, because she had to stay close to the Council office.

She was unhappy about the prospect of Jamie being out of her sight, away from public officials she controlled, near single girls she couldn't track or intimidate. And she seemed to be blaming me for Jamie's abandonment, since I had spent months helping Jamie wade through forms, releases, background checks, and other paperwork that vampire students had to file with their applications.

And Ophelia was my new boss.

For someone with above-average intelligence, I didn't always think my decisions through.

"I can't wait," he said. "I'm so excited. Thanks for making this happen for me, Geeg."

"All I did was help you with the paperwork." I scoffed. "You're the one ducking tradition and your bloodmate in order to major in sports medicine."

"Former jocks have to major in something," he said. "And I'm not *ducking* my bloodmate. I am simply following my sire's advice and getting an education. Ophelia understands." When I made an indelicate horselike noise, he added, "She will understand, eventually."

"Yeah, that should make work less awkward if and when Ophelia ever decides to make eye contact with me," I muttered.

"OK, as happy as I am for you, Jamie—congratulations—can we change the subject back to my sister's near-death experience?" Iris interjected. "Are you sure you don't need to go to the emergency room or something, Geeg?" She fussed with my disheveled hair. "Did you bump your head or—internal bleeding! You could have internal bleeding and not even know it. Let's just load you into the car and pop down to the hospital for an MRI."

"I'm fine," I insisted, shaking Iris gently. "Can we all just please go inside? I'd like to get out of this pantsuit and into some natural fibers."

I walked through the front door, shrugging out of my jacket and tossing it into the closest waste-basket. Cal and Iris had made the house more vampire-friendly after Iris's transition. Cal's histori-cal presence was represented in the ancient-but-somehow-in-museum-condition bronze shield over the fireplace in the den and a marble bust of harvest goddess Demeter on the entryway table. But Cal had also made serious structural changes with Sam Clemson's help, from heavy-duty sunproof shades mounted under the window shades to a security system that made Fort Knox look like the Bank of Mayberry. And the access door to the basement had been replaced with a much sturdier solid steel ver-sion, painted to look like wood but able to stand up to several grades of explosives.

I would call Cal paranoid, but the scuff marks on my face made it hard to poke fun at him.

The moment I walked into the parlor, I got a face-ful of British vampire for my trouble. Cool, sandy-haired Collin Sutherland, with whom I'd been on a strict handshakes-and-firm-nods-only level for years, swooped in and threw his arms around me with so much enthusiasm that I was once again swept off my feet. It was nice to know I was loved, but the undead tackle-hugging was starting to become a little much.

"I'm so sorry, Gigi," Collin whispered. "So, so sorry."

His girlfriend, Miranda, who worked for Iris in Beeline's vampire-transport department, approached us with a bemused but concerned expression on her puckish face.

"As the only other human here, I'm counting on you to be the voice of reason," I told her solemnly.

"Who do you think kept them all here?" Miranda said, blowing a strand of dark hair out of her eyes. "Iris tried to rally the others to go to the parking lot and follow the scent trail of whoever hurt you. It was like a small, angry mob with fangs instead of pitchforks. Also, Zeb told me that he's sorry he couldn't be here to represent the other human voice of reason, but the twins are going through a gnawing phase. He didn't want Iris's furniture to get ruined."

I shuddered, picturing Jane's very human childhood best friend, Zeb Lavelle, and his gorgeous werewolf wife, Jolene, trying to corral their adorable but destructive twins. I babysat the kids once so Zeb could take Jolene on a date night. I babysat them *once*. That was enough to make me question the wisdom of reproduction.

"What's wrong with him?" I asked, pointing to Collin, who, for the record, was still holding me several inches off the ground.

"Collin's feeling a little guilty," she said. "He thinks he should have seen this coming. You know, with his—" Miranda waggled her fingers around her head in a way that I assumed represented Collin's precognitive gift.

Right. Collin had had a vague and barely helpful premonition over the Christmas break about me being attacked by a vampire. He had predicted that while none of the undead members of my circle of friends would hurt me, a vampire would eventually come after me. It was part of the reason I cooperated when Cal arranged my *Hunger Games* training.

Poor Collin. He hated to be right.

"Collin, I'm fine," I assured him. "It's not fair to beat yourself up over visions. And technically, you did see it coming while I was home for Christmas. And you took the time to warn me. You just didn't have a lot of details. You did all you could."

"I never get enough details," Collin grumbled. "And I could have followed you around in the ensuing months so I could protect you from what I saw."

"That would have become annoying really quickly," I assured him. "And we never would have reached the stage in our relationship where we hug for socially inappropriate amounts of time."

Collin blanched and retracted his arms, dropping me to my feet, while Miranda snickered. By this time, the other vampires had trooped into the living room for what I could only assume would be a debriefing.

"It's really not a big deal, guys. I got grabbed from behind by a vampire, who probably saw me as an easy midnight snack. I proved him wrong. I don't have any serious injuries. I call this one a win. Who wants something not-bloody to drink? Miranda?"

"Gigi, do not make light of this," Cal said, putting his arm around me to prevent my retreat to the vampire-friendly kitchen.

"Making light of things is how I process," I retorted. "Besides, who could blame the guy for trying? I'm awesome. What self-respecting vampire wouldn't want a piece of this?"

"And you're so modest, too." Iris sighed. "You're quitting that job."

Well, at least she'd skipped "I told you so."

"I will not have you in and out of that parking lot every night, risking another attack," Iris said. "You're going to find a nice, safe office job, far, far away from vampires, werewolves, zombies, ghosts, or any other supernatural creatures. I don't care if you have to become a telemarketer. I will keep you safe."

"I am not quitting that job, Iris," I told her calmly. "This is a dream job for a programmer. More money and perks than I could make anywhere else, and I haven't even finished my degree yet. I'm an adult, and if I choose to work somewhere, as long as it doesn't involve pasties or a Webcam, you should respect that."

"We'll talk about *that* later," Iris said, snorting.

"It could have just been a random attack," Dick suggested. "It's never happened in this group. But it is possible that Gigi crossed paths with a vampire with bad feeding habits, even outside the Council office,

where Ophelia made it clear that such habits will result in quick, bloody, permanent death. Some vampires
don't listen and do what they want . . . I'm not helping,
am I?"

Andrea patted his arm. "You're trying, sweetie. It counts."

Now that my heart rate had finally settled down long
enough to let me think clearly, my feelings were more
than a little hurt. Why had my vampire tried to hurt
me? Before, he'd merely followed me around, skulking
in parking lots, all broody and observant. And when
he kissed me, it was like something out of a really
good old episode of *Buffy*. Passionate and urgent, just
a little bit filthy. I could practically hear the carefully
selected indie rock playing in the background.

Was it all a setup? Or had he just wanted to amuse
himself by playing with his food? I'd spent all of this
time thinking about him, hoping I'd meet up with him
again someday. And now I felt like a first-prize idiot
for not seeing what was right in front of my face. I was
the human equivalent of a cat toy. And through this
cloud of brooding and gloom, I heard Cal say, "So I
called Nikolai. He can accompany Gigi to work starting tomorrow night."

My head snapped up, suddenly able to follow the
conversation. "Wait, what?"

Clearly, I wasn't *hearing* what was right in front of
my face, either.

"Cal's called in a favor from an old friend," Iris said.
"He will be following you to work every night and

then home and anytime you leave the house at night. For . . . ever."

"That giant hamster ball I bought Jane for Christmas is also an option," Dick suggested.

"Dick, stop helping," I begged him. "And Cal, what do you mean, 'old friend'? As in you exchange occasional Christmas cards, or 'remember that time we sacked Constantinople because we were peckish?'" Cal leveled an exasperated look at me, which I ignored. "It's a valid question."

"Please take this seriously, Gigi."

"It's hard to take this seriously, because I do not need a vampire bodyguard!" I exclaimed. "Don't you think this is just a little bit of an overreaction? It could have just been a random attack, like Dick said. I may never see this vampire again. Besides, people in this little group have been attacked and kidnapped and had deer parts left on their doorstep, and they never hired a bodyguard."

"Well, do you notice that all those people are dead now?" Jane nodded toward Andrea and Iris. "OK, they're vampires, but still. I think Cal is trying to get ahead of the situation, which is something this group has struggled with in the past."

"How did you even manage to arrange this so quickly?" I asked Cal, who was looking up at the ceiling, being careful not to make eye contact. Something was up. "Unless you'd already made the arrangements and were just waiting for the excuse to call him?" My brother-in-law was still studying the track lighting. "Cal, don't make me get the flamethrower."

"I knew he was in town and may have mentioned to him that we might need the help of a vampire you couldn't manipulate," Cal said defensively when I smacked his arm. "You can't protect someone properly if that person has you wrapped around her little finger."

"She doesn't have *me* wrapped around her little finger!" Collin protested. "I am an impartial bystander!"

"Inappropriately long hugs, Collin," Miranda reminded him.

Collin wrinkled up his face in the most undignified expression I'd ever seen him make. "Curses!"

I took a deep breath and reminded myself that the concern Iris's vampire friends showed for one another was part of the reason I loved them so much. Threatening them all with Cal's silver spray would be a poor return for that care.

But seriously, one more hug, and I was going to snap.

"Cal, bringing fanged personnel to the office with me is only going to make me look immature and incapable to my coworkers, who don't show much respect for humans anyway. It's going to make my job that much harder."

"Yes, because keeping up appearances is so much more important than your personal safety," Cal muttered.

"Look, you've done everything you can to prepare

me for hostile interactions with a vampire, including finding a martial-arts instructor who shouted incorrect Sun Tzu quotes *and* 'Mercy is for the weak' at me while he tossed me around the mat like a rag doll," I said. "And the good news is that it worked. Thanks to what I learned and the bag of tricks you gave me, I was able to defend myself. The worst injuries I sustained tonight were from falling on my face after the guy ran off. So unless you can protect me from gravity, I'd say you've done all that you can. So I don't need some vampire version of the Rock following me around, checking the bathroom stalls for potential assailants."

"Actually, a vampire version of the Rock doesn't sound that bad," Miranda murmured. "Can one of you get on that? For the greater good?"

"Gigi, you have made a series of cogent and intelligent points," Cal said, his head cocking toward the front door as if he was listening for something. "And you may be right . . . in some small way. I might have jumped the gun in calling in my friend for support."

"Thank you."

"But none of that matters now, because he's standing on our front porch," he said, dashing around me to answer the knock before it was even finished.

"What?" I spat. "Damn it, Cal!'"

I heard Cal at the front door, conversing in hushed Russian with a somewhat familiar second voice. I reached into my purse so I could at least wipe some of the smeared lip gloss from my cheek. The moment our guest stepped through the door, the hair on the back of my neck stood up. There he was in all his blond glory, the guy who had been following, kissing, and, most recently, attacking me.

"Motherfudger!" I yelled, dropping my purse and holding my stake hairbrush in a stabby position.

Iris frowned. "Gigi?"

I clicked the silver stake into place and demanded, "I didn't smack you around enough the first time, jackass? You had to come back for seconds?"

Mr. Tall, Blond, and Bite-y stared, tilting his gorgeous head and staring at me as if I was a particularly interesting specimen at the zoo. He was wearing different clothes, jeans and a thin green cashmere sweater that brought out the lighter amber flecks in his stupid, beautiful eyes.

It was difficult getting past the "so damn cute" to focus on the "violent possible sociopath" of this situation. But I would do it, for puppies and feminism and for no other reason than that I'd already committed to this road by pulling a stake on a guest.

"Gigi, what are you doing?" Iris asked through a tightly wrought, awkward smile. All of the other vampires stood cautiously, not quite sure why I appeared to be losing my mind in front of our guest. "Kind of being rude to Cal's friend."

"This is the vampire who attacked me."

Cal scoffed. "Don't be silly, Geeg, this is my friend, Nikolai Dragomirov. Nik for short, because no one needs that many syllables."

"Well, I'm telling you that your 'friend' Nik tried to

bite me in the parking lot tonight. Which I think means he is no longer a friend but an acquaintance, at best. I don't care what you did in Constantinople."

Nik wandered closer, towering over me, completely oblivious to the fact that I was pressing the tip of a silver stake to his chest. Seriously, I had time to adjust my placement two or three times to make sure I had the heart, and he didn't even glance down.

"I know you," he said. "I have seen you before."

"Of course you have," Cal said, and when Iris sent him a questioning look, he hastily added, "I sent pictures of the wedding."

"Which probably helped when you were following me around Half-Moon Hollow during Christmas break. Also, you saw me earlier when you were *attacking* me. How is that not breaking through?" I asked, digging the stake in just enough to make him wince. And yes, I was still willfully omitting the kissing part, because I wanted to escape this situation without Iris trying to ground me to my room like a preteen.

"What about Christmas?" Iris asked, frowning.

Double damn it.

I tried to cobble together a coherent, plausible explanation for what I had just said, but all I could produce was a series of increasingly twitchy facial expressions that communicated guilt or nausea. Or maybe both.

"Gigi, what aren't you telling us?" Iris asked, her voice deceptively calm.

I locked eyes with Nik, who seemed just as confused as Cal and Iris. Because he wasn't aware that I'd omitted a large portion of our less-than-adorable "how we met" story. And neither was Jane, because she immediately piped up, "Of course he's seen her. One of the first clear pictures I got from Nik was of him standing near Gigi at McDonough's Tree Farm, watching her and wanting to talk to her and . . . judging from the expressions on your faces, I should just stop talking right now, shouldn't I?"

I cringed and nodded. Sometimes it really sucked to hang out with a mind-reader. "Jane, maybe you shouldn't go poking around in Nik's head. It seems like a violation of a lot of different civil rights."

"Let's worry about vampire Fifth Amendment issues when you're not attracted to a man who seems to have Gigi-based rage blackouts." Iris snorted. "Also, you were seeing him over Christmas break, and you didn't think to tell us?"

"I wasn't seeing him as in dating him. I was seeing him as in possibly hallucinating him!" I cried. "And I don't know how that is relevant to the current conversation."

Nik's smile was indulgent as he stepped closer to me. "I am certain I would remember attacking someone as pretty as you, *sladkaya*."

"What did you call me?" I asked, arching a brow as Iris pushed Nik back a step away from me.

"He called you 'sweetheart,'" Cal said, glaring at the back of his friend's head. "He's Russian. He calls every woman he meets under the age of seventy 'sweetheart.' It doesn't mean anything." Cal's glare intensified. "It *doesn't* mean anything, right, Nik?"

"Why wouldn't it mean anything?" I growled, though I wasn't sure who was on the receiving end. "Look, you actually spoke to me this time, don't you remember that?"

Nik turned back to Cal, completely ignoring the question. "You said she was a bit of a genius. Does that mean she is also a little bit . . ." Nik made a hand gesture near his head that was considerably less flattering than the "little off" gesture Miranda had made for Collin.

"Oh, I'm crazy now?" Seething, I reached down and squeezed his thigh, right over the spot where I'd stabbed him with silver. He didn't even bother defending himself. In fact, he looked downright intrigued when I reached toward his thigh. But when I applied the pressure, he yowled and backed away. "Do you remember how you sustained this limp? Because that's how I left you, Skippy, with a gaping, difficult-to-heal silver wound."

He looked almost amused by the fact that I'd left a big wound on his leg. "*You* stabbed me?"

"What?" Cal watched, his expression horrified, as a bright bloody patch spread across the leg of Nik's jeans.

"I told you, I stabbed him in the thigh with my hairbrush stake. Am I the only person in the room following this conversation?"

I heard several murmurs of "Possibly" and "Probably."

I was more worried about the intensity of Cal's glare, which, by rights, should have melted Nik's forehead.

"Cal, was this one of your training exercises gone wrong?" Iris demanded, as Cal slid between me and Nik and gently shoved me out of striking distance. "Did you send your friend to attack Gigi in a parking lot? I can appreciate that you want her to be prepared, but I think you've gone too far."

"Of course I didn't!" Cal exclaimed. "Nik, did you attack Gigi in a parking lot?"

"No, I came here as soon as I rose for the evening," Nik insisted, the faint Russian accent growing deeper. "She looks familiar, I will admit. But Cal, you know I would never hunt a random human, especially not this close to the Council office. It would be professional suicide."

I would try not to focus on the "professional suicide" qualifier, I really would.

Cal checked his watch. "You just now rose at two a.m.?"

"I rose late. I have been working longer hours lately. I did not know I was going to need an alibi."

"OK, how did you end up with that wound on your leg?"

"I do not know."

"What *do* you know?" Cal asked.

Nik nodded toward me. "I know that I have seen her before. I do not know how or when or where, but I have seen her before."

"Of course you have, you idiot. I sent you to her school months ago to 'talk to' that boy in her class who wouldn't stop making unwanted advances on her!" Cal cried, exasperated.

"That was you?" I exclaimed.

"Oh, Cal, you didn't." Iris sighed.

"I do not remember that." Nik shook his head, still staring at me as if I was some precious, fascinating gemstone. A girl could get used to being stared at like that . . . minus the patchy memory and the occasional attempted mugging. And despite the situation, I could feel a little smile forming on my lips.

"Do you remember following me when I was home over Christmas break?" I asked.

Nik shook his head. "No."

"What?" Iris exclaimed. "What the hell is going on here? Has *everyone* gone nuts?"

"Do you remember kissing me in front of Jane Jameson's bookshop?" I asked, ignoring my sister's growing distress.

"No, but I wish I did remember, truly," Nik said, grinning cheekily. "You have certainly built up an elaborate pretend relationship between the two of us. I am sorry I missed it."

"Gladiola Grace Scanlon!" Iris yelled, catching my arm as I surged forward to smack him. Or at least poke him really hard. "You were followed and kissed by a strange vampire, and you didn't think to tell anybody about it?" Damn it. She broke out my full birth name. That meant I was really in trouble.

"Let's just focus on the problem at hand," I told Iris, my violent intent temporarily redirected.

Iris pointed her finger in my face. "We are so going to revisit this."

Meanwhile, Cal had Nik pressed against the wall by his collar. "You kissed my little sister?"

My stake swung dangerously close to my vampire companions as I threw my arms into the air. "Oh, come on, *that* you believe, but I'm crazy when I say he attacked me?"

"I don't know if we should be here right now," Andrea whispered to Dick.

"If we leave now, we'll miss a lot, and we'll just have to catch up later," Dick whispered back.

"Everyone can hear you," Jane hissed over both of them.

Suddenly, Nik started laughing and pointing at Dick, who was wearing one of the few shirts Andrea had missed in her legendary purge of his inappropriate T-shirt collection: "Home is where the pants aren't." When he realized everybody was staring at him, Nik cried, "What? Is funny, yes?"

Jane slapped her hand over her face. "Oh, God, it's Russian Dick Cheney."

Gabriel shuddered. "There are two of them."

"Hey!" Dick exclaimed. "That hurts my feelings!"

"Let's get back to the point. Did you kiss my sister?" Cal demanded, shaking Nik back and forth hard enough to make fangs rattle.

"If you say that you don't remember kissing me, I will choke you out," I told him.

The room went silent. Even Cal was looking over at me with a doubtful expression that I found insulting.

I amended, "I would try real hard."

"All right, all right, yes, there is something going on here," Nik said, clearing his throat and removing Cal's hands from their locked position around his neck. "And I do not understand what it is. But I do not think that choking me is going to help the situation."

Somehow, the overly formal language, the precise pronunciation of every syllable without contractions or slang, the mark of someone who'd learned English as a second language decades before, reminded me so much of Cal it made me smile. That sort of sucked, because I was supposed to be all pissed off and bad-ass. It was hard to be badass when you were smiling like a goof.

Nik smiled back at me, a big, beautiful, open smile, and it set a whole flock of condor-sized butterflies loose in my stomach. And all that doubt about where Nik landed on the fairy-tale-monster line of violence didn't seem to matter so much anymore. In that moment, forgiving him for that little life-or-death scuffle in the parking lot seemed like a totally reasonable thing to do. Hell, climbing into his lap and nibbling his ears seemed like a totally reasonable thing to do.

I might not have been the authority on what was reasonable, at that moment.

Maybe Nik's secret vampire power was like Dick's "female persuasion"? Dick could persuade a woman to shave her own head and do the Macarena in the town square if he flirted enough with her, something he rarely put to use because he didn't consider it sporting.

"Why do I not remember you?" Nik asked me, as if we were the only ones in the room. He reached for my face, like he was about to cup my cheek, only to have his hand diverted by a slap from Cal. "I should remember you."

"I don't know." I chuckled, despite the incredible weirdness of the situation. "But could you maybe say hi from now on? Instead of the skulking and the lunging?"

Nik leaned just a tiny bit closer, his blunt white teeth dragging over that full bottom lip. "I think that could be arranged."

Cal cleared his throat. And then I realized I was inappropriately infatuated with someone who shared an uncomfortable number of similarities with my surrogate brother-slash-father-figure, and my goofy smile melted away like magic. And then I remembered the parking-lot roughhousing, and I took another step back.

"This is a very sweet moment, but I would really like you to get out of my house," Iris said, somehow outmuscling her husband and pushing Nik toward the door. "Cal will be in touch. Stay away from Gigi."

"What if I do not want to leave?" Nik asked, his voice a low, threatening growl, as Cal hovered in front of Nik, preventing him from getting closer to me.

My eyes widened as a ripple of that same fear I had felt in the parking lot zipped down my spine. Jamie moved in front of me in a protective stance, while Iris leapt forward at her inhuman speed and practically tackled Nik to force him out the door. She slammed the door in his face. His beautiful, beautiful face. I would analyze my rapid shifts in attitude toward parking-lot assailants at a later time.

"I do *not* understand what is happening right now." I sighed.

"You are making very poor decisions," Iris told me.

"You are not to see that boy again," Cal said in an authoritative, fatherly tone that was frankly terrifying.

"I am not twelve," I told him. "And he's hardly a boy. If he's an old friend of yours, that probably means he's, what, four hundred years old?"

Cal muttered something under his breath.

"What was that?" I asked.

"I said it's closer to five hundred," he grumbled. "Give or take a decade." And Iris buried her face in her hands.

"I told you we should have left earlier," Andrea whispered to Dick. "Now it's super-awkward, and they're standing in front of the door."

**You are not Norma Rae. Sometimes standing up for what
you believe in should take a backseat to survival.**
—*The Office After Dark: A Guide to Maintaining a
Safe, Productive Vampire Workplace*

I would like to say that Cal, Iris, and I bade our trapped
guests good evening and had a mature, thoughtful discussion about my options before forming a coherent
plan for how to handle the Nik situation.

But instead, they sent me to my room.

This was what I got for not renting my own apartment for the summer.

The next morning, the whole hit-by-a-truck feeling
still lingered. Because I couldn't explain what the hell
had happened the night before or how it was going to
affect me in the long term, I decided to just continue
as if it hadn't. I restocked my purse with antivampire
weapons, packed my own lunch, and drove to work
early. Oh, and I downgraded to a business-casual outfit
of a pair of khakis and a dark blue cardigan, because I
would never wear poly-blend again.

I didn't know how to process all of the truth explosions lobbed at me in the parlor. There were so many elements to be upset over. Cal sending Nik to my college campus to threaten the mouth-breather from my history class. The fact that Nik couldn't remember coming to my college campus to threaten said mouth-breather. Nik taking this as an invitation to follow me around the Hollow while I was home for Christmas vacation. The fact that he couldn't remember following me around the Hollow while I was home for Christmas vacation. Nik attacking me in the parking lot. The fact that he couldn't *remember* attacking me in the parking lot. And he forgot the kissing. I couldn't seem to get past that.

This was not normal vampire behavior. What with their immortality and superhuman eye for detail, vampires had awesome memories. So why did Nik have a big blank spot when it came to me? I'd assigned all this meaning and excitement to my interactions with him, and he couldn't even recall anything beyond *Hey, I think your face is familiar-ish*. Was I really so unmemorable?

In the most basic terms, I was hurt and sad, and I felt very foolish. I'd used those few seconds with Nik, that first kiss of all kisses, the silly whirlwind romance of it all, to assure myself that breaking it off with Ben hadn't been a mistake. I'd told myself, *See? You're going to be OK. Mysterious hunky vampires dig you.* To find out that it was all some bizarre possible setup by my brother-in-law that resulted in a memory fugue state was, well, disappointing.

On top of that, I was not used to fighting with Iris, so my internal level was way off-bubble. Between the age difference and losing our parents at such an early age, Iris had always been more of a mother to me than a sibling. After a disastrous attempt to try to blend me into her life in the big city, Iris had given up college and the career she'd planned to bring me back to Half-Moon Hollow and live in our parents' old house. She'd even started Beeline, a "daytime concierge service" and event-planning business for vampires so her schedule would be flexible enough to work with mine.

I knew exactly how hard Iris worked to keep our parents' house, pay the bills, and make me feel I had some sort of normal life. There were times when seeing the dark circles under her eyes and the worry on her face made me feel so guilty I wanted to run away just to relieve her of the burden of me. And then I resented her, for making me feel that way, for taking our parents' place so readily. And then I realized what a stupid reaction that was, and I went through the whole guilt cycle again.

Tripping over Cal while dropping off a service contract at his house had seemed like some sort of karmic reward for her suffering. Cal, an investigator who occasionally worked for the Council, made her happy. She didn't have to prove herself to him. She didn't have to do anything for him. She just loved him, and that was enough.

My love for Iris and my gratitude to Cal helped keep

us on the same wavelength through my teenage years. We rarely disagreed, and when we did, we'd always been able to work through it with lighthearted teasing and minor threats of Tasering.

I knew they had to be worried if they were acting so flipping loony. Now that Iris had leveled up to her vampire state, she hated the idea of me being out in the world without superpowers to defend myself. Every day that I walked around as my weak human beta version made them both twitchy, but Iris was still holding out the hope that I could have some sort of normal life, with kids and the white picket fence.

I didn't have a lot of experience, romantically speaking, but it seemed weird to be so focused on Nik. Was it because I'd suddenly made contact with him again after building up such an epic imaginary relationship in my head? Or because I'd been alone since breaking up with Ben and needed to latch on to any man who'd shown the slightest interest in me, even if it was lunge-y, bite-y zombie interest?

Was one option better than the other?

Defying Iris by continuing at my job wasn't like me at all. I hoped that at some level, it communicated to her how important this was to me. And the fact that I was still thinking about Nik at all was a sign either of my own desperate, self-destructive loneliness or that I could possibly be feeling the first twinges of grown-up emotions toward a completely unsuitable man.

And Nik was just that, a *man*. Ben was sweet and kind and an awesome boyfriend, but he was a *boy*.

Even though John, the evil teenage vampire con man who'd duped me into helping him hurt Iris and Cal, had been a teenager for hundreds of years, he'd never matured past the petulant egomaniac stage. But here was Nik, a man, not a guy, not a boy, a *man*, with all of the power and appeal that implied. He'd been around long enough to see the world several times over. He'd been a witness to history.

And for a split second—well, two of them, actually—this man found me interesting enough to kiss me, and while I knew that I was, in general terms, pretty awesome, I just didn't understand why. Then again, he was interested in me in a sporadic fashion that he didn't even seem to remember, so . . .

OK, yeah, the universe made sense again.

I used my shiny new employee pass to get past several levels of security beyond the Council office's employee entrance. I felt very official and grown-up, flashing my little plastic badge around to get to the inner sanctum of vampire archival information. I sat at my bare, personality-free desk and took a deep breath.

"Focus on work," I told myself. "Just focus on doing a good job, and everything else will work itself out."

It occurred to me that my new life philosophy matched that of the super-tense Michael Bolton character in *Office Space*.

I logged into my department's server and opened my first window. Cracking my knuckles, I tried to picture the end result of what would be months, if not years, of work by myself and my coworkers, the largest, most comprehensive archive of vampires' living descendants in the history of the world.

No pressure.

Vampires had been dragged out of the coffin in 1999 by a cranky undead accountant named Arnie Frink. Recently turned and not quite comfortable with his daytime hours, Arnie requested evening hours so he could continue his job at the firm of Jacobi, Meyers, and Leptz. But the evil HR lady, as ignorant as the rest of the world about the existence of the undead at the time, insisted that Arnie keep banker's hours, because she had concerns about him messing with the copy machine.

Arnie countered with a diagnosis of porphyria, a painful allergy to sunlight, which would make him burn and peel and generally be unpleasant to work around, but the HR lady insisted that he could just wear a hat or something. So Arnie responded by suing the absolute hell out of Jacobi, Meyers, and Leptz.

When the allergy-discrimination argument failed to impress a judge, a sunblock-slathered Arnie flipped his proverbial feces in court, stood up, and yelled that he was a vampire, with a medical condition that rendered him unable to work during the day, thereby making him subject to the Americans with Disabilities Act.

After several lengthy appeals, not to mention a *lot* of testing by mental-health professionals, Arnie won his lawsuit and got a settlement, evening hours, and his own Internet following. When the furor died down, the international vampire community eventually agreed that it was more convenient to live out in the open anyway. Blood was easier to get when you could just ask someone for it, without the drama of stalking and body disposal.

An elected contingent of ancient vampires officially asked the world's governments to recognize them as legitimate, nonmythical beings, asking for special leniency in areas such as, say, income taxes that hadn't been paid in two hundred years. I don't remember much of that first year. I was too young to understand much beyond the snippets of stories I picked up before Mom rushed to turn off the evening news for being too scary. Iris called it a dark chapter in human history. Mobs of people dragged vampires out into the sunlight or set them on fire for no reason other than that they just didn't understand the new world they were living in. All I knew was that my classmates' mothers were feeding them garlic supplements with every meal, and all of my junior league soccer games got canceled because the government said we weren't allowed to leave the house after dark.

The same international contingent of vampires, who called themselves the World Council for the Equal Treatment of the Undead, appealed to the human governments for help. In exchange for providing certain census information, the Council was allowed to establish smaller, local bodies within regions of each state in every country. The Council was charged with keeping watch over newer vampires to make sure that they were safely acclimated to unlife, settling squabbles within the community, and investigating "accidents" that befell vampires. We were fortunate enough to have one of these offices in our backyard, a coincidence that Iris took full advantage of when she started her vampire concierge business.

This familiarity was what made Iris nervous about my working for the Council. She'd witnessed the vampire officials' by-any-means-necessary style of management firsthand and the intimidation, cover-ups, and otherwise dirty dealings it involved. Well, she hadn't actually witnessed the dirty dealings—that was how you disappeared. But she'd seen enough that she didn't want her baby sister on the Council payroll, which, when you think about it, is a little hypocritical.

In the years since the Great Coming Out, a lot of vampires had taken on "reverse genealogy" as a hobby. Instead of searching for their ancestors, they searched for the children and grandchildren they'd never met. In many cases, they wanted to share the wealth they'd accumulated over the years or pass on heirlooms. Or they simply wanted to assure themselves that their loved ones had fared well without them. Personally, I think they just wanted to assure themselves that they had been human once, that they'd once lived in the daylight.

Dick Cheney did his own version of this when he lingered around the Hollow to keep an eye on the family started by his "youthful dalliance" with a laundress. He posed as a helpful but secretive uncle, providing discreet help with rent, food, and even college tuition when his several-times-great-grandson, Gilbert Wainwright, became the first of his family to even consider higher education. Oddly enough, Jane ended up working for Mr. Wainwright at his bookstore, Specialty Books, and continued to run it after Mr. Wainwright died. The undead circles in the Hollow ran like a really small social Venn diagram.

The Council wanted to limit the criminal activity that inevitably popped up whenever vampires started trending, so they'd started an international movement to establish a user-friendly private search engine of vampires across the country, allowing the undead—and only the undead—to track their living descendants. It would work like ancestry.com but with more shadowy vampire connections and not-quite-legal documents than would be available to nice, law-abiding humans.

That was where teams of programmers like myself came in, organizing the information and building the engine from the ground up. To keep too much sensitive information from being stored in the same location, we were working out of Council offices all over the country. Each team handled a different piece of the puzzle, working for a regional team supervisor, who answered to a big, scary board of national vampire officials.

The coding would be only half the job. Some teams worked on the security angle, making it difficult for unapproved users to access the records. Others set up the registration features or did graphic design. (We called them the "lame teams.") Our portion of the puzzle involved finding the best way to link genea-logical documents and make them easily searchable, and then, because we were interns and our eyesight was considered expendable, scanning, keynoting, and cross-referencing the aforementioned shadowy docu-ments provided by vampire volunteers was an addi-tional "side duty" for our team. Other materials would have to be culled from public records. And then, of course, the engine would have to be tested, launched, updated, and maintained over the years, which, for the right people, could be long-term, lucrative employ-ment. And as someone who would like to move out of her sister's home in the near future, I considered long-term lucrative employment very important.

Yes, very important. And yet . . . instead of, say, open-ing the programming application and poking around a bit to get settled in, I was opening the server shared by the entire office complex—and opening employee records. Because the IT department, whose members weren't nearly as up-to-date on security measures as they thought they were, hadn't assigned us login cre-dentials yet, my entire department was working under the group "new employee" ID, which meant that open-ing employee histories in the personnel server couldn't be traced to a specific person. A terminal, yes, but not a person.

Nikolai Dragomirov's folder was listed in the "Spe-cialized" directory, right next to Cal's. I tapped my fin-ger against the mouse, mulling over what I was about to do. This was probably a bad idea. I was breaking several policies already, some of which could get me severely disciplined, *and it was my second day*. And reading Nik's files behind his back was definitely a violation of his trust . . . which I assumed I had. OK, not really; I barely knew the guy.

And that was the point, really. I knew *nothing* about Nik, and what Cal knew, he wasn't telling. Given the circumstances, looking through Nik's employment records was the responsible thing to do, right?

Right?

"Argh," I groaned, batting at my mouse. I clenched both eyes shut, clicking randomly, hoping that maybe fate would open the folder for me without my having to aim for it. I opened my eyes.

No dice.

"Fine." I grunted, opening one eye while opening the folder.

Nik's file was empty.

No work history, no sire/turning history, no case files, nothing to indicate that he'd ever stepped inside a Council building, much less worked for the agency for years. Part of me was relieved, because it kept me from learning anything disturbing. But at the same time, what the hell? According to Cal, Nik had been working for the Council since before it was officially formed. Why wouldn't they have any information on him?

What the hell was going on here?

I flopped back into my desk chair, contemplating what Nik's blank personnel folder could mean. Was it that his history was just so secretive and badass that it wasn't meant to be recorded, like a vampire James Bond? Or had someone—namely, Nik—erased his file knowing that he would come under scrutiny as the newest freelance investigator to work under Ophelia? (She did seem to go through a lot of them.) Was there a master hard copy I could find somewhere? Contacting the Council's international archives to request such a file would probably be difficult to overlook, right? Like checking his Facebook message folder but exponentially increased to the power of eleventy?

Maybe this was standard procedure for the Council's operatives? Maybe Cal's folder was empty, too? I hovered the cursor over his folder, flexing my index finger. Then again, there were a lot of things I didn't know about my beloved brother-in-law. And I didn't need to know most of them if I wanted to make eye contact with him over the dinner table.

"Nope, nope, nope." I closed out the folder while flailing my free hand. I would remain in my protective little bubble of ignorance, thank you.

I took a deep breath and closed my eyes, willing my brain to empty of all concerns about vampire attacks and sisters who may or may not show up at my workplace and attempt to drag me out of my office by my hair. I would not do this to myself. I would not lose my job because of my adolescent crush on an inscrutable vampire. I clicked on the sample programming text issued by the regional supervisor and began building an index. Slowly but surely, my brain relaxed into the task, and I felt more like myself than I had in days.

Everybody had a calling. This was mine. And I'd almost missed out on it. I'd started off majoring in nursing at University of Kentucky, inspired by the hospital staff who had treated Iris after Waco Marchand's henchman (also known as my ex-boyfriend, Creepy John) nearly turned her into a person pretzel. And as much as I wanted to succeed, it turned out that anatomy and exposure to actual internal parts were a bit beyond me. Computer science? That clicked for me. I discovered the aptitude in an Intro to Computers class that I'd only taken because Ben needed it for his major and it was the one time slot I had open on my schedule for a shared class. (It was either that or get him to join my women's self-defense class.)

The professor had us type command prompts, and it just made sense. All of the seemingly random numbers and letters weren't so random. I could see what they were supposed to be. It was as if the codes had always been tucked away in my bloodstream, and putting my fingers on the keyboard set them free to create and build. So the girl who had trouble loading music onto her iPod without violent cursing was suddenly able to write her own programs. It was enough to make me wonder what I could have accomplished in high school if I'd actually applied myself to my classes instead of coasting by while flinging myself around the volleyball court.

So I was now heading into my senior year, majoring in computer science, with a 3.8 grade-point average and the support of almost every professor who mattered in my department. I'd already written several programs and apps of my own. They were nothing worth selling but enough to keep my roommate—who believed every "You have won!" pop-up ad she saw—from destroying my hard drive with inadvertently downloaded viruses.

In an hour, I had a basic "sketch" of what I thought the records index should look like, when Jordan and Aaron marched into our windowless corral. They were arriving at exactly 1:56, just minutes before their shifts started. They stopped in their tracks when they saw me already clacking away at my keyboard.

"You're already here," Jordan said, lifting an eyebrow. "And you've been working."

"I just wanted to get started early," I told them, carefully avoiding motives involving uncomfortable conversations with overprotective vampire siblings.

"Project leader!" Aaron declared.

My head popped up. "Wait. What?"

Aaron whipped his messenger bag over his head and dropped it onto his desk. "Oh, you know that they're going to eventually ask us to elect a project leader. And by virtue of being early and working before our first day of real work starts, you are hereby elected. Jordan, any arguments?"

Jordan shook her rainbow head as she set up a mini-TARDIS play set next to her phone. "Nope."

"Majority rules!" Aaron crowed.

"What if Marty wants to vote?" I asked.

"Trust me, Marty will vote for you," Jordan muttered.

"I'll vote for what?" Marty asked.

"To make Gigi project leader," Aaron said. "To start off our time at the Council right, I think we should be proactive in shunting responsibility off on one of our own."

"Oh." Marty gave me a shy smile. "Sure. I think Gladiola would do a great job."

I caught sight of Jordan rolling her eyes behind Marty's back.

I laughed. "OK, well, as your dubiously elected leader, I say everybody should sit down and get to work. The Council wants a beta version of the program by the end of next year. If we want our portion to be ready by the end of next summer, we're going to have to get cracking."

"Wow, give a girl a little authority, and she goes straight for the dictatorship," Aaron muttered.

"Shut it," I said, smacking his shoulder with my files. "Now, if you guys want to look at the basic sketch I saved on the server and let me know what you think, I'd appreciate it. Make suggestions. Make changes. Make up your own, and we'll let them fight it out cage-match style. But according to this scary timeline tacked up on the wall, we need to have something to show the regional supervisor in weeks."

"Workplace violence!" Aaron cried, rubbing at his shoulder. But he turned toward his monitor and logged in. Jordan shrugged and did the same. Marty gave me one last big smile and set about organizing his desk. He was the last to get to work, but eventually he started tapping away at his keyboard.

I was cautiously proud of myself. Project leader for less than an hour, and my team was already on track. Maybe it was some sort of great karmic repayment for everything in my personal life falling to crud.

To test out how the information would be sorted, I needed to enter data from one of the hundreds of genealogical files the archivists were so eager to off-load into the corner of our office. I ran my fingertips over the madly tilted stack of manila folders. Opening any one of them could open my brain up to secrets that some vampire could decide were worth killing me over. It felt as if Pandora's box had been reduced to office debris. Determined to choose at random, I shoved my hand into the pile—and promptly knocked half of the stack onto the floor.

"Let me help you with that!" Marty sprang to his feet and dashed over to help me gather the displaced files from the carpet. In fact, he was so eager to rescue me from my clutter that his knee knocked my feet out from under me. Only quick reflexes and a well-placed hand against the broad side of my cubicle kept me from taking a dive.

Marty winced. "Sorry."

"That's OK. You were just trying to help." I sighed, pushing up from the floor. "Thanks."

"Are you sure we're ready for data entry?" Marty asked, eyeing the mess I'd made.

"Oh, no, I just wanted a random family file to scan," I said. "And I managed to create a file avalanche."

"It could happen to anybody," he told me, giving me a lopsided grin.

"I'll stack the rest of these. You go do your thing."

"You sure?"

I nodded while balancing the last few files on top of the stack. "I think I can be trusted not to destroy the rest of the records."

Marty laughed and sauntered back to his desk. I carefully patted the folder edges back into place, noting a bold flash of color among all that beige. I pulled the red folder from the stack, careful not to cause another collapse. The folder tab was marked "Linoge."

That seemed random enough.

I dropped back into my chair and cued up some Lorde on the music system, sliding my headphones into place. I opened the folder and found that most of the paper inside had been carefully blacked out with marker. This was not a genealogical archive folder. This was a disciplinary file. A really old disciplinary file. The paperwork inside was a photocopy, but the original had been old wrinkly parchment. What little text remained on the first page described a Pierre Linoge, a vampire who'd briefly lived in northern France in the eighteenth century but had been permanently disciplined by an earlier incarnation of the Council when his violent feeding frenzies threatened to expose the region's vampire population. And while the names of his descendants had been redacted, the good news was that the heavy editing left only the barest facts visible, making it easy to pick out the vampire's basic information that I needed to enter into the biographic program. I could at least give the index a test run.

There was one strange footnote at the bottom of Linoge's report. It was just a few lines of text: "Linoge's feeding excesses are described as contrary to his character by other vampires of good reputation. His friends note that the attacks started after he parted company with [redacted], a human known for practicing magicks both light and dark. It is possible his indiscretion was due to her influence."

"Oh, sure, blame the girlfriend," I muttered, tapping the keys.

Something about the file bothered me. Why the hell would they give us a file full of information on a dead vampire? In general, the "living" vampires were the only ones interested in tracking their descendants. And why bother giving us a file with so much information missing? Hell, the descendant information was redacted. What was the point? Maybe it was just thrown into the archive pile by mistake? It seemed unlikely, since the Council had put so much emphasis on securing the genealogical information.

"Is it working?"

Marty appeared at my elbow, making me jump, knocking a binder on top of the file. Marty was oblivious to my clumsiness, staring at me intently. I shoved the file into the binder and slid the binder into my bottom desk drawer.

"Oh, yeah, sure."

"Great job!" he exclaimed. "Guys, we made the right choice for team leader!"

Aaron and Jordan had their headphones in place and their hands on their keyboards. We probably wouldn't hear from them again until they ran out of Twizzlers.

"I'm sure they're very proud," I assured Marty.

Slowly but surely, I was coming to realize that having a grown-up job mostly meant saying things I didn't mean.

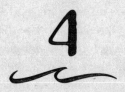

4

Until you gauge the mood of your first staff meeting, it's best just to keep your mouth closed and your head down.

—*The Office After Dark: A Guide to Maintaining a Safe, Productive Vampire Workplace*

My third day of work was momentous, not because my team managed to outline a programming proposal to submit to the regional director or because I saw Nik again but because I took part in one of the scariest freaking staff meetings in the history of employment.

Around nine p.m., just as we'd hit our stride work-wise, frumpy, prematurely gray Margaret Coggins appeared in our office and informed us that our presence was required in the conference room, immediately. But she didn't tell us why, which was ominous and super-unhelpful.

Margaret was a human clerical worker who served as Ophelia's assistant. She dressed like my fourth-grade Sunday-school teacher and seemed to have no measurable sense of humor. That made her exactly like my fourth-grade Sunday-school teacher. So far, our interactions with Margaret had been limited to her delivery of Ophelia's "best wishes" and various signed employment forms, nondisclosure reminders, and parking validations. Since she didn't mention my "little problem" in the parking lot—and my co-workers didn't seem to know about it—I supposed part of Ophelia's best wishes included the discretion she'd promised the night of the incident. I found that comforting.

Jordan was reluctant to leave work while the code was flowing, so Aaron threatened to delete all of the Gaslight Anthem from her playlists and then lured her away from her desk with a trail of Twizzlers.

"I don't like things that make me uncomfortable!" she cried plaintively, as Aaron dragged her into the hallway.

Marty shook his head at their antics while I grabbed a notebook. I wasn't sure what sort of information session or potential massacre we were being summoned to, but surely someone should be taking notes.

While we expected to be shown into the grim, windowless conference room of our orientation, we ended up falling in step with the herd of office drones past that door to a subfloor we hadn't explored during the orientation. We entered a sort of shallow amphitheater, large enough to seat the sixty or so people shuffling about awkwardly, but not so spacious that you couldn't make direct eye contact with the people standing on the dais at the front of the room. And those people happened to include Nik, who was standing behind Ophelia, a silent, expressionless tower of Russian, like Dolph Lundgren in *Rocky IV*.

While Nik's face remained impassive, I froze at the sight of him, stopping short so that Marty bumped into my back.

"Oh!" I exclaimed, as Marty grabbed my elbows to keep both of us from toppling over. "Sorry, Marty."

"This seems to happen a lot," Marty said, laughing as we dropped into our seats, just a few rows away from Nik and Ophelia.

Nik's lip drew back in the slightest of snarls, his eyes flitting toward Marty and me.

"I'm a hazard to myself and others," I confessed, giving Marty an awkward little smile, while not quite breaking eye contact with Nik.

Aaron and Jordan were already sitting with their heads bent together, whispering, speculating about the subject of the meeting.

Nik's narrowed amber eyes stared a hole through Marty, who was blissfully oblivious.

When all of the employees, humans and vampires alike, were seated, the lights dimmed, and Ophelia cleared her throat pointedly. I couldn't imagine what had prompted her change from her usual "innocent teenage extra who wandered off the set of *Mad Men*" wardrobe choices, but she was wearing a tight black silk blouse and black leather pants tailored so close I could have counted the change in her pockets—if she'd had pockets or bothered carrying cash, which she did not. With her hair slicked back in a high pony-tail, she looked like a really classy dominatrix.

The employees' murmuring came to an abrupt halt as Ophelia crossed her arms and tapped the toe of her knee-high black leather boot. I glanced at Nik, whose eyes rolled ever so slightly toward the ceiling at Ophelia's dramatics.

"Good evening. I'm so sorry to have disrupted your work to call you here," Ophelia announced, in a tone that suggested she wasn't sorry at all. "Especially since our summer employees are just now finding their footing in our little family. But it seems that some of our staff are not as appreciative of our trust and generosity as I hoped they would be."

Marty and I shared a confused side-eye. It was natural, I supposed, to wonder whether your boss was talking about you in a situation like this. I tried to remember anything I might have done in the last two days of employment that might have provoked this response. But all I'd done was stab someone in the parking lot. No, wait, I had also looked into server folders that I wasn't supposed to—which was definitely a violation of the Council's trust—on my first full day of work. But surely all the Council officials knew about was the stabbing.

No, wait, that sounded bad, too.

I squirmed in my seat as Ophelia announced dramatically, "Someone in this room abused the resources of the Council. Someone here used his or her position to steal from us. One of the people sitting in this room is a thief."

I relaxed ever so slightly. Of stabbing and snooping I was guilty, but I definitely wasn't a thief. I would worry about my shaky morality scale later.

"I would like to introduce you to my associate, Nikolai Dragomirov," Ophelia continued, gesturing to Nik with a flourish. "Mr. Dragomirov is here as a consultant to help us find the thief. And trust me when I say there will be no lying to Mr. Dragomirov. He will find you out, so it would be better for you to just come forward now in hopes of a lesser chastisement."

Nik nodded, back to "gorgeous Russian statue man" mode. Somehow I didn't think Ophelia's idea of a chastisement would be a rap on the knuckles with a wooden spoon and a scolding. What exactly was this "thief" supposed to have stolen from the Council? The World Council for the Equal Treatment of the Undead had considerable resources, but I didn't think much of the vampires' vast worldwide fortune was being stored here in Half-Moon Hollow. Then again, this complex had about ten subfloors that we weren't even allowed to talk about, so I supposed a Smaug-style treasure room wasn't out of the question.

And how exactly was Nik supposed to help ferret out the thief? Cal had mentioned that Nik was an old friend, and Cal had served as an investigator for the Council for years. Did Nik do actual police-type investigative work? Or did he have some sort of special vampire power? Was he a mind-reader, like Jane? Considering the thoughts I'd had around him, I sincerely hoped not.

Suddenly, Nik glanced toward me, as if he *could* hear me thinking about him.

My eyes went the size of a venti lid.

Damn it.

"I need Sandra Matthews, Elliot Reyes, Su Tran, and Joseph McNichol to come up to the dais, please," Ophelia said.

Slowly but surely, four Council employees made their way down the aisles to the stage. Sandra Matthews and Elliot Reyes were humans. But Su Tran and Joseph McNichol had the pallor and sharp features of the undead. McNichol, in fact, seemed paler than the usual vampire, but I supposed that could be an illusion caused by his pale blond hair and eerily gray eyes.

All four wore the same suspicious expression and ID badges that marked them as members of the "operations" department. They were in charge of ordering supplies, processing the center's mail, and keeping us all in creature comforts such as fresh magazines in the waiting room.

"In the past four months, someone has stolen more than nine thousand dollars in copier paper, thumbtacks, and other office supplies from this office and sold them on eBay for a deeply discounted price. Imagine our shock and disappointment when the Web site's fraud-management unit traced the account user's IP address back to a computer in the operations department."

I snorted. I couldn't help it. All this fuss over copier paper? From the way Ophelia was carrying on, I thought someone had stolen the crown jewels. Nik eyed me and gave me the slightest shake of his head. I hid my giggles with a cough. If Nik was concerned, this was the time to engage my little-used discretion function.

"And since all four of you have access to that computer, we decided to be egalitarian about this process." Ophelia held up a small parcel and opened it, fishing out a large box of binder clips. "We ordered this gross of binder clips through the unscrupulous user's account and had it shipped to a local post-office box. This shameless, greedy thief thought nothing of using the Council's own shipping supplies to mail the package across town!

"Mr. Dragomirov will be able to identify the person who handled it—" Ophelia broke off as McNichol bolted from the stage, vaulted over the end of the first row at vampire speed, and tried to escape through the back exit. Unfortunately for him, Peter Crown was waiting at the top of the amphitheater. Crown caught him by the throat and slammed him to the ground.

I shuddered. I did not like Mr. Crown. Turned in his mid-forties, during an age when young people shut up and did what they were told, he was by far the crankiest member of the local Council. He reminded me of every math teacher I'd had in high school. And I definitely didn't envy poor Joseph, whose throat was now under Mr. Crown's shiny, stylish shoe.

"I do so hate to be interrupted." Ophelia sighed. "Well, since Mr. McNichol seems to have confessed by cowardice, I suppose the rest of you are dismissed. Unless, of course, you were accomplices in Mr. McNichol's scheme." She looked to Nik, who shook his head. Ophelia rolled her eyes. "Sit down."

Meanwhile, Mr. Crown had dragged Joseph to the dais. Nik took a step back, separating himself from the spectacle now that his role seemed obsolete. Crown dropped a cowering Joseph at Ophelia's feet. I glanced around the room. While the other interns seemed as confused as I was, the long-term employees were restless, uncomfortable, unwilling to look at the stage. What the hell was going on?

"Joseph McNichol, you are six hundred and forty-two years old," Ophelia hissed, as Crown grabbed Joseph's fair hair and yanked his head back. "Old enough to know better than to steal from the Council. Did you think I wouldn't find out? Did you think I wouldn't see you taking what was mine from under my very nose? I see everything. Nothing escapes my notice. You would do well to remember that."

Ophelia produced a pair of flat-nose pliers from her boot, a perfectly ordinary-looking household tool. But Joseph started thrashing around in Mr. Crown's grip, howling when Crown gripped his jaw and forced his mouth open. Crown took a vial of red liquid—blood—from his pocket and waved it in front of Joseph's face. His fangs popped out with a *snick*.

"You know the punishment for stealing from the

Council," Ophelia intoned. In all this commotion, Nik didn't move a muscle, either to help Joseph or to help Mr. Crown contain the office-supply thief. He didn't seem at all bothered by what was about to play out just a few feet away from him. What had he seen over the course of his life that this didn't give him the slightest pause? Hell, my teeth were perfectly safe, and I still had my jaw clenched in sympathy for Joseph.

"Noo!" Joseph shouted. "N—"

But Ophelia stopped his protest, gripping his left fang in the pliers. I'd expected her to yank the canine out of his mouth by force, but instead, she squeezed the handle brutally, crushing the tooth into powder. Almost everyone in the room seemed to wince at once, ducking away, covering their mouths with their hands. Joseph howled in pain, screaming as Ophelia took the other fang in hand and smashed it, too.

"Why not just pull it out?" Jordan said quietly.

I shook my head. "Later," I murmured. Jordan nodded and leaned back in her seat, keeping her mouth clamped shut.

Thanks to a youth misspent around vampires, I knew exactly why Ophelia didn't yank the fang. Crushing it was more painful. The nerve ending in the root would remain, but since fangs were the one part of the vampire that didn't regenerate, the tooth would never grow back. The exposed nerve would remain raw and alive, flaring painfully with every brush or bump. And when he was hungry or stimulated, his "phantom" fangs would extend, which would be even more excruciating. Unless it was capped—which I was sure Ophelia wouldn't allow—it would go on for years, an eternity of relentless, throbbing pain.

Over copy paper.

My new boss was evil. Pure, unadulterated evil.

"That will be all, Mr. McNichol. You will be continuing your employment, without pay, for the next six months. At the end of the six-month period, we will review your performance. If it is considered subpar, you will be terminated."

"Somehow, I don't think she means 'fired,'" Marty whispered sotto voce. I shushed him, patting his arm. When I looked up, Nik was frowning again.

Mr. Crown dragged a groaning Joseph from the dais. Ophelia turned a relatively pleasant smile on the audience, and all of the summer employees practically recoiled in their seats. "Now, just a reminder, please respect the assigned parking spaces. If you do not have an assigned space, there's a reason. If you don't like the situation, work harder. Do not touch items in the office refrigerators that do not belong to you. If it's not your blood, don't drink it. Friday is College Shirt Day. You will be permitted to wear a T-shirt or sweatshirt advertising your alma mater, and blue jeans, which is an exception to our usual dress code. I know you will all gladly participate in this frivolity. That will be all. Please have a pleasant, productive evening."

The auditorium was completely silent. None of us dared move, afraid it would draw Ophelia's attention.

"Get back to work!" she barked. "Now."

Suddenly invigorated, we rose from our seats and scrambled over one another to get back to our offices.

"Well, I guess I should take that red stapler out of my messenger bag, huh?" Marty joked.

I jostled his arm. "Shh, Marty, now's not the time for snark. The creatures with the superhearing will not appreciate your special brand of coping humor."

"What did we just see?" Aaron whispered fiercely. "What the hell was that?"

I pressed my finger to my lips again and shook my head, because discretion was necessary and because I just didn't know. Why the spectacle over stolen office supplies? Why not just handle Joseph's theft in a less humiliating fashion? Was it some sort of demonstration for the summer kids? Was Ophelia trying to show us what happened to Council employees who stepped out of line? Or was this more personal? Ophelia had mentioned over and over what happened to "people who take from me." Was she referring to Jamie in a none-too-subtle way? Was she planning to crush my teeth with pliers for helping her boyfriend fill out college applications?

That seemed like an overreaction.

I glanced over my shoulder down the hall, to where Nik stood, watching as I herded my teammates into our office. His expression was the very definition of inscrutable. I couldn't tell if he was upset or intrigued or trying to figure out a way to jump me again. Either way, I shut my office door in his face, which was probably rude, but I was team leader. I felt an obligation to protect my underlings and their canine teeth.

Marty seemed completely unmoved by the display in the amphitheater. He plopped down in his office chair and slipped on his headphones as if nothing had happened. Aaron and Jordan, on the other hand, were shaky and pale. Jordan leaned against her desk, arms crossed, chewing nervously on her thumbnail.

"Is it wrong that I'm on the verge of freaking the hell out and walking away?" Aaron asked. "I mean, what the hell was that? We joke around about vampires, 'Haha, they'll kill you if your parallel parking offends them.' Because for years, that was supposed to be how they solved their problems—violence, violence, violence. But that was . . . over office supplies? That just seems petty and weird."

"I know that guy was a thief, but I felt so bad for him," Jordan said. "I don't know if I feel safe here now. What if I accidentally eat someone's Hot Pocket? They might waterboard me."

"Look, you two, I understand that you're shaken up. That's normal, expected, evidence that you have a soul—which, as someone who shares a very small office space with you, I find very comforting. But this, this imbalanced, paranoid thing, this is exactly why Ophelia pulled that stunt. She wants you to worry, to overanalyze every decision you make for fear of stepping the tiniest bit out of line. She wants to scare you into being a model employee. You know how they say that on the first day of prison, you should find the biggest guy in the room and kick his ass, for intimidation's sake? Well, this is like prison. We are working in a version of *Oz* with no full-frontal Christopher Meloni but better AV equipment. You just have to decide if that's something you can tolerate."

"How are you so calm about this?" Aaron asked.

"I've lived with a vampire for the past couple of years. Some of my best friends—and family—are vampires. I'm used to their tendency toward violent hyperbole. I don't necessarily like it, but I've learned to deal with it, because, overall, vampires are people just like us. And while some of them are card-carrying psychos, some of them are pretty awesome. You just have to tread carefully around them until you figure out which type you're dealing with. But you have to decide for yourselves what you're willing to accept. If you have any questions or concerns, I'm here for you. At least, I will be, after I go and get you some morale-building caffeine."

"You're getting us coffee?" Jordan asked.

"Yeah, my treat. There's a good place across the street, far superior to the swill they serve in the break room," I said, grabbing my purse from my desk drawer. I'd become quite familiar with the Perk-U-Later, the little independent coffee shop adjacent to the Council office. After she'd started Beeline, Iris had parked me there on the rare occasion she had to stop by the office while I was with her. She didn't want teenage me anywhere near the vampire hierarchy.

Which, of course, turned out to be pointless, because I was sort of a pain in the ass, in terms of little sisters.

"We face a moral crisis, and she's getting us free coffee?" Aaron muttered.

"We definitely picked the right team leader," Jordan whispered back.

Balancing a purse on one arm and four not-cheap coffee drinks in a flimsy foam carrier with the other wasn't as easy as it sounded. As I made my way across the darkened downtown street, I was convinced that the weight of Jordan's drink, which was more than half sugar, was throwing off my equilibrium. I'd almost made it to the staff entrance when a voice sounded from a startlingly close distance behind me. "Miss Scanlon."

I jumped, dropping the coffee carrier. Nik's hands shot out with lightning speed and caught it without spilling a drop. He grinned down at me, his stupid perfect white teeth lighting up his whole stupid perfect face. And I felt all of those reasonable, nonsuicidal instincts melt like the now nonexistent whipped cream on my coworkers' coffees. He was towering over me, trapping me between his body and the grimy brick wall opposite the staff entrance. He wore a blinding-white button-up shirt that perfectly framed the hollow of his throat. It had been easy to stay somewhat emotionally neutral when he was up on the dais, but now, up close . . . I felt badass for not swooning.

I wondered if it would send the wrong message to trace a near-stranger's throat-hollow with my tongue.

Probably.

More than likely.

These lattes were never going to make it to my co-workers.

"I'm not supposed to talk to you," I told him in the sternest tone I could muster.

"Do you always do what you are supposed to do?"

"When advice involves warnings like 'Stay away from the guy who assaulted you in a parking lot,' I give it a courtesy listen. Particularly after I see you standing in as Ophelia's guard dog at the world's scariest staff meeting."

"I am no one's dog," he said, his voice a low purr.

"You're right. Dogs are loyal, guileless creatures. You strike me as more of a cat person," I retorted.

"I do not know how to interpret that."

"Good. After all the messed-up, potentially scarring things I've seen today, I think leaving you confused and off-balance is the only thing that has the potential to make me happy."

"You are prickly when you are flustered, are you not?"

I stared at him, wondering whether I could get to my hairbrush stake before he realized why I was digging around in my purse. And yes, I recognized that this was a wide swing of the pendulum from wanting to lick his Adam's apple. I blamed hormones and mild dental PTSD.

"So what are we going to do?" he asked. "With you barred from speaking to me and me unable to remember you?" When he saw my eyebrows shoot up, he hastily added, "To my overwhelming regret."

I honestly didn't know. I didn't trust him. Obviously, I found Nik interesting. I wanted to know more about him, without having to break Council computer-use policies. So I was willing to spend more time around him, as long as I was heavily armed.

"Have you had episodes like this before? Memory loss, blackouts, random fits of violence against an unsuspecting and undeserving target?"

"No."

"Do you think you're sick? Or brain-damaged?"

"You know, in five hundred years, you are the first human to ask me that," he growled, his voice gravelly and low.

"Oh, don't try to pull the hostile-vampire routine now," I told him. "Once I stab you, it sort of takes away your mystique."

"I doubt I am brain-damaged," he deadpanned. "But it is not as if I can get a diagnostic scan. My brain does not run on the same electrical impulses as yours. Besides, this whole situation stinks of the supernatural. So where does that leave us?"

"I have no idea," I said, shaking my head. "This is a situation that defies even your twisty vampire logic."

He smirked. "True. I do not know how it is possible that I do not remember being sent to your college campus to, er, intervene on Cal's behalf. But I read back over my letters and found—"

"Wait, did you say letters?"

"Yes, letters. Correspondence. It is what people have used to stay in contact for centuries."

"Yes, but now they have this thing called the Internet, and we use it to send the electronic version of letters. They're called e-mails. They work faster and kill fewer trees."

"I know about e-mails." He sniffed. "I do not trust them. You never know if they have arrived, and they are too easy to access by hacksters."

"Hackers," I corrected.

"I have adjusted to modern conveniences enough to buy a cell phone. That is enough."

"So you haul around a huge briefcase full of letters with you." I snorted. "That makes way more sense. Let me guess, you run Netscape Navigator on your laptop, huh?"

Nik frowned.

"You don't have a *laptop*?" I cried. "Even *Cal* has a laptop! What are you, a Luddite?"

"My work requires more hands-on involvement. I manage my professional and personal life with less fuss and fewer means to track me. We are wandering away from the point," he reminded me. "According to my *letters*, Cal requested that I visit your campus, and there is a reply from me, promising that I would, so I must have done it. I would not have broken my word to Cal."

"So you don't remember anything about me?"

"I do not remember anything about the month of

December," he said. "Nothing. And that is not normal. Usually, I spend Christmas tucked away at some remote cabin with a . . ."

There went my eyebrow again. "Yes?"

"A carefully selected, special lady friend," he said, clearing his throat. "But I do not remember that. I do not remember anything around that time. I do not know what is happening to me. But I think you are the key to finding out."

"So that's why you want to spend time with me? So you can figure out your Swiss-cheese memory? That's flattering."

He didn't answer. Instead, he was looking at my earrings, the little flowers made of moonstone, the same earrings I'd admired in a shop window right before my forgotten kiss with Nik. The same earrings that mysteriously showed up on our front porch on Christmas, right *after* my forgotten kiss with Nik. The same earrings I'd worn almost every day since, because I thought they meant something. His brow furrowed, as if he was concentrating on them. "Those are pretty baubles. Were they a gift?"

"You don't remember them?"

He frowned. "No, should I?"

My heart sank. "No."

I'd assumed that he'd given me the earrings. But what if it had been someone else? What if it was Cal or Jane, and I just hadn't thanked them? Now I felt foolish *and* rude.

"Why does that make you so sad?" he asked. "I hate

that I could be the one putting that heartbreaking expression on your face."

"It would be really hard to explain," I told him. "And it would cost me a lot."

"How?"

"In terms of my dignity?" I laughed. "How would you like it if you'd had this knee-trembling, paradigmshifting kiss with someone, and they didn't even remember it?"

"In my defense, you know nothing of my life, my history. And I doubt very much that Cal has told you anything of interest."

I nodded. "I know that you enjoy biting people, and your name sounds Russian."

He smirked. "Maybe that is all you need to know."

"That wasn't an answer." When he gave me a blithe, maddeningly confident smile, I poked him in the ribs—really hard.

He yowled. "And you complain about *my* fits of violence?" But he grinned—a real, amused expression of joy—and his face looked vaguely human.

"How about, for everything you tell me about yourself, I will grant you information." Said smile became downright filthy, so I added, "Nothing dirty. And just one question, because I have to get back to work."

"Who was that boy you were sitting with at the meeting?"

"That's the one you went with?" I asked, leaning closer to him, not entirely unaware that it made the dip in my camisole fall open just a little bit, exposing a hint of cleavage. "Of all of the depths you could have plumbed, of all of the dark secrets you could have asked me to share, you picked 'Who was that boy?'"

"Well, now that you mention it." His tongue swept over his bottom lip as if he was reconsidering, and then he added quickly, "Yes, that is what I want to know."

We engaged in a facial-expression standoff, in which I squinted at him and he did not appear to be affected by my scrutiny at all. This would be so much easier if he was some alpha-male tool. But here he was, being all charming and rakish, and rakish vampires seemed to be my kryptonite.

I blamed Iris and her stash of romance novels for my even knowing what the word "rakish" meant. I rolled my eyes and told him, "'That boy' is Marty. He works in my department. And for wasting your request on a boy who doesn't mean anything to either of us, I should be allowed to silver-spray you again."

"Or, instead, we could do this," he said, bending his head toward me, and gently brushed his lips across mine. I stiffened, lips parting as I gasped against his mouth. He took advantage, sliding his tongue between my lips and teasing my own into a slow, tangling dance.

After a long moment, I pulled back. "You remember anything yet?"

He shook his head, ducking to recapture my mouth. He pulled my bottom lip between his teeth, nibbling lightly. I moaned, wrinkling the hell out of his shirt as I gripped it and pulled him closer to me. I could feel his fangs growing into sharp little points, scraping against my lip. My breath caught as a tiny bead of blood welled up and he lapped it away with his tongue.

He growled, palming my hip in his hand and pushing me against the wall. My cardigan rode up, and my back scraped against the brick, but that only put my nerves on edge. Every neuron seemed to fire at once, making everything I felt ten times more intense. His mouth worked at the little wound on my lip, his movements becoming quicker and more frantic.

I couldn't do this, right? I couldn't just make out with a vampire right outside my office door. I was sure there were security cameras around somewhere, and this was not the sort of thing I wanted getting back to Ophelia. Not to mention, I didn't want to get a reputation as a willing fang-bunny among my undead colleagues. Plus, the man didn't even own a laptop. How was I going to find common ground with someone who was neither a PC *nor* a Mac guy? We were doomed.

Right, OK, I'll push him away in three . . . two . . . just one more kiss . . . Seriously, this is the last one. The next-to-last one.

Finally, I pushed him away, and he was panting, staring at my mouth with the sort of hunger that tested my knees' resolve all over again.

And the repeat performance of the paradigm-twirling kiss was interrupted by the screech of tires. The Dorkmobile, Iris's bright yellow minivan, emblazoned with the Beeline logo, was barreling down the street toward us.

Dang it.

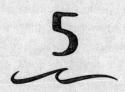

5

Little annoyances will build up in any workplace. Keep the big picture in mind when filing complaints with HR. Is that stolen stapler *really* worth the hassle of a severed jugular?

—*The Office After Dark: A Guide to Maintaining a Safe, Productive Vampire Workplace*

Even in the dark, I could see Iris fuming behind the wheel of the van.

"Oh, hell." I sighed as Nik shoved me behind his back, his body silhouetted against the headlights of the Dorkmobile.

Cal and Iris climbed out of the van. Cal was eyeing the security cameras warily, while Iris slammed the driver's-side door. She was dressed in her usual work outfit of a slim black pencil skirt and a sage-colored cardigan but somehow managed to look intimidating as she stormed toward us.

"Gigi!" Iris cried. "Seriously?"

"What are you even doing here, Iris? This is not normal sibling behavior."

"We were bringing you dinner," Iris said, holding up a yellow Beeline lunch cooler, which the drivers typically used to transport vampire clients' blood. "To try to make amends for crossing a few lines the other night. But now we find you doing exactly what we asked you not to do! Where is your head, Gigi?"

"Argh," I groaned, thumping my head between Nik's shoulder blades.

"It is rather sweet that they are concerned for you," Nik whispered over his shoulder. I jabbed him in the ribs, making him add, "Though clearly annoying and very wrong."

Iris dashed around Nik and pulled me toward the car before whirling around to stick her finger in Nik's face. "You stay away from my sister, do you hear me? You stay away from her, or I will end you. I will find a way."

"You are very young, and you are Cal's wife, so I will forgive the finger-pointing," Nik said. "But do not presume to threaten me."

"Hey, let's not escalate this beyond what we can salvage with apologies," I insisted.

"And you are very old," Iris said, her voice going deadly quiet, as if I hadn't even spoken. "And I think you are underestimating the resourcefulness of some-one who worked with your kind for years before she was turned and knows exactly how to sneak into a sleeping vampire's home to use a *variety* of tricks to make sure that vampire never wakes up again."

"Aaaaaand now it's gone too far." I sighed, rolling my eyes toward the moonlit sky.

"So, Gigi," Iris said, pursing her lips, "is your death wish so strong that you've decided to lie to us full-time now?"

"It wasn't so much lying as—" I began.

"It was lying. You left out major chunks of truth. The effect is the same. Listen, I'm trying to stay calm. I'm not going to yell or act like a banshee. But this can't continue until we figure out what is happening to Nik," she said, her voice quiet and more Iris-like than I'd heard her in days. "I don't think I'm being unreasonable here, Geeg. It's not like you're madly in love. You barely know each other."

Ouch.

I looked up at Nik, hoping for some reaction from him. But his face was inscrutable. Stupid handsome vampires capable of suppressing their facial emotions.

"Just 'barely know each other' for a few more weeks . . . or months. Maybe years. Just until we know what's going on. Or, you know, you meet someone else."

"Subtle, Iris," I muttered.

"Nik, we have been friends for a long time, but I cannot allow you near Gigi," Cal said, urging Iris back toward the car. "Also, we've talked about you kissing her. I believe the words 'ass-kicking of an immortal lifetime' were used."

"I would not hurt her," Nik insisted.

"Not consciously, but I can't trust you not to lose control over yourself again."

"Well, that is going to be difficult, considering that Ophelia has hired me on for a long-term assignment at the Council offices, where Gigi will be working."

Before Iris could even open her mouth, I told her, "I'm not quitting!"

"Well, you are not to see Nik outside of the office," Cal told me. "And when you are in the office, you must have at least one vampire chaperone to watch over you."

"Cal, you can't ask me to—I'm an adult. I am not sixteen years old anymore!" I cried.

"No, but secretly associating with a vampire when you were sixteen didn't work out for you, either, did it?" he asked.

My eyes narrowed while Nik sent a questioning look my way. "That was a low blow, Cal."

Cal raised his hands. "You're right. You're right. I'm being unreasonable." He suddenly grabbed Nik by the collar and tossed him toward the open van door.

"Where are you taking him?"

"Away!" Cal said.

"You can't do this!" I exclaimed.

"It will be fine, Gigi," Nik said, sounding almost bored as Cal slung the van door shut. "Go back to work. I will see you soon."

"No, you won't!" Iris yelled, and pulled the van out of the lot with a squeal of rubber.

As the Dorkmobile's taillights disappeared into the

night, I tilted my head up to the sky and prayed for patience and the strength not to smack all of my vampire loved ones with a tack hammer. I glanced down at the Styrofoam carrier, which was resting safely on the little concrete pad outside the employee entrance.

I hoped my coworkers liked cold coffee.

I was hiding under my covers, because that's what grown-ups did when they were faced with problems, right?

I'd managed to finish my workday with some dignity, delivering coffee to my grateful coworkers and doing some actual work. And I'd avoided having any of my teeth forcibly pulled, so I considered that a win. Coming home and avoiding contact with either Iris or Cal, who were both working in their office because three a.m. was the middle of the workday for vampires, was another mark in my victory column.

I put on my softest, comfiest pajamas and climbed under the covers, pretending the previous twelve hours were a surreal and upsetting dream. All except for the second kiss with Nik, which, again, made the old paradigm its bitch.

And I could not explain that in a rational manner, endorsed by a sense of self-preservation. Nik was the opposite of every person I'd been attracted to in the past. From what I could remember, John had played up the wounded, soulful, brooding creature of the night thing. Ben was the poster child for boys you'd gladly allow your daughter to date. And Nik was kind of, well, untrustworthy, but at least he was up front about it.

I liked it. I liked his weird, dry sense of humor. I liked that he called me on sassing him. I liked that he seemed to take my threats of violence seriously, instead of considering them cute, like the other members of Team Vampire did. He was the one vampire in Half-Moon Hollow who hadn't seen me go through my awkward adolescent Gigi phase.

The irony that I'd mocked Iris's fascination with paperback romances for years—and I was basically infatuated with the template for every "naughty duke" cover hero she'd ever swooned over—was not lost on me.

The last thought I had before drifting off was that once she got over being wicked pissed at me, Iris was going to mock me mercilessly. And I was indeed drifting, floating in that unstable twilight space between sleep and waking, where everything is formless and quiet and dizzy. Images floated freely through my head. My desk at the office was perched on the edge of an abyss, and unless I continued working, I would fall off. Then the desk became a table at Jane's shop, Specialty Books, where stacks of file folders loomed over my head. Nik's wry grin became Marty's strangely confident face as we shuffled out of the staff meeting. My delicious midnight coffee was thick and metallic in my mouth, like sucking on pennies. I threw the cup away from my lips and watched it splatter the walls of my bedroom in thick rivers of red. The very sight of the mess was enough to send me running. But now I was sprinting down the hallway at the Council offices with an athame, a double-edged ceremonial blade, clutched in my hand, the gray walls melting all around me into fog. And even though I couldn't see anyone in the offices, I could hear the *click-clack* of computer keys. Someone was typing, and from the sound of it, the code was angry. *Click-clack-clackity-clack-click.* I turned corners at random, searching for a door, an elevator, anything that would get me away from some invisible menace that seemed to be hovering closer and closer at my heels. *Click-click-clack-click-clackity-clack.* I was afraid to look back, afraid to see what might be chasing me. I turned again, and there was Nik, standing at the end of the hallway, in front of the staff exit, and he was roaring with rage, baring his bloodstained fangs.

Clack-click-clack-clack-clackity-click.

I bolted up from bed, clutching the comforter to my chest, sucking in deep, gulping breaths, as if I'd been shoved underwater. I threw the covers aside and rubbed my hands over my face.

Click-clack-clackity-clack.

What the fracking frack?

I turned toward the source of the noise and saw Nik, with his knees propped up on the planter box outside my window, tapping his fingernails lightly against the glass.

"Ni— Wha!" I hissed, clapping my hand over my mouth so my shouts wouldn't draw attention from Cal and Iris.

Now that he had my attention, Nik waved casually, as if it was totally normal to be balancing on a planter outside a girl's bedroom window. Using every trick Cal had taught me, I crept noiselessly over to the window. My room was the only one in the house without sunproof shades, but it also required its own keypad and a thumbprint scanner to open from the *inside*. So Nik had to wait a while for me to negotiate with my brother-in-law's insane security system.

"Good evening, *sladkaya*." He smiled as I opened the window, as if butter wouldn't melt in his mouth. His soft, sensual, filthy mouth.

"Are you nuts?" I hissed. "My surrogate parents have superpowers!"

He hopped gracefully through the open window, landing catlike on silent feet. "I only wanted to see if you were sleeping well after the stressful events of this evening."

"Shh!" I hissed, pressing my fingers against his lips. He parted them ever so slightly and gently bit down on my fingertip. I used my free hand to tweak his nose, making him shake his head.

"Do not worry about being overheard. Cal is currently distracting your sister with a very thorough massage."

I recoiled as if I'd been slapped in the face with a salmon. "Gross. And it should have been clear to you the minute you looked through my window that I was sleeping just fine," I told him. "And if you think you are going to sneak into my room to watch me sleep, I am not above stabbing you again."

"It did not look as though you were sleeping just fine at all," he told me, with an innocent expression far too practiced to be natural. "You were tossing back and forth and muttering to yourself. What were you saying?"

"I don't know, I was asleep," I murmured. "Now, get away from my window before we get into trouble."

"You are not what you would call a 'morning person,' are you, my Gigi? How long would I have to wait after you wake to have a civilized conversation with you?"

"Well, if you keep up that condescending tone, it could be a while," I told him. "And if you make enough noise to draw Cal or Iris up here, a lot longer."

I was suddenly very self-conscious of my room, which had not changed since my senior year of high school. It was the one area of the house left untouched during Cal and Iris's remodeling rampage, because Iris knew I needed to come back to a space that was familiar. While I loved that she knew me so well, for the first time, I wished that she'd updated the denim-blue walls, the quilted blue-and-white bedspread, the beaten-up bookshelves containing my old beaten-up paperbacks. And then there was my pinboard, which also hadn't changed since high school, with the same pictures of me with my friends at volleyball games, parties, and dances. And pictures of Ben. What felt like an inordinate number of pictures of me with Ben.

Aw, hell.

Why hadn't I pulled those down? Stupid ex-boyfriend clutter blindness. I thought I'd gotten rid of all of those.

"I pictured something a little more genie-in-a-bottle, big, round bed covered in pillows and scarves." He scanned my pink checked pajama pants and tank top. "And I pictured you wearing less."

I grinned. "Oh, you did?"

"A lot less," he said. "And I have imagined it frequently over the past few days, fantasized about it shamelessly."

I ran the tip of my tongue along the blunt edges of my canine teeth. They weren't as brilliantly white or razor-sharp as his, but the action certainly caught his attention, if the dilated golden glow of his eyes was any indicator. "Did you, now?"

"Shamelessly," he said again, bending to kiss me.

"No, none of that," I told him, dodging him. "We need to talk without the distraction of your sexy mouth."

He frowned with said sexy mouth. "That does not make any sense."

"You know what I mean."

"No, I do not. But I would like to. Why do we not go outside for a conversation, so you feel more comfortable speaking at full volume?"

"Eh," I said, letting the corners of my mouth tug down as I glanced out the window.

"It is a lovely night," he added, in a lilting, crooning tone.

"This is literally how every horror movie starts. Also, you've attacked me before. I know it seems petty to harp on that, but . . . I think I will anyway."

"Are you always this stubborn?"

I nodded. "Yes."

"If you are worried about getting out of the house unnoticed, I can hold you as I jump to the ground from the window."

I arched an eyebrow. "My brother-in-law put me through ninja training. You don't think he taught me how to land safely from a second-story jump?"

He grinned. "You do not like being patronized, do you?"

"No, which is why they call it 'patronizing,' with the negative connation."

"I know the connotation. I have spoken English for many years," he insisted, more than a little affronted.

I shushed him. "I know, that's not—OK, I'll jump, but maybe hop down there and be ready, just in case."

"Excellent," he said, swooshing out of my room like a gust of wind.

I peered down from my window at the handsome blond man beckoning with a fang-tipped smile. Like many a damsel before me, I wondered at the wisdom of joining my moonlit paramour. A smart woman would have smiled, waved good night, and *not* joined the man who'd recently attempted to maul her on a midnight stroll.

And yet . . .

"I am not a smart person," I muttered, slipping into

my sneakers, which were a lovely complement to my pink gingham pajama pants and tank top. I braced my arms against the windowsill. It was maybe fifteen feet to the ground. I cut the difference, dangling from the planter box ever so briefly and dropping to the soft grass on both feet with a quiet *oof*.

Oh, thank Cthulhu that worked, because otherwise, I would be very embarrassed.

I wriggled both ankles to make sure they were intact. I listened for some weird alarm from Cal to sound or for Iris to come screaming out of the house.

Nothing.

Nik smiled and offered me his arm. It was all I could do not to hold my pajama leg up like a hoop skirt.

"I think I owe you information," he said, as we sauntered through Iris's elaborate garden. In high summer, her beloved flower beds were bursting with night-blooming plants: delicately scented jasmine, proud, trumpetlike moonflower, and night gladiolus (in my honor, thank you very much). Cal and Sam even dug a small pond in the center of the yard so she could plant night-blooming water lilies, in bright pinks and white. Thanks to Cal's influence, it reminded me of Persephone's garden, delicate and beautiful but still shrouded in the darkness of the underworld. Iris, a lifelong gardener, was careful to mix some color into her palette, the sturdy pink evening primrose and flaring yellow of narrow-leaved sundrops, to remind her of the joys of daytime living even while the moonlight reflected, bright and brilliant, against the petals.

Even though she clearly loved her life with Cal, even though I knew that vampirism was the only option if she wanted a long-term commitment with him, I couldn't help but feel a little sad for my sister, having lost the sun, cut off from the growth cycle that had meant so much to her. I wondered if I would be able to make the best of it, as she had; if I would be able to give up feeling the sun on my face, the crackle of popcorn on my tongue, the velvety softness of chocolate. Probably not; Iris had always been better at adapting.

For now, I was grateful that the scents and colors gave me something to cling to, to focus on, rather than the pounding of my nervous heart. I was counting on the droning of crickets to drown it out for Nik's sensitive ears.

Nik folded his arms behind his back as we walked, with a strange, almost military stance that made me wonder whether he was used to more formal "walk-and-talks" or he just didn't know what to do with his hands. We wandered closer to the edge of the woods, ducking into the trees.

I stopped just a few feet in, far enough that Iris wouldn't be able to see us if she glanced out the window but not so far that I couldn't see the lights of the house. That counted as some semblance of common sense, right?

Nik cleared his throat, leaning back against a tree. Despite my desire to look just as casual, I did not want to risk bark scrapes or getting my hair caught in low-hanging branches. Nik tilted his head, studying me. "If I recall, the last time we were together, you were interrupted before you could ask me anything."

"I suppose my first question would have to be, are you an evil vampire hell-bent on my death and/or destruction?" I retorted with more snark than I probably deserved to use.

"I am not evil, that I am aware of," he said evenly, though he sounded as if he was about to laugh. "And I do not think I am hell-bent on your destruction, though my actions apparently lead you to believe otherwise."

"Which, I suppose, is your way of saying that you don't know why you're going into anti-Gigi fugue states," I muttered.

"I really have no idea. But for now, can we pretend that we are two normal people on a normal outing, in which we are exchanging the background information one would expect to learn when one of them is not blacking out large portions of his history?"

"You mean the kind of conversation that usually takes place *before* getting to second base with somebody?"

He leaned forward, trapping me against the trunk of a large oak tree by placing a hand on either side of my head. "I am not familiar with the base system, but I am fairly certain we did not get to any of the interesting ones. As a man, I insist that I would remember touching a body like yours. The sense memory alone would be enough to carry through to my conscious memory."

He flashed that megawatt grin at me, and my lady bits did a little happy dance. It just wasn't fair. The man should come with a warning label. "Caution: May Cause Panties to Spontaneously Combust."

OK, Scanlon, you are a grown, modern woman, with plenty of practice controlling your hormones. This is no different from any date with any attractive man. You just have to set boundaries and keep the blood directed above your waist. You'll be fine. Now, keep him at a distance, so you can concentrate on producing words of more than one syllable.

I reached up to toy with the collar of his shirt. "Well, I'm combining the lovely languid kisses with the aggressive biting attempts, which rounds up to second."

Traitorous lady bits!

Clearly, the parts of my brain not controlled by pheromones had lost the fight. They were probably tied up and shoved into a storage space somewhere in my oculomotor section, the part of my brain that controlled eyelash fluttering and giving Nik the "come closer" looks. Stupid trampy brain parts.

Nik's nose brushed against the curve of my forehead, running along my hairline. "What do you want to know?"

Nik knelt to the ground, silent in the dry, rain-deprived grass. Fear flared through me like a warning bell. What if this was some weird sex thing I wasn't ready for? What if he sank his fangs into my thigh? He slid off the rubber ballet flats I used as house shoes and dropped them to the ground. Yeah, that didn't make me feel much better, in terms of potentially weird sexual things.

Even in the moonlight filtering through the overhead canopy of leaves, I could see the iridescent red polish on my toes, with little golden House Lannister lions painted on my big toes and *R-O-A-R* written on the others. His eyebrows rose in surprise.

"I noticed these before, in your bedroom. As much as I want to use my question on something profound, this begs explanation," he said, waggling my foot.

"Jane and I paint our toes with the different house sigils while we watch *Game of Thrones* reruns," I told him, slipping my foot back into my shoe. "Last week, we had House Tully trout swimming across our feet. Jane's got a much steadier hand with the polish than I do. I'm more of a House Stark girl, but we don't play favorites."

He stood, pulling me gently as we went deeper into the woods. "You are an interesting group."

"We find ways to enjoy our time together," I said, as he threaded my fingers through his. He compared the size of our hands. The verdict? His were huge, even compared with my long, tapered fingers. The same flaring feeling thrilled through my belly, but it was less fear-based and more giddy nerve-giggles. "Iris can't watch *Game of Thrones* anymore. Every time she starts to like a character, that character dies in some spectacularly horrible way. So she sticks with nice, safe network comedies that don't feature regular beheadings. But Jane likes the show, so she comes over to watch it

and get a little time away from the testosterone cess-
pool at her house."

Nik took a lock of my dark hair and twirled it
around his long, deft fingers. "I envy your closeness.
It has been a long time since I have shared that sort
of camaraderie with anyone, even Cal, whom I would
consider a close friend. And I have not seen him in
centuries."

"Still, to come running when he asked you to harass
my classmate on my behalf, that's a pretty tight bond,"
I said. "Also, before we *really* start the Q-and-A portion
of this evening, I need to tell you something. Because
I don't want you to find out some other way and get
upset. I may have gone into the office server last night
to look for your employee file."

He stopped to stare at me, golden eyebrows at full
mast. "You did what?"

"I didn't know if I would ever get to see you again,
and I had all of these questions that Cal refused to answer. And I'm sorry. I didn't mean to violate your privacy. I just wanted to know more about you. I thought
I should tell you myself."

"How did you find my employee file?"

I winced. "Technically, I didn't. I found what was
supposed to be your employee file, but it was empty."

He laughed and pulled me against his side, tucked
neatly under his arm. "The fact that you were able
to find the empty file was impressive. My actual file
fills most of a storage room at the Council archives in
Prague."

I would take time to be frightened by that later. "So you're not mad?"

"Mad that the girl who has occupied most of my waking thoughts since the moment I remember meeting her is equally curious about me? No, I am not angry, quite the contrary. I am glad you want to know more about me. And I am intrigued that you have the skill and cunning to accomplish your goal. All wrapped up in that sweet, deceptively guileless package. You surprise me, Gigi."

"Well, I'm glad you appreciate my sexy curiosity, because I have questions galore. What's your origin story? And as a follow-up subquery, how do you know Cal?"

"Are you allowed a 'subquery'?"

"Yes, I am," I said airily. "Entertain me, Nikolai."

"Oh, I could *entertain* you for hours," he teased me, rubbing his thumb in tight circles around my palm. "But for now, I will tell you that I was born in the 1500s," he said. "I was the youngest of three sons in a fairly well-off family, for the time. We did not have a title, but we had a very rough version of what could be considered a castle. It was mostly a fortress, deep in the Romincka Forest. My father tended faithfully to his tenants in the village. He made sure they had enough to eat, medicine when they were sick, firewood when they were cold. He was a good man, educated and kind, and so were my brothers. But as the youngest, there was little for me to do or look forward to unless one of my brothers died. And that wasn't the way I wanted to make my way in the world.

"So one day, when a traveling Romani circus drove past the village, I jumped on the nearest wagon and joined the caravan."

I hooted. "You ran away with the circus?"

"For a time," he said, looking pleased that he'd made me laugh. "They were not pleased that I had stowed away on their wagons and made me work for every crust of bread they threw my way. It was a rude awakening for a boy used to servants and soft sheets. But I earned my place."

"Were you ever a clown?" When my alarmed tone caught his attention, I added, "It's a fair question."

"No, I was more of an 'advance man,'" he said. "I went into the towns before the caravan arrived and was sure to tell the locals of my woes down at the nearest tavern. My pretend farmhouse had burned down, my pretend cows had dried up, my pretend wife had left me for my brother, that sort of thing. Conversation would naturally lead to commiserating about similar mishaps in their village, and I would take what I learned back to Mama Katya to use in her palm readings."

"And no one ever caught on to you?"

"I wore disguises," he said. "I blackened my hair with boot polish, rubbed walnuts on my teeth to stain them. I learned about subterfuge and sleight of hand.

The circus folk may have stolen and lied, but they were very open about it."

"Once again, your vampire logic is not like my human logic."

"I suppose it is not," he said, sliding a cool hand over the delicate bone of my wrist. "I enjoyed myself with the circus. I learned who I was and what I was capable of, and I picked up many of the skills I still use today." He held up his hand, which was currently dangling my stainless-steel cuff bracelet, inscribed with a swirling *G*.

"Hey!"

"You did not even feel me take it off," he said smugly.

"You could have used your vampire speed to do that," I said, snatching it out of his hand and hooking it around my wrist.

"But I did not," he said, and somehow, he had managed to get the dang bracelet back and was dangling it from his fingertips again.

"Stop that!"

"When it stops being funny," he said with what almost sounded like contrition. "I toddled along that way for years, until I sent a very superstitious fellow—who I didn't know was a vampire—for a palm reading. Katya predicted a long and lonely life for him, and he lashed out, turning me to prove her wrong. He told her that he would keep me with him for all eternity."

I was not able to suppress my shudder. All of the

vampires I knew, with the exception of Andrea, had been turned by people they knew and trusted, or eventually came to know and trust. And Andrea's horrible sire had been given the Trial, the triple whammy of vampire capital punishment, making way for her husband to take his place as a mentor. I couldn't imagine being turned by someone who was basically an emotional albatross. "Did that work out for him?"

Nik shook his head. "No, I rose three days later, and the moment he turned his back, I staked him and ran."

"Seems fair."

"There are certain benefits to being turned by a vampire who is not particularly smart," he said. "Or fast."

"And then what happened?"

He waved his hand in a dismissive gesture, as if all that history was boring. "Eh. Enough about me."

"But your story is so much more interesting than mine," I protested. "My life story is sadly lacking in circus folk."

"To you, it is less interesting, maybe. But I have so many questions about a girl named Gladiola Grace and her strange vampire upbringing."

"We're coming back to your awkward vampire adolescence," I told him, but when I pointed my finger at him, I realized my bracelet was missing again. "Damn it, Nik!" I snatched it back from him.

He asked, "So what was it like, growing up with one human parent and one vampire?"

"I didn't grow up with Cal," I said, closing my bracelet around my wrist. "He sort of swept in under the wire and filled that big-brother role right before I flung myself out of the nest for college."

"You are going to have to learn to use fewer metaphors."

I pulled his hands into mine, so I could study them, trace the outline of his scarred palms with my fingertips. How could hands that still seemed so young and strong have survived for so long? How many countries had these hands touched? How many lives? Trying to estimate made me a little dizzy. How could he stand to see so much, to know so much? How could he drum up enthusiasm for each new stage in history? And how could I seem at all interesting compared with any of that?

I cleared my throat and shook off those crippling feelings of inadequacy, because I refused to be *that* girl in this strange undead love story. "Our parents died when I was around twelve. A drunk driver hit their car on the way home from a party. Iris was already in college and she tried to fold me into her life so she could finish up her degree. But that didn't work. It was hard enough to try to get along, just the two of us, without adding the stress of living in a big city, no connections, no help. Iris gave up school so she could take care of me. We moved back to our parents' house in the Hollow. For the longest time, it was just Iris and me. We were together, and we were as content as you could hope to be under the circumstances, but it was so hard on Iris, being the only adult in the house. And there was always this fear nagging at the back of our minds. We never talked about it, but I knew it was there, the fear that at any moment, we could lose it all. One bad accident, one slow month with Iris's business, and we could teeter right into financial disaster. We could have lost the house. We could have ended up living in our car. And then Cal came along with his 'grrr, I must protect all of the womenfolk'-ness and endless pots of money. And for the first time, we felt safe. So many of our worries seemed to just melt away. We could enjoy each other's company in a way we hadn't before. And then there was the added fun of freaking Cal out whenever we could. I mean, the man fought in the Trojan War, but seeing a bra hanging over a shower-curtain rod makes him stammer like a choirboy."

Nik burst out laughing. "I will have to remember that."

"Cal was the kind of big brother you always wanted, but he was kind of a nightmare at the same time. He loved us fiercely, but it was always just a little twisted. I mean, he decided he wanted to do an Easter egg hunt the first spring we were all together, and he filled all of the eggs with twenty-dollar bills. But then he *buried* them because he thought it was funny. He scared the hell out of Ben, even though he liked Ben, just because he could. There was a boy in one of my classes at UK who wouldn't take no for an answer when I didn't want to go out with him, and I didn't know what happened, but I figured Cal threatened him with something, and then next thing I know, this kid runs across the campus when he sees me coming. And then he dropped out of school . . . which I suppose you already know about because you were there. Do you often do favors like that for Cal?"

"When I am not doing business for the Council, I occasionally offer my services to friends, yes."

"Business like attending terrifying staff meetings where fangs are crushed with pliers?" I asked wryly.

"That was a special favor to Ophelia," he said. "I am in the Hollow because Ophelia requested my assistance with a series of thefts from vampires in the area. My special talent is well known among vampires. My presence at the meeting gave her intimidating claims more credence. To be honest, I hoped that I would not have to demonstrate in front of the room. I do not particularly like performing in public, even after my circus years."

I nodded. Almost all vampires had some sort of special talent, like Jane's mind-reading or Dick's gift of persuasion. Iris had yet to discover her special vampire gift, which Cal assured us was perfectly normal. It could take years to cultivate a special talent. And even then, it could be something completely off the wall like finding lost objects or talking to woodland creatures. Though, personally, I think the lost-object thing would be kind of cool.

"So far, we haven't figured out what Iris's is yet. I am really rooting for that ability to talk to squirrels thing, because that would be weird and awesome. Oh, wait, let me guess yours. Is it wearing clothes really, really well? Or sneaking up on people in locations where they park cars?"

He lowered his head until we were nose-to-nose and growled softly, reminding me once again that I had a bad habit of poking at predators. But then he grinned broadly, and I felt all off-balance again. He was *really* alarmingly good at that. "My vampiric gift is psychometry. I touch an object, and I get images of past events that occurred around the object."

"So why don't you use your gift to try to recover your memories of me?" I exclaimed, smacking his arm.

"I have tried!" he said, batting my swinging hands aside like harmless flies. "Have you not noticed how often I touch you? I am not getting any sort of read from you."

"But how does it work?"

He thought about it for a long moment, as if trying to find an explanation I could handle. That made me nervous. "Every time you touch an object, you leave fingerprints behind, yes? You also leave an echo of your soul."

I frowned. "Like a Horcrux in *Harry Potter*?"

I would never get tired of seeing him rub his hand over his face like that. "No," he said. "You leave a little bit of the emotions you are feeling when you touch an object. If the emotions are strong, whether they are positive or negative, the echo is much stronger. When I pick up an object, that echo bounces into my head and shows up like a movie on a screen. Only the movies are always unpleasant."

"Always?"

"Almost always. People seem more open to feeling strong negative emotions than positive ones."

"Well, that's depressing." I stuck my bottom lip out in an exaggerated pout.

"I can see what they saw, feel what they felt, hear what they heard. If the echo is very strong, I can hear their thoughts in my head. It takes me away from myself, out of my own head."

Suddenly, his not needing a laptop for his work made much more sense. He literally had to be "hands-on" while conducting his research for the Council. Not much use for Google there. I tilted my head at a curious angle. "Does it work with people?"

"People have too many emotions going on at once. It is almost impossible to get a clear reading. It is like white noise. If I opened my mind up to it, I would go insane."

"Well, I'd hate for you to risk that," I admitted.

He took my hands in his. "I hate the idea that I could not remember our first moments together. I hate that you might feel alone in this. I never want you to feel anything but—"

He stopped, jerking his head toward the house, as if he was hearing something I couldn't. Which was likely.

"Cal and Iris are moving upstairs," he said. "Dawn is coming, and I must rest for the day. I will walk you back to the house."

"Wait, you were going to say something," I said, as we moved out of the trees. "Something about feelings?"

"Some other time, Gigi. The wonderful thing about being undead is that I have all the time in the world."

"Well, I don't. I am a human. I have a limited shelf life," I protested quietly as we neared my window. Without so much as a by-your-leave, he picked me up bridal-style and leaped up to my open window. He employed the whole catlike-grace thing again, landing with no effort on the windowsill and passing me through the open window. We entered the room noiselessly so as not to provoke my undead housemates.

"You do not have to have a shelf life," he whispered. "I am sure there are any number of vampires who would be willing to turn you."

I laughed, even though I knew he was right. Though Iris still held out hope that I would grow up to be a happy, well-adjusted soccer mom, I knew that if it came down to my dying or becoming a vampire, she would turn me. Or Cal would. Jane, Dick, Jamie, or even Gabriel would turn me if I needed help. And frankly, the prospect didn't scare me. Yes, I recognized that there were things I would have to give up, if and when I was ever turned. Motherhood, graceful aging, a natural death, though, given my circle of friends and family, that was probably unlikely. But I'd had several years to ponder these sacrifices, and as far as I was concerned, they were worth it if I got to live out my days with the people I loved. And of course, being faster, stronger, more attractive, and more likely to win a fight weren't exactly downsides, either.

Besides, between working for the Council and my usual all-night coding parties, I was basically keeping vampire hours and sun exposure levels already. But these were not issues that I was ready to share with Nik just yet.

"If we can't have the feelings conversation due to time constraints, we are definitely not having the 'do you want to be turned' conversation," I whispered back. "You just take your Old World charm and frustrating conversational tactics and remove your person from my room, sir."

He chuckled, brushing my hair back from my face. "Will you see me again?"

My eyes narrowed. "Are you asking me on a date?"

"This does not count as a date?"

"No. This was a walk. In the dark. In my pajamas. Dates include leaving the house for a planned activity. And I didn't say I would go out with you."

He grinned at me. "I think I could persuade you."

Before I could gather my forces of snark, Nik yanked me close, sweeping me into one of those swoony, back-bending kisses also featured on the covers of Iris's romance novels, all soft, sliding lips and clever flicks of the tongue. My eyes went wide, and I couldn't help but notice, at this intimate distance, that Nik closed his eyes. Five hundred years on this earth, countless kisses with countless women, and he still closed his eyes when he kissed. I didn't care if he was potentially evil. My heart melted a little, even when his hands slipped down my back and cupped my ass through my pink pajama pants.

"Still not persuaded," I told him cheekily, when he finally pulled away.

"I will have to dig deeper into my bag of tricks."

"I look forward to it."

"Because you are a perverse, sly creature." He pecked me on the lips, a quick, mischievous kiss, before he ducked out of the window and back-flipped onto the grass.

I peered down from the open window, shaking my head at his antics. "Good night, Nikolai."

"Good night, my Gigi."

6

Arguing with a vampire over office policy is generally pointless. They can outlive you, and really, when one party is alive and the other is dead, right or wrong doesn't matter much.

—*The Office After Dark: A Guide to Maintaining a Safe, Productive Vampire Workplace*

Three days later, Sammy Palona, a permanent "coffee and sandwich" guy, was appointed to keep us humans from needing to leave the office during work hours. He set up a mini-deli in the human break room and kept a constantly circulating batch of espresso flowing to the overnight crowd. Also, there were several new video cameras installed in the parking lot, but I wasn't sure if that was Nik's doing or Cal's. Neither one of them wanted me wandering around darkened streets at night.

But Sammy was a perfectly nice, enormous Samoan guy who knew his way around a skinny peppermint mocha, so I wasn't going to complain about my brother-in-law and/or vampire crush's possible interference in my workspace. Sammy's genius did not extend to sushi, however, so I continued to bring my own vampire-prepared California rolls from home. I even kept a bottle of soy sauce with my name on it in our office's "nonblood" mini-fridge. I liked to think of it as marking my place as an official Council staffer.

Of course, Ophelia had refused to meet with me twice so far when I'd asked to talk to her about my position as project leader. Both times, she had been unavailable. I tried to tell myself it was because of her busy schedule, but I was sure it had more to do with Jamie than a jam-packed day planner.

Oddly enough, her assistant, Margaret, had wandered in every night, shuffling through our archive files. She seemed to be looking for something. But when we asked her if she needed help, she got this weird deer-in-the-headlights look on her face and scuttled out of the room.

The project seemed to be flowing easily into the initial stages. We'd divided up our tasks and were scheduled to start testing that Friday using a program created by our regional manager. And as much as I enjoyed my work, I hadn't seen Nik in almost a week, and frankly, I was getting a little twitchy. After his initial, blatant violation of the embargo, he'd kept his word to Cal, not calling, not coming by the house or ambushing me outside my office. And even though he'd had a meeting with Ophelia, he'd managed to get in and out of the office without seeing me. I lived in a Nik-free bubble. This, of course, meant that he occupied most of my waking thoughts. I wondered where he was, what he was doing, where he was staying in the Hollow.

I threw myself into work for a distraction. My skin went paler and paler as I spent my nights glued to my monitor, music blasting into my headphones as I wove coding magic. I was living on fancy coffee and sushi. And despite the fact that I was getting plenty of sleep during the day, the disruption of my circadian rhythms left me with dark circles under my eyes. I was starting to look like a vampire, albeit a vampire of below-average hotness. And no, no matter how many folders I searched through, I did not see information on living descendants Nik might have.

Meanwhile, I was getting past that awkward "I think we might get along, but you could also secretly be a colossal jerk" phase with my new coworkers. The problem with working in the IT field was that when you grouped a bunch of superintelligent people used to being the "weird kids" in their classes, they tended to try to outdo one another in their "out-there-ness." Marty was on a "brain-boosting" diet of quinoa and wild-caught salmon and therefore refused to eat anything that his mother hadn't packed for him. Aaron kept zombie-apocalypse supplies in his desk, just in case. Jordan regularly waged war between her My Little Pony and Dr. Who figurines on her coffee breaks. The Ponies always won, crushing the pretend sonic screwdrivers under their ruthless plastic hooves.

Fortunately, I'd spent most of my formative years as a member of the jock semipopular crowd, so I was used to the sort of diplomacy required to navigate interpersonal insanity. Pony carnage aside, I enjoyed spending time with Jordan. At first, I thought she didn't like me, based on her multiple eye rolls on the first day. But I eventually figured out that was her basic mode of communication. One eye roll meant she thought something was a good idea. Two eye rolls meant she was doubtful. A full three eye rolls meant she thought you were an idiot.

But since she only gave me two eye rolls when I told her I was a Ninth Doctor girl, I considered us friends.

Marty was a mixed bag. Sometimes he could be downright sweet, dropping a handful of my favorite mini Reese's peanut butter cups off on my desk or bringing me a *Wired* article he thought I would like. He friended me on Facebook and occasionally left me links to funny YouTube videos on my wall. And there were other times, like when he called me Gladiola or when he insisted on walking me to my car, even when I asked him not to, when he was sort of irritating. I figured it was all part of the grown-up workplace experience, finding ways to cooperate with people who grated on your nerves, even though you spent more time with them than you did with your family.

Aaron had this thing where he pretended to be lazy and sketchy, but he was actually a very talented programmer. He managed to cut through the layers of bull to find the real problem before the rest of us could grasp what was going on. He just didn't want to be in a leadership position. It took up too much time when he could be doing actual work. I had to admire that about him.

Besides my warren mates and Sammy the coffee god, I didn't see many of our coworkers on a daily basis. Each office had its function and seemed to work as its own little biosphere of productivity. I ventured out of my office for runs to Sammy for coffee and to the copy room, and that was about it. On one such expedition, I was scurrying down the hall from the copy room and happened to pass Ophelia's partially open office door.

"What do you mean, it's 'missing'?" Ophelia shrieked.

I stopped in my tracks. She sounded displeased, and by displeased, I mean volcanically angry. As scary as she was in everyday interactions, it was pretty unusual to hear her raise her voice. Ophelia was more of a "let your anatomically elaborate threats do your talking for you" kind of gal.

"I don't know where it could have gone, Miss Lambert," Margaret whimpered. "The last time I saw a red file, it was on your desk, waiting to be returned to the archive. That's the only one I've seen since I started working here. Normally, they're kept in the special archives."

"I know that they're normally kept in the special archives, Margaret. The fact that the folder is *red* indicates that it's a record of some importance. You find that file, Margaret. I won't even bother to threaten you with the consequences of not finding it. Just have it on my desk before you outlive your usefulness."

Cringing, I backed away from the door, hoping I could escape before Margaret emerged and I had to make awkward "I heard you getting your ass handed to you" eye contact.

"How was it spelled again?" Margaret asked, her voice quivering.

"Linoge," Ophelia spat. "L-I-N-O-G-E."

I froze.

Linoge, as in the red folder I'd found in the archive stack on my first day of work? As in the file folder still tucked away in the recesses of my desk, Linoge? As in the vampire who was executed for "excessive feeding" due to his girlfriend's evil magical influence? That Linoge?

A familiar sensation buzzed through my brain, the click of puzzle pieces falling into alignment. Linoge was executed for violent, out-of-character behavior linked to magic. Nik was experiencing violent, out-of-character behavior, which, frankly, stank of magical whammy. Could the two vampires be linked? Could I get some clues to Nik's memory issues if I could figure out how Linoge was cursed?

I needed to get back to my desk. Now.

I motored down the quiet, gray hallway as quickly as I could, while still appearing casual. I opened the door to find an empty office. All the desks were empty. The muffled strains of Sia rang out from Jordan's abandoned My Little Pony headphones.

Well, this was incredibly creepy. Maybe my team members had decided to take their own simultaneous smoke breaks . . . after simultaneously suddenly deciding to take up smoking? Still, I was grateful for the chance to retrieve the folder from my desk without making my coworkers liabilities . . . I mean, witnesses.

That still sounded wrong.

I opened the drawer where I'd stashed the binder containing the file. I scanned the paperwork, but it was just as skimpy with information as it had been the first time I read it. Basic information about Linoge only, no hints to who or where his descendants were. I wasn't even sure if it was worth holding on to the file, except that it irritated Ophelia, and that was sort of fun. But something told me to hide it away, to keep it as some sort of leverage against my mercurial boss, just in case. I wasn't dumb enough to steal Council property and take it home, so I shoved it into a drawer, under my lady supplies and contact solution, and prayed that no one would see it.

Right, so where did this leave me?

I needed to find more information about Linoge. Given the somewhat, let's say, "creative" information-storage methods used by the Council, it was more than likely that there was another file on Linoge on the server completely unrelated to his kin, probably something to do with taxes or flossing habits or something. I couldn't use my own computer now that the network administrators had assigned us all IDs and done away with the generalized "new employee" login. I would imagine that the IT staff would ask why I was looking at areas of the server I had no business opening, searching for a file I shouldn't know existed. And using my coworkers' stations was weasely and mean.

Right, accessing scary vampire networks without it being traced back to me or my computer. Something to ponder. For now, I needed to do some actual work so I didn't get fired before I could do something that could get me murdered or, at least, scolded in a stern fashion.

I'd no sooner logged back into the server when I felt a tap on my shoulder. I jumped about a foot, throwing my coffee cup aside and knocking it into my wastebasket. And somehow I did it without spilling a drop. God bless lids.

"Whoa," Aaron said, jumping back from me, hands raised. "You're right. It was bad coffee." Aaron sent a mocking glare into the wastebasket. "Bad coffee."

"Sorry, a little too much caffeine today," I said, laughing nervously. "What's up?"

Aaron brushed his hair out of his eyes long enough to look distinctly uncomfortable. He opened his mouth as if to speak and then stopped, dashed over to the office door, and shut it. "I don't want to break the unspoken rules about office tattling."

My eyes went wide. Crap. He knew about my file hoarding.

I cleared my throat, willing my blood to go back into my facial muscles so I could appear nonchalant. "I don't think those are an actual thing."

He grimaced. "It's just that Marty accidentally saved a copy of the file he's been working on in my folder on the server. And I was curious."

Relief flooded through me, like sipping a hot drink after feeling cold for days, and I was able to smile and appear truly nonchalant. "Because you're competitive and wanted to know if you're better than he is," I said, my tone teasing.

"No comment," he said primly. He nudged me aside gently to open his server folder on my computer.

"If you give me a virus, there will be consequences," I told him.

Aaron snickered. "Anyway, I went over this section of code that Marty just finished, and it's not working. It's like he isn't even using the same language we are."

"What?" I scoffed. "That can't be right."

I opened Marty's work and ran it through the test program that would show what the final results would look like live. And the result was gobbledygook. Just a bunch of random letters.

"Wow, that's a steaming-hot mess," I marveled. "Maybe he's just nervous? Sometimes when I'm feeling uneasy, it puts me off my game."

Aaron shook his head. "Almost every file in his work folder is like this."

"What are you doing opening all of his files?" I asked him seriously.

"No comment," he said again, clicking as many server folders as my monitor would allow.

"You've got to wonder how he got the job," Aaron murmured, as each piece of Marty's work failed the testing program.

"Uh, yeah, I barely got the job, and I'm competent," I grumbled. Beyond the initial test to prove that I'd mastered basic programming, Ophelia had locked me in an outdated archive and asked me to find the living descendants of Geraldine Dvorak, who was not, in fact, a vampire but the actress who played Dracula's bride in the Bela Lugosi classics. I was only allowed to use the resources in the room, which did not include a computer—which I'd found a little odd, considering that I was being hired for a programming position. I'd only managed to find the answer because Ophelia failed to pat me down for my smartphone. "Hey, speaking of which, how did you get past Ophelia's insane test?"

Aaron shrugged. "All she asked us to do was Google a few names and find some descendants' addresses and then pass a basic programming test. I basically got the job based on my professors' recommendations."

"You were allowed to use a computer?"

Aaron's sharp black brows furrowed. "Yes."

"You didn't have to complete her insane challenge?"

"What are you talking about?"

"Nothing." I clenched my fist and shook it at the ceiling. "Ophelia!"

"Well, insane tangents aside, if Marty keeps this up, we're going to have to redo his work on top of doing all of our own. It's going to put us way behind on our schedule and make it impossible for us to meet the deadline."

"That sounds like the voice of a mature, involved employee, and yet I am distracted by the Bieber haircut," I said, shaking my head as I saved copies of Marty's work to my folders.

"This is not a Bieber cut," he insisted, pointing at his carefully shagged, inky black hair. "I had this haircut way before Justin Bieber."

"A *hipster* and a Bieber!" I gasped.

"OK, now I'm giving you viruses on principle," he told me.

"I'll talk to Ophelia about Marty."

He crossed his arms over his chest. "When?"

"What time frame will prevent you from uploading cyber-herpes into my hard drive?" I asked.

Aaron gave me a scathing mock glare. "This is a 'get ahead of it' situation, Miss Project Leader."

"Ugh, emotional discomfort." I groaned, printing out the results of Marty's work and shoving them into a file folder (a real manila specimen, not a digital one). "This is why you voted me into the job, isn't it?"

Aaron grinned at me and slapped me on the back. "Yes, it is."

"Let me look over the file history, make sure this isn't some misunderstanding, and then I'll go to Ophelia. I'd hate to tank this guy over some sort of mistake. But if you do see any other files from him with issues, let me know."

"You have twenty-four hours," Aaron told me solemnly.

"Really?" I deadpanned.

Aaron pulled a dispassionate face. "Yeah, that always sounds cooler in the movies. Just do something about it soon, OK? Or I will do something regrettable to the files you hold most dear."

"You realize that if you do, in fact, give me a computer virus, I'll fix it so every time someone Googles you, your name will come up as the author of articles in *Cannabis Quarterly*!" I called after him as he returned to his desk.

"It already does that!" he called back.

Just then, Marty came through our office door bearing a disposable coffee cup with the red Council logo on the sleeve. He beamed brightly at me. "I brought you some coffee, Gladiola. Sammy said you were partial to peppermint mochas."

He glanced into my wastebasket at the discarded mocha cup and frowned.

"Thanks. There was an incident with the last one," I said, accepting the cup and cringing on the inside. Because only hypocrites accepted gift coffee from the people they were about to run out of the office on a rail labeled "incompetent as hell." I cleared my throat and tried to keep my tone as friendly and nonjudgmental as possible. "Hey, Marty, are you having any problems with the programming language? We're not exactly using a standard here, so if you have any questions, just let me know."

"I don't need any help," he said stiffly. "Why?"

"Well, you saved a file in the wrong folder, and I opened it to take a look," I said, as Aaron cringed and disappeared into his cubicle. "There were a few problems with your work."

Marty scoffed. "Oh, I'm sure that was just something I was tinkering with, like a doodle on scrap paper. I don't have any problems with the language," he insisted. "I don't need any help. Now, how's the coffee?"

"It's fine, Marty, thanks."

"It was pretty hot," he added. "I almost burned my hands carrying it."

"Thank you again."

"Let me know if you want another cup," he said.

I pressed my lips together and nodded. "OK, then."

My eyes narrowed as he ambled back to his desk. He knew something. He had to know something; otherwise, he wouldn't be sucking up to me like this, trying to keep me from going to Ophelia. Had he overheard Aaron telling me about his issues? That was a socially terrifying thought.

I mentally reviewed the conversation and tried to remember whether we'd said anything personally insulting about Marty or limited our comments to "he sucks, let's get him fired." His overhearing either would be pretty damn embarrassing. Or maybe he knew he was failing miserably at the job and was trying to butter me up to prevent an explosive and embarrassing termination? Was he trying to play on my ingrained female tendencies to play nice and smooth ruffled feathers?

That was insulting. It was condescending. And worse yet, it was working, because I was trying to find any reason to justify keeping Marty on as a coffee fetcher.

While I was at it, I checked Aaron's and Jordan's files, which passed testing with flying, functional colors. I supposed I should be thankful that Ophelia hadn't saddled me with a completely incompetent team.

Ophelia. I cursed inwardly and made another little hand-shaking gesture at the ceiling, hoping no one else noticed. Had she planted Marty on my team on purpose? Was she trying to sabotage the project so I wouldn't be hired full-time by the Council? Or was she just messing with me because she could?

I stared at my monitor, but for once, it didn't have any answers for me. Would Marty ever catch up? Did he really not know what he was doing, or was this some sort of boundary-testing thing with his new project leader?

I took a deep breath and closed my eyes. I needed to stop asking myself questions and find a solution. No more panicking and self-doubt. It was time to be a hard-ass and be *awesome* at it. Just like I did in most craptastic situations, I asked myself, "What Would Iris Do?"

My big sister would put on her big-girl underpants and deal with the situation, no matter how eye-twitchingly awkward the solution might be. She would figure out the extent of her employee's incompetence and then address it with her superior, even if it made her very uncomfortable.

I scrubbed my hand over my face. Why couldn't I have just taken a job at the Apple Store?

I could not get out of the office fast enough. I grabbed my purse from my now-empty cubicle farm and bid Margaret a cheery good night. She did not return it, giving me a shallow imitation of Ophelia's stink-eye. As I walked into the employee lot, I pulled my silver spray out of my purse, as was now my habit, and snagged my car keys. I'd promised Cal that I would take more care with parking-lot safety, and honestly, if I got attacked again, I'd never hear the end of it. He'd probably follow through with Dick's giant-hamster-ball idea.

I rounded the car nearest the Dumpster and jumped at the sound of angry hissing.

"Shitballs!" I yelped, jumping back three feet as an angry possum swiped at my ankles, obviously upset with me for interrupting its dinner of garbage. I dropped my silver spray, and the can skittered across the pavement, under the Dumpster.

"Really? I need the scare factor of an angry marsupial?" I sidestepped the still-agitated possum and backed toward my car. "I'm going to have a heart attack before age twenty-five."

I had only dodged a possum once before. I didn't have a lot of practice. That was the only justification I had for running smack into Nik's chest.

"Gah!" I exclaimed, bouncing off my vampire's considerable pectorals like a bumper car and smacking into a nearby Honda. "Come on, Nik, there's only so many scares I can take in one night!"

But Nik didn't respond, not a word, not even a facial twitch. His eyes were glazed over, filmy and hazy blue. His mouth hung open, and he was breathing heavily, even though, technically, he didn't need to breathe at all. He shuffled toward me, zombielike, without really seeing me.

"Nik?"

I backed away, edging my way along the Honda's body to an open space. "Nik, is this a joke? Because it's not funny."

He lumbered closer, his expression dead. It would have been almost comforting if he'd snarled or leered or even looked vaguely confused. The blank, lifeless face was just unnerving. I faked left, then darted right. Nik lunged, snapping his jaws where my neck had been just moments before.

Nik dove at me, arms flung wide and teeth bared. I sidestepped him, wrapping my arms around his waist and shoving his weight to the left. He flew face-first into the Honda and dropped to the asphalt like a sack of potatoes, groaning. I grabbed my hairbrush out of my bag and clicked the stake into place.

Nik staggered toward me, moaning softly. He was moving slowly, I realized, like someone who was sleepwalking. It was probably the only reason I stood half a chance when he attacked me. He didn't have all of his vampire wits together, or I would already be girl-hamburger.

And why the hell wasn't anybody watching the security live feed so they could send in some backup for me?

I held the stake out straight, like a dagger, aiming it at Nik's chest. Could I do this? Could I stake him? Could I hurt him at all, now that I knew him and had kissed him and had the not-so-tiniest of crushes on him?

No. A world of no.

This wasn't Nik. This empty, violent shell of a vampire wasn't the Nik I knew. I couldn't hurt him when he wasn't in control of himself. He wasn't to blame. I would have to find some other way. I backed up a few steps, dropping the stake to the asphalt.

I slipped my hand into my purse as Nik followed. At the very bottom, I found Old Reliable. Mr. Sparky. The very first Taser that Cal had ever given me, now rewired and more powerful. And it was pink.

Nik shuffled forward, hunching down as if he was getting ready to spring at me.

"Nik, I am really sorry about this." I sighed, wincing as I pushed the trigger. A bright white arc of electrical current jumped between the prongs. Scrunching up my face, I jammed the prongs against Nik's ribs. He yowled and dropped to his knees.

I kept the Taser pressed against his side even while he flopped against the pavement like a hyper fish. The strange gray fog drained from his eyes as he twitched. His brow furrowed, and his jaw clenched, but I couldn't tell if it was from confusion or electrocution.

"G-G-G-Gigi!" he stuttered. "Stop T-T-Tasering me!"

"You attacked me!"

"S-s-s-still Tasering m-m-m-me!"

I yanked the Taser back and pulled my finger off the trigger. "Sorry."

Nik groaned and let his head flop back onto the asphalt. "Ow."

"This can't be healthy, domestic-violence-wise," I said, as he sat up and shook his head, as if he was checking for a rattle in his skull. "We're going to end up in some horribly ironic PSA."

"What happened? The last thing I remember was sitting at home, doing some work. And now I am here. I do not even remember driving here."

"You were waiting for me in the parking lot. Again. And you attacked me. *Again*. This is a pattern with you."

"Did I hurt you?" he asked, sitting back against the tires of the damaged Honda. He cupped his hand around my jaw, searching my face for bruises, then my wrists and arms.

"No, I pretty much whooped your ass," I assured him, as he pulled me into his arms. It surprised me how easy it was to let him. He'd tried to exsanguinate me just moments before, and now I was letting him hug me. It made no sense, but somehow it seemed right, which just spoke to my spotty sense of self-preservation.

"I do not know how to feel about being with a woman who can beat me up," he murmured into my hair.

"Well, stop going all *Walking Dead* on me, and you won't have to worry about it."

He frowned. "Would that make you the Daryl Dixon in this relationship?"

I tried to contain the silly little thrill in my belly at his use of the word "relationship." Also, he got special bonus points for understanding my pop-culture references, which was always a risk with non-Jane vampires. I nodded. "Get me a crossbow, and I'll be the most badass lady redneck you've ever met."

His shoulders sagged. "I knew it."

"Come to think of it, I wonder why Cal hasn't gotten me a crossbow yet."

"It is probably in the public's best interest."

7

Older vampires are more prone to office intrigues than humans. Centuries of living under the human radar and negotiating vampire politics instill a strong need for the rush of subterfuge. Frankly, it's better to let them get it out of their systems as long as no one gets hurt. A bored vampire is a dangerous vampire.

—*The Office After Dark: A Guide to Maintaining a Safe, Productive Vampire Workplace*

"**G**et up." Nik was shaky, but he helped pull me to my feet. He seemed to be looking around the parking lot for his car. "I am kidnapping you."

I groaned, stretching and gingerly testing my bruised arms. Nik nodded toward a black SUV and clicked the keyless entry. "Shouldn't you be using an unmarked white panel van and some candy for this?"

"Very funny," he grumped, rubbing at the side I'd Tasered. "Now, call your sister and make some excuse that will keep her from activating the LoJack chip she installed in your neck while you were sleeping."

"She was only kidding about that," I huffed, pulling out my phone. "I'm ninety percent sure."

I was never so grateful for a call to go through to Iris's voice mail. Because I'm sure that the presence of her vampire superpowers on the other end of the line would have resulted in Iris guessing that I was lying about going out for a late breakfast with my coworkers. I could lie to a machine, but I couldn't lie to my sister.

Nik opened the passenger door and handed me inside. Honestly, he offered me his hand and helped me in, as if I was climbing into a horse-drawn carriage. The elegance of the gesture—compared with guys my age who not only walked through doors before me but didn't bother holding said doors open long enough so they wouldn't smack me in the face—touched that part of my heart that secretly enjoyed Jane Austen movie night with Iris and the girls. There were definitely perks to this "Old World guy" thing.

We were silent on the drive down the Hollow's country roads to . . . I wasn't sure where. And that's when it occurred to me, once again, how potentially stupid it was to drive anywhere with someone who had been lunging for my jugular just moments before. But somehow, with Nik, it made sense, in a way I would never ever explain to Cal, because the mocking would be extreme. Zombie Nik and my Nik weren't the same person. And so far, I'd been able to handle zombie Nik pretty easily.

I needed answers. I needed time to figure out what

was happening and what was going on inside Nik's head. And to do that, I needed to trust that he wasn't going to space out and try to kill me again . . . despite all evidence to the contrary.

I'd just guaranteed my own "dumb human trick" hashtag on Twitter.

And still, I stayed in the car. I didn't employ the *Charlie's Angels* roll that Cal had taught me to escape a moving vehicle. Information—I needed it, and Nik had it, or at least, he had more of it than I did. So I would just have to trust, while keeping my hold on Mr. Sparky.

I'd expected him to live in some vampire-friendly extended-stay hotel or one of the renovated condos downtown, but he took me to the old Victorian house where Nola lived. The duplex was owned by Dick Cheney and had been split into two rental units years before. Nola and Jed lived in one half. And apparently, Nik lived in the other.

"Ophelia arranged a short-term rental for me," Nik said, as he handed me out of the car. "My neighbors were out of town until a few days ago, and Dick was eager to have at least half of the house occupied while they were gone. Something about invasive possums."

"They are aggressive," I said, nodding.

"Well, it is not much, but it is definitely more luxurious than some places I have stayed over the years," he said, as he unlocked the door.

Nik's half of the house was comfortable but impersonal. The door led into a large parlor and, beyond that, a small beige dining-room-turned-kitchen. The polished living-room floor was covered with an extra-large faded blue rag rug. The furniture was sturdy, manly, no-nonsense. Several large bookshelves flanked his windows, but they were empty. There were no personal touches, no pictures, no personality. And *no laptop*. It might as well have been a hotel room.

Stairs led to a second story, but I wasn't sure I was ready to see that part of the house, because if I did, I would probably end up losing all of my clothes. They would just spontaneously fall off. And that would be embarrassing.

"Can I get you something to drink?" he asked, crossing into the kitchen.

"That's always a loaded question, coming from a vampire," I said, leaning against his counter. "I am not one for O positive."

"I have human drinks. I arranged for my Beeline representative to stock them. I thought you might be coming by." He opened the refrigerator door to show me a stunning array of sodas, juices, mineral waters, and wine coolers mixed in with his bagged donor blood. My mouth fell open at the sheer quantity of beverages weighing down his fridge shelves.

"I did not know what you would like."

"That's kind of adorable." I tried my hardest to keep my smile in check, but I failed. "Diet Dr Pepper is my favorite."

"Do not patronize me," he grumbled. "Why not get more comfortable, and we will talk? I will get your drink. We will sit down and have a normal talk, like two normal people."

I turned toward the living room but hesitated as I surveyed the seating options. A recliner and a couch. If I sat in the recliner, it was a pretty clear message that I didn't want to sit anywhere near him. Or that I had a bad back. If I took the couch, he might think I was angling for snuggle time. If I continued standing, it was going to get weird.

It was already weird.

Nik stepped closer and rubbed his palms along my arms, his gaze intent and absent of any sort of glaze-y hostility. Before I could adjust to this new proximity, he yanked me against his chest and zipped across the room at vampire speed. I yelped as he gently dropped me at one end of his couch. I bounced a little, but before I landed, he had arranged the cushions behind me in the perfect vegging-out position and spread a soft blue chenille throw over my legs. I opened my mouth to protest, but he'd already disappeared into the kitchen in a blur, retrieving my soda and placing it on the coffee table. On a *coaster*.

If Iris ever got over her irrational "attacking Gigi" hang-up toward Nik, she would love him.

"See?" he said, dropping gracefully against the opposite end of the couch. "Perfectly normal."

"Not quite," I told him. "But it was a nice effort."

There was an awkward silence as I paused to open my drink. How exactly did you start a conversation like this? Someone should write a book about upsetting conversations with undead potential boyfriends with memory issues. Note to self: Talk to Jane to see if she has any books about upsetting conversations with undead potential boyfriends with memory issues. If not available, force her to write said book at stakepoint.

A curious, slack expression crossed Nik's face. He reached for me, tracing the curves of my face with his hands like a blind man. His thumbs ran rings around the moonstone earrings at my lobes, and his eyes went hazy. It looked like his zombie phase, only his pupils retained their color. I scrambled back across the couch, perching on the arm, just in case he was phasing into zombie Nik. I could make the ten-foot dash to the door as long as he was stumbling around.

This was a really weird relationship.

"Cal did not threaten that boy." His voice was odd, as if he was just remembering the words as he spoke them.

"Yes, we have established this," I agreed.

"Cal did not threaten that boy. *I* did."

I nodded, pursing my lips. "Once again, this is not exactly news."

"Cal knew I was in the area, on a job. He called me, said he needed a favor, and asked me to visit your college campus. He gave me your schedule and told me that you were not to see me. He did not want you to know he was interfering. He told me the boy's name and the nights when he would be walking around campus. I tracked him down and told him that if he so much as looked at you in a way that you found discomforting, I would remove the parts he held most dear."

"You would have done it, too, wouldn't you?" I asked, unsure whether I really wanted the answer to that question.

He nodded, a precise and decisive movement. "Without a second thought. One, because it was a favor for Cal. And two, because he was bothering you. And that made me angry enough to want to see him hurt, very badly hurt."

I slid back into my seat and crossed my arms over my chest. "Suddenly, everything makes sense."

"That was the first time I saw you," he said. He looked so pleased, scooting closer to me and shoving the throw out of the way so he could pull me into his lap.

"How are you remembering this?"

"I do not know," he said.

He kissed me, once and then twice, my breathy little laugh lost against his mouth as he sealed his lips over mine. I'd dreamed of him as a historical hero, but there was nothing chaste about this kiss. Nik wanted me—badly, if the hardening bulge against my thigh was any indication. And the only thought my brain—a brain my professors touted as brilliant and innovative, I might add—could cobble together was *Naked, yay!*

"You were walking across a courtyard, with a friend, and you were smiling." He slid his hand into my hair and made a makeshift bun at my crown. "Your hair was piled up on top of your head. I heard you laugh. It sounded like music that only I could hear. It made the hair on my arms stand up." Another kiss, lingering and open, teasing his tongue against mine. "And all I wanted to do was follow you so I could hear more. I have been on this earth for hundreds of years, but I have never wanted something so much in my whole existence as I wanted to make you laugh."

Speechless. For the first time in my short but relatively remarkable life, I was speechless. He remembered me. He'd *admired* me. And my laugh. No man, living or dead, had ever said anything so magical or sweet to me.

"But I knew that following you would make Cal unhappy, so I left."

That was less magical. "It would also make me unhappy, because that would be very creepy behavior," I murmured against his mouth, before leaning away from him and adding testily, "Also, it didn't keep you from following me when I came home for the holidays. You just kept popping up at random times, like a vampire *Where's Waldo?*"

"I came to the Hollow over Christmas to discuss the position at the Council. I did not mean to see you. In fact, I was trying to avoid you." With every sentence, he sounded more and more excited, and his speech sped up. He pulled me closer, tracing the lines of my collarbone with the tip of his nose. "But then you came to the Council office, for your interview, I suppose, and there you were. I knew I should not have followed you. I did not mean to scare you. But I could not find a way to talk to you without sounding like a madman."

He licked a soft, wet path up the hollow of my throat, kissed my chin, and claimed my mouth. I threaded my fingers through his hair and ground my hips down.

He moaned, pulling away, staring up at me with wide, shocked eyes. "I have kissed you before."

"Of course you have. Earlier this week, in fact. If you tell me you don't remember *that*, I will be very hurt."

"No, I have kissed you before!" he exclaimed. "It was cold. And your cheeks were bright pink. And you were looking at something in a window that made you smile . . ." He glanced up at my ears and cupped my jaw. He let out a long breath, and his forehead crinkled in concentration. "I kissed you."

"Ran across the street and kissed me, like some thief in the night," I told him, as his hand slipped under the tail of my shirt. His thumb stroked the base of my spine, making my hips jerk toward him. "A—a kissing thief. And then you ran away, and I never saw you again. Until you jumped me in the parking lot. You really hurt me. It hurt that you didn't remember me."

His eyes cleared to their usual golden brown, and he pressed his forehead just over my heart. "I wish I had. Really and truly."

"Do you remember why you didn't just talk to me then?"

"Because I was not supposed to," he said. His hands worked their way around my waist, tugging my shirt loose and pulling it over my head. I might have objected, but at some point, I seemed to have unbuttoned his shirt, too. And I was pushing it from his shoulders, revealing smooth white skin and a muscled torso that tapered down to narrow hips.

I was not intimidated by his marble-toned damn-near-perfection. I was not self-conscious about my body. I'd always been athletic, but training with Cal's people had put a considerable amount of muscle on my frame. I actually had abs and definable tone in my thighs, not to mention a rack I was pretty darn proud of. As far as I was concerned, Nik and his godlike physique could bring it on.

"Cal asked me not to contact you directly because he did not want you to realize you were being followed," Nik said, pushing me back onto the couch and cradling my legs around his hips.

He trailed his lips from the lace connecting my bra cups, down my stomach to ring my belly button.

"But when you returned from school, I found that I missed seeing you. I tried to keep you from seeing me. But you have solid instincts for a human; you picked up on my cues. That is all I remember, admiring your ability to sense me, even when you could not see me."

"Why?"

He shrugged, resting his chin on my sternum. "Probably because you have spent a lot of time around vampires and do not let fear cloud your ability to process the environment around you."

"No, not that!" I cackled. "Why wouldn't you just ignore Cal and come to see me anyway? It would have saved us some drama. Also, I wouldn't have spent months thinking I was nuts and had imagined the whole thing, which would have been nice." I pulled him closer, looping my legs around his and locking them in place.

He frowned and tried to sit up, but I held fast, and he took me with him. We landed against the beige upholstery with a thud. "You will not pull away from me that easily. Consider me the giant squid of potential romantic partners." When he snickered, I said, "It's an unsexy but illustrative thought."

He let out a long breath and pressed his ear against my heart, listening to its erratic beat. "I told you, I killed my sire. I did not have any supervision as a young vampire, and I enjoyed my adolescence a little bit too much. I have done things, Gigi, that make even other vampires uncomfortable. I have killed many people, and in some cases, I enjoyed that killing very much. And I make no apologies for that. I am what I am."

"You're the vampire Popeye?"

He groaned, dropping his forehead against the hollow of my throat. "You make it easy to forget you are so young, and then you say something like that. Even though I want you for myself, I am sure that I am no good for you. And even more sure that I do not care."

"News flash, Skippy, everyone on earth is young compared to you," I told him, digging my knuckles into his ribs. He yelped, and I cupped my hand around his jaw. "So you get that noble, self-sacrificing bullshit out of your head right now." I traced the lines of his pecs with my fingertips, barely brushing over his nipples. "I have seen more in my short lifetime than a lot of vampires you know. I've lost people I loved." I skirted my hands down his ribs and settled them over his hips. "I've been threatened and seen people hurt because of my bad choices. I've loved someone enough to put their happiness before my own comfort. I am walking into this with my eyes wide open. I have accepted the risks and am really, really looking forward to the rewards." I popped the button on his jeans and slipped my hand against the sensitive skin over his pelvis. He gasped and thunked his forehead against my collarbone. "Now, admit that I'm a very mature person, or by all that's holy, I will give you a purple nurple."

His smooth white shoulders were shaking, but I wasn't sure if it was because he was laughing or because I was still teasing my fingers just under the band of his shorts. My free hand skimmed up his torso and mercilessly tweaked his nipple. "Ah!" he yelled. "You are a very mature person!"

"That's more like it." I preened.

"Centuries of spreading terror and bloodshed across the globe, and I think I just became the girl in this relationship," he muttered.

"Yep," I said, letting my lips pop over the "p" sound.

Nik let out an indignant snort. "Oh, you think it is funny, do you?" He poked his fingers into my ribs, tickling me at vampire speed.

"Hilarious!" I giggled, trying fruitlessly to push his hands away. "Side-splitting, even!"

My giggles were interrupted by a series of sharp raps on the wall Nik shared with Nola and Jed.

I clapped a hand over my mouth, which barely muffled a whole new wave of laughter. "Whoops."

"You are a vicious, bloodthirsty creature to treat your vampire so," he murmured against the skin of my throat, even as his hands teased and plucked at my ticklish places. My pulse skipped at the mention of him being "my" vampire. Nik's ears must have picked up on the change, because he spread his hand over my heart to feel it thrum.

"I'm so sorry," I said, though I was still laughing, and he was pulling my slacks over my hips with his free hand. "We're going to get you kicked out of your apartment."

"Worth it," he assured me, while nibbling on my ear. "After what I overheard the other night, they deserve to lose some sleep. It sounded like an obscene nature special over there."

I shoved his jeans down his thighs with my feet. "Nola and Jed are good people. They just got back from Ireland, and they're probably just jet-lagged." Then I gasped and sat up, sending Nik toppling off the couch.

He landed on his hands and knees, because of the

whole vampire-reflexes thing, but he didn't look very happy about it. "You know, if you want to slow down, you just have to say so."

"Nola!" I yelled. "We need to talk to Nola."

Nik glanced down at the pants bunched around his ankles. "Right now?"

"Right now!" I insisted, yanking up my slacks.

"No, wait, do not do that," he said, as I slid into my black shirt. He groaned. "You did it."

"Put your pants on, and let's go meet your neighbors."

I was careful to make sure that we were both buttoned and zipped properly before we left Nik's apartment. I felt bad for not having a bottle of wine or a Bundt cake or something while knocking on Nola and Jed's door in the wee hours with supernatural problems. Then again, we never knocked on each other's doors in the wee hours with natural problems, so she should expect it by now.

It took a few knocks, but eventually, the porch light clicked on, and an enormous bipedal shark creature opened the door. Rows and rows of razor-sharp teeth glinted in the moonlight from under the creature's conical nose. Its dead black eyes narrowed as a low, menacing growl rumbled from its humanoid chest. Nik stumbled back, grabbing my arm and dragging me away from the threat.

I rolled my eyes and patted Nik's hand in a comforting gesture, completely ignoring the walking fish-man.

"Damn it, Nola, I told you not to let him watch *Shark Week*!" I called over the creature's shoulders. "You know it gives him weird ideas."

"Gigi!" Nola's voice rose from behind evil bipedal Bruce. A slender woman with coffee-colored hair and wide brown eyes appeared in the doorway. She shoved the drooling shark creature aside. "What in blazes are you doing here at this time of night?"

It was always a bit of a shock to hear Nola's accent, a mix of Irish lilt and nasal Boston drawl, a by-product of her international upbringing. Nola was the last of Dick's line, the previously unknown granddaughter Mr. Wainwright had left behind in Ireland. She was also the leader of a very large, very talented coven of witches. She'd come to the Hollow a few years before on a sort of supernatural scavenger hunt, searching for magical items that would settle a generations-long interclan feud. But since the late Mr. Wainwright had some hoarding tendencies and Jane had some compulsive organizing tendencies, those items were spread out all over the Hollow, and it took a bit longer than she'd expected, giving her time to be adopted by Jane and Company. She and her boyfriend, Jed, now spent several months each year in Ireland, running her family's clinic in Kilcairy, and the rest here in the Hollow, working for the local free clinics in both spots.

Nola saw Nik standing next to me, and her dark eyes narrowed. A low, threatening hiss issued from the shark's maw. "Oh, Jed, seriously, can you *not* be a mutant land shark right now?"

A bluish shimmer of light rippled along the shark's skin, and the outline of the creature gave way to a handsome, shirtless, shape-shifting redneck who looked like a Greek statue and pouted like a grumpy panda. "You never let me be a mutant land shark."

"I'm not saying you can't shapeshift. I'm just saying, why not a giant badger or a were-bear? The shark doesn't make any bloody sense!" she exclaimed, pulling her robe closed over her skimpy green sleep shorts and tank top. "We're hundreds of miles inland. How are intruders supposed to be afraid of you when they're too busy asking themselves how the bloody hell that mutant shark wandered so far from the ocean? Unless there are six-foot-tall, walking shark creatures living in Barkley Lake now, and the local media has neglected to report it because of tourism concerns."

"Are they insane or magical?" Nik asked, pulling me closer to his side, as if he expected Jed to shift into another scary sea-creature hybrid at any moment.

"A little bit of both," I whispered back. "Uh, guys? I'm sorry to interrupt the shark debate—Jed, it's awesome but implausible—but there's a reason we knocked on your door at this time of night."

"Also, could he put on a shirt?" Nik asked, pointing to Jed's broad chest, tanned and well muscled from the construction work he did for Sam.

"You came knockin' on *my* door, bud. I'll wear what I want," Jed said, snorting, but he did grab a T-shirt from the couch while Nola hustled us inside.

"Is this Nik, then?" Nola asked.

"Nik, this is Nola Leary of the McGavock clan. Nola, this is Nikolai Dragomirov," I said. Nik beamed at me. "What?"

He shrugged, but the silly smile didn't fade. "It just sounds nice, hearing you say my full name like that."

"I think Cal would want me to shift back into the land shark right now," Jed whispered to Nola. "For the sake of brotherly honor."

"Jed, please be the one person I know and love who doesn't threaten my special vampire gentleman friend."

And there went the pouty-panda face again. Jed protested, his strange Cajun-meets-backwoods accent growing thicker with every syllable. "Everybody threatened him without me?"

"We have been out of town, sweetie," Nola said, soothing him.

"But he's a vampire, and he's clearly dating Gigi. Cal is going to destroy him!" he exclaimed. "I should get to join in on the hazing. I've paid my dues. I'm a full-fledged member of the group!"

"Well, you've missed a lot," I told him. "And for right now, can we maybe not tell Iris that you saw us? Together?" I pulled a spare dollar from my pocket and pressed it into Nola's hand before she could object. "Also, please consider me a paying client and therefore subject to any confidentiality that as a medical professional and a magical practitioner you would offer any patient."

"Is that how it works?" Jed asked.

Nola's eyebrows rose, and she tucked the dollar into her pocket. "I'll put the kettle on."

Nola and Jed's side of the house was a much more colorful, personalized mirror image of Nik's apartment. The pictures and tchotchkes that were missing from Nik's shelves were found in abundance here: a framed photo of Jed and Nola smiling together from rolling green hills, white candles inscribed with Celtic knot symbols, a green glazed ceramic bowl filled with dried herbs, a photo of Jed holding an empty pint glass aloft as two men who bore a stunning resemblance to Nola seemed to be shouting in good-natured protest. Despite being from two wildly different backgrounds, they'd made a comfortable home together. And even though I couldn't help but feel a little envious of them, it gave me hope that Nik and I could find that kind of common ground.

As far as I was concerned, Nola was the coolest among our little family-friend-undead circle. Sure, vampires and werewolves were all right, but Nola could heal wounds and light candles from across the room. I begged her to teach me how to do stuff, but she said magic was the sort of thing you had to be born with. If I tried the wrong spell, I could permanently remove my eyebrows or something. And I liked my eyebrows right where they were.

Over tea, I explained my brief history with Nik, his spotty memory and occasional bite-y states, plus the various developments she'd missed over Christmas.

Nola sipped her peppermint tea and quietly absorbed the information, while Jed looked at Nik with more and more hostility. Oh, goody.

Nola poured another cup of the jasmine green tea I favored and pressed it into my hands. "That doesn't sound like normal vampire behavior."

"Tell me about it." I snorted.

"Why are we telling her about it?" Nik asked, eyeing Jed warily. He hadn't touched the warmed bottled blood Nola had served him, as if he suspected that the land shark might have snuck into the kitchen to tamper with it somehow. "This seems like an odd conversation to have when we should be worrying about the approaching sunrise and the fact that they could report us to Cal and your sister for violating the unofficial no-contact order."

"Nola wouldn't do that. It would violate her ethics as a nurse. And as a medical empath. Medical empaths have ethics, right?" I asked. Nola shrugged. "Anyway, ethical quandaries aside, Nola can sense a medical problem just by standing near someone. Jane couldn't sense anything wrong with your brain; maybe Nola can sense something going on with you medically, or magically."

"It's hard for me to get a read on vampires," Nola said. "Different systems."

"So maybe you can sense some sort of evil whammy," I said. "This whole situation reeks of misused mojo. And if you can sense what sort of mojo, maybe we can undo it."

"I've told you, there is no magical control-Z."

"Everything's negotiable," I told her.

"I'm a little uncomfortable with this, Geeg," Nola said. "If Iris doesn't want you spending time with this guy, maybe you should do as she asks. No offense, Nik."

Nik waved off her concern. "I am getting used to it."

"Please, Nola, I wouldn't ask if it wasn't important," I said. Then I amended, "If *Nik* wasn't really important to me. And as much as I respect Iris's opinion, who I see is my business. What would you have done if someone had told you that you shouldn't be with Jed because he could shift into a porcupine creature in the middle of the night?"

"That's not really the same thing!" Jed protested. "I couldn't hurt Nola. My claws and quills aren't real. They're projections. His fangs are very real and right in front of my face."

"OK, what if your family told you not to live with Nola because she could turn you into a toad?"

"Actually, he did have an aunt who told him that," Nola noted.

"And how did that make you feel?"

"Like turning her into a toad," Nola muttered.

"OK, so get with the empathing!" I cried. "The sooner we figure out what's going on, the sooner we can fix it, and the sooner I can stop acting like the tragic, put-upon teen waif in a reimagined Shakespearean rom-com!"

"Did you understand that one?" Jed asked Nik, who shook his head.

Nola looked to Jed, who shrugged his shoulders. She sighed, though she was warming up her hands, clearly intent on examining Nik. "Fine, but we're doing this now, before I change my mind."

"Doing what?" Nik asked, sounding more than a little alarmed as Nola crouched in front of him. "What is she going to do?"

"Relax," Nola said. "This isn't going to hurt in the slightest. But if Iris asks, I dug through his aura like a Roto-Rooter."

"Roto what?" Nik's indignant grunt was cut off as Nola placed her hands on his and closed her eyes. She winced but seemed to push through whatever discomfort she felt, blowing out a low breath. She stayed still and silent for a long while, so long I worried about Nik being caught in the rapidly approaching sunrise.

Nola's eyes snapped open. There was this strange moment when I felt as if I was waiting at the doctor's office to find out whether my husband had a serious disease. She shuddered and gave Nik's hands a squeeze. "Well, I have good news and bad news. The good news is that you've been cursed. There is a pall hanging over your energy, like a cancer, eating away at your intentions, your memories. It's like little gray moths surrounding your head, blinking in and out of focus."

"How is that the good news?" I asked, as Nola pulled a black medical bag from her end table and prepared what looked like a syringe and a vacu-tube.

"Because the curse means that he's not a psycho who slips into altered states to give him an excuse to brutally drain you?" she suggested, swiping at his inner elbow with an alcohol pad.

"That is good news," I agreed.

"I think that hurts my feelings," Nik said, wincing when Nola inserted a needle into his arm. "On several levels."

"The additional good news is that if it's a curse, there has to be a way to break it. Those are the rules." Nola attached a test tube to the needle and drew an alarming amount of Nik's blood with quiet competency. The fact that I didn't want to look directly at the needle slipping into Nik's skin was yet another sign that I'd made the right choice in not going into nursing.

"Who makes up the magical rules?" I asked.

"We have a big meeting every year at a Hyatt in Jersey City."

"I'm going to assume you're kidding but accept that you might not be." I watched Nola fill one tube and then another with Nik's blood sample and asked, "OK, Nik's cursed. What do we do about it?"

"Well, that's the bad news. I don't know what kind of curse it is. While you're setting off a very strong *ping* on my magical radar, Nik, you're not giving off any particular magical signature, which is rather clever on the caster's part. Unless I was with you and the caster at the same time, I probably wouldn't pick up on him or her as the originator of the spell. There may be a way to pick up on the caster's energy without Nik or me being present, but I'll have to look into it, give my cousins a call and see if they have any ideas. And I'll test his blood, see if I can spot any abnormalities or poisons. It would help if I had Iris's cooperation on that front, considering that she quite literally wrote the book on vampires and organic poisons."

Despite myself, I smiled proudly at the mention of Iris's book, which she wrote after her experience with Cal and got published through a small academic press. *Bitten Botanicals* hadn't exactly set the bestseller lists on fire, but the profits were enough to allow Iris to pay her own way through finishing a vampire-friendly PhD program, something she'd always regretted abandoning.

"Could you ask her on behalf of a troubled but un-named neighbor?" I asked.

"Sure," she said. "And I won't tell you to stay away from each other, because I think you should be the one to make that call."

"Thank you, Nola, that means a lot."

"Also, because I know you wouldn't listen either way," she noted, pulling the syringe out of Nik's arm with a practiced air. Nik rubbed absently at the wound, which was already closed up.

"You're probably right," I conceded. "Nola, could a human cast a curse on a vampire?" I asked.

Nola shrugged. "A magical human or a regular human?"

"Regular."

"Probably not. She could hire a witch to do it for her. But a nonwitch couldn't pull this kind of power."

"And is there a way to figure out whether someone's a witch? Since you're magical, can you tell just by look-ing at her?"

She shook her head. "No, she would have to do magic somewhere near me. You could have Jane listen to her brain, but that won't work if she's handy with a mental shield."

"Can't I just do some sort of forensic test, like swab her for magical residue?"

"On the next episode of *CSI: Half-Moon Hollow*?"

"Come on, there has to be something," I wheedled.

"I'll look into it."

"It is possible that someone in my life is behind this phenomenon," Nik said uneasily. "When you do the work that I do for the Council, you make enemies. If someone sensed that Gigi was important to me, they could have placed this curse on me."

"Can you think of anyone specific?" I asked, even as the chill of dread crept up my spine.

"It would take a while to make a list," Nik said. "A very long while."

"Well, for now, let's focus on the field that's not so wide it terrifies me, OK?" I suggested.

"I am sorry, my Gigi," he said quietly. "For a long time, I have lived without a thought to how it might hurt the people closest to me. I have not had people close to me. I am sorry you are caught in the crossfire. I can change."

"I wouldn't want you to change," I told him. "Much."

Nola slapped a Hello Kitty bandage on Nik's arm, which was completely unnecessary, and pronounced him "all done."

"Is it not customary to get a lollipop after you have been poked and prodded?" Nik muttered.

Nola ruffled his blond hair, which Nik did *not* appreciate. "Do they make blood-flavored lollipops?"

Nik blanched. "If there is any justice in the world, no."

She smiled sweetly. "Then, no."

8

There will be days when you will be tempted to pull a stunt of unbelievable incompetence to escape your vampire employer and collect unemployment benefits. Do not pull this stunt.

—The Office After Dark: A Guide to Maintaining a Safe, Productive Vampire Workplace

The Linoge file was missing.

Missing. Absent. Mislaid. Gone.

I will admit that over the last couple of days, my desk had gotten a little messy, but I didn't make a habit of losing incredibly important super-secret files that could potentially incriminate my employer. Someone had gone into my desk, moved my box of tampons, and taken the file I rightfully stole! I felt so violated.

My options for recovering it were limited. I looked around and under my desk. I very discreetly asked Jordan and Aaron if they'd seen a red folder marked "Linoge" lying around, but they said no. I waited for Ophelia to bust into my office and kneecap me for hoarding inappropriate information, which didn't happen. And so, since I couldn't exactly go into the archives and steal the file back, I pretended the whole thing had never happened. (Because wondering who'd rifled through my desk and found the file would eventually drive me mad.)

And that theory worked for almost a week. I kept my head down. I did my work. I tried to find a way to discuss Marty's competency issues that didn't sound like I was accusing him of being incompetent . . . which was difficult. I did nothing to draw attention to myself. And since I was not, in fact, fired or kneecapped in that week, it helped justify my decision when I noticed that Waco Marchand's office was still empty. Mr. Marchand had been killed a few years before, and he had never been replaced. Of course, he'd been killed by Cal after he attempted a nationwide vampire poisoning in order to make a fortune providing the antidote for said poison, tried to kill Cal in order to prevent Cal from investigating the poisoning, tried to kill Iris for helping Cal, and tried to kill me because I happened to be there. I chose to believe that the vampires didn't want to replace him because they were afraid they would get another like him. But it was more likely that the paperwork had gotten held up because some thousand-year-old vampire administrator refused to learn to fax.

I even wore black slacks and a black eyelet blouse to add an extra layer of un-noticeability while I committed my office cat burglary. With my colleagues occupied, I made an excuse to visit Sammy, sneaking down the hall to Mr. Marchand's empty office. I shut the door behind me and didn't bother with the light. I had some illumination from the streetlight outside, just enough to creep around Mr. Marchand's dark, baroque furnishings.

I felt a pang of guilt when I saw the antique painting of Mr. Marchand's family in front of their Civil War–era mansion. With his resemblance to Colonel Sanders and his chivalrous ways, Iris had once considered him the epitome of genteel vampire manners. And then, of course, he tried to murder us. So while I felt sort of bad for breaking into his office, he had been kind of a dick.

By some miracle of poorly supervised office equipment, Mr. Marchand's computer was sitting on his desk, untouched since the last time he'd used it, if the accumulated dust was any indication. The administration's solution to keeping us out of "forbidden" areas of the server was to limit our access through our user names. As IT drones, we were granted more access than most, including enough authority to create user names without linking them to our work stations. I checked the employee handbook for some sort of ironic punishment for taking advantage of this counterintuitive loophole but found nothing.

The computer roared to life, blowing out a bit of burned dust as the tower's fans started up. But the monitor showed updated programs from the office server, so I clicked on the ADMIN logo and created a user name for Dominic Purcell, the actor who played Dracula in *Blade: Trinity*. Because it would take them *years* to catch on to that one. Using the dummy user name, I searched for files that included the word "Linoge."

A big red "RESTRICTED" message flashed across my screen, demanding a password.

"Bitch, please." I snorted, tapping a few keys that allowed me around the restriction.

One file folder popped up under a directory labeled "Watch List." That seemed promising. The folder was labeled "Renart." I opened it and found a list of names and birth/death dates and locations. All women with the last name Renart, starting with a woman named Marie Renart, who lived near Rouen until her move to America just before the Louisiana Purchase.

The Renarts were not a particularly fecund bunch. Once they landed in Louisiana, the family tree was more of a bush, sticking with one or two kids in every generation, and not all of those kids carried on the family name. But the list abruptly stopped in 1968, which wasn't super-helpful. Also, I didn't see the Linoge name anywhere in the document. Anywhere. When I opened the metadata for the file, there it was in the keyword section, which, again, not helpful. Curiouser and curiouser, but ultimately, I'd learned . . . not that much.

I was missing something. All of the pieces were right there. I just couldn't make them fit.

Wait. The Renart line started near Rouen, which was in the north of France. Linoge was executed for rampaging across the north of France. Could Marie Renart be the girlfriend whose bad magical influence the early Council blamed for Linoge's feeding issues? Was that why they'd tracked the family over the years, because they were afraid the Renarts would mess with more vampires?

I took out my phone and took several shots of the screen. Logging off the server, I cleared the computer's history and shut it down.

I listened at the door for anyone walking down the hall outside the office, then stuck my head out to check for passersby. I hustled down the hallway, careful to avoid the range of the security cameras mounted near the ceiling. And I managed to snag a mocha from Sammy on my way back to our office, so I wouldn't look completely suspicious . . . to the empty office I found upon my return.

Well, I could at least succeed at not getting caught.

"Gladiola?"

I jumped in my seat. Honestly, I needed to keep a mirror on top of my monitor so people would stop sneaking up on me.

I turned to see Marty leaning against the wall near my desk, car keys in hand. "I was thinking I should walk you out to your car. Our shift ended a few minutes ago."

I sat back in my desk chair and tried not to let my annoyance show at his use of "Gladiola." Aaron and Jordan had left just a few minutes earlier, in keeping with their barely-there punctuality. And I couldn't help but notice Aaron's hand slipping into Jordan's as they walked into the hall. Aw, nerd love.

Even though I was ready to jet home, I needed to stay late and check Marty's work from that day one more time, just in case he'd gone back to fix his multitude of errors. But I couldn't tell him that, so I stuck with "Marty, I've told you, I prefer to be called Gigi. I don't go by Gladiola."

"Well, Gladiola is a much more mature name than Gigi," Marty said, a faint expression of distaste wrinkling his mouth. "So I'm going to call you Gladiola. Besides, I like that I'm the only one who calls you Gladiola. It's like I have my own cute little nickname for you."

"Yes, a nickname that belongs on the door of a nursing-home suite," I muttered, refraining from pointing out that as his superior, however technically, I could file a disciplinary action for insubordination for his use of a too-familiar and embarrassing birth name. But I figured that would be an abuse of power.

"Now, can I walk you to your car?"

"No, thank you, Marty," I said. "I'm not ready to leave just yet."

"Oh, I can wait," Marty assured me, dropping his messenger bag next to my chair.

"No, really," I insisted. "You go on home. I have paperwork I have to finish, all part of the project leader thing."

There, a very subtle reminder that I was higher on the office food chain. And if he continued to call me Gladiola, the reminders would become less subtle.

"Are you sure?" Marty said, placing a hand on the back of my chair. "I don't mind."

"No, please, go on home," I said, waving him away. "I need time to come up with the correct wording for my own job description. I think Ophelia wants to double-check that I understand what I'm supposed to be doing."

"I can stay to help," he offered.

"Go home, Marty," I said, just a little sterner than I should have been, because Marty pulled this wounded-puppy expression that made me feel like a jerk.

"All right." He sighed, moving very slowly to pick up his bag. "Good night, Gladiola."

I thunked my head against my chair. Great. I was the office ogre. And I was sticking around to sabotage the wounded puppy's chances of gainful employment. So I was a vengeful ogre. Being a grown-up kind of sucked.

I gave Marty a few minutes to come back and check one more time if I wanted to leave with him. When I was sure he was gone for the day, I ran every example of his work through the testing program one more time, just in case. It was still garbage. Unusable garbage that failed to meet even the basic standards of coding, much less the version we were using. I was starting to wonder if Marty walked me to my car most nights to make sure I wouldn't stay behind and discover this dickery.

I logged off my computer and noticed that Marty hadn't bothered doing so before leaving for the night, which was a major security-policy violation. I shut down his computer, too. After gathering up the print-outs I needed, I walked with purpose down the hall toward Ophelia's office. Her dowdy human assistant, Margaret, sat outside the closed double doors, stapling papers with such economy of movement that it was practically surgery.

Over the last week, I'd learned that Margaret was a bit of a blood bunny trapped inside a schoolmarm's body. She turned her big brown calf eyes at any vampire who crossed her path, simpering and smiling and constantly craning her neck so that the vampires were sure to notice her long, swanlike jugular. But it was hard to complain about her, since she was also a consummate professional when it came to answering questions, responding to e-mails promptly, and juggling Ophelia's schedule. She also didn't seem to like me much, but I think that had more to do with my attitude toward her boss than anything else. Much like Jordan, I had a hard time containing my eye rolls when Ophelia was mentioned in the break room.

When she saw me approaching, Margaret threw herself in front of Ophelia's door, her gray-streaked blond hair flopping over her face. She blew it out of her eyes and told me sternly, "She's not available."

"Margaret, I've worked here for weeks, and I haven't met with my supervisor. That's not reasonable. Also, I have something I need to discuss with her. I can wait right here until she's available."

"I meant, she's not in," Margaret said quickly. "She's been out for hours."

Just then, I heard Ophelia's voice on the other side of the door. "I have neither the time nor the patience for your excuses, Serena. I expect results, and I expect them immediately."

I tried not to look too smug when I smiled at Margaret. I really did.

"I demand results!" Ophelia yelled. "Concrete proof that you're actually making some effort on my behalf!"

"Fine." Margaret sighed, her florid face taking on a very put-upon expression. "I'll buzz you through when her call is over. But I'm not responsible if she takes your head off."

I was aware that she was possibly talking about actual decapitation.

I heard Ophelia bark, "You have thirty days, Serena!" and something plastic shattered against the office door. It was always nice to know you were walking into a room where office supplies were aerodynamically sound.

"Fine." Margaret sighed, pulling a petulant face while flopping into her desk chair.

I straightened my sweater, shuffled my papers, and knocked on the door.

"Enter, Margaret!" Ophelia yelled.

Before Margaret could warn her, I walked through the door and shut it behind me. Iris had warned me before my initial interview, but really, nothing could have prepared me for the array of crystal-encrusted Hello Kitty desk accessories before me. It was always a shock to walk into Ophelia's spacious pink office and see the sheer number of cartoon kitty-cat heads, from the rug to the mouse pad to the giant mural on the wall behind her. It was like reporting to an aggressively adorable Tony Montana.

And once again, I couldn't help but be unnerved by the portrait of Georgie, the beautiful blond, gray-eyed child who also happened to be Ophelia's vampirized biological sister. Still, I'd met Georgie. And as creepy as it was to speak to the living embodiment of that supersentient little girl from *Dune*, I still found the Hello Kitty shredder way more upsetting.

Ophelia was wearing an indecently red pencil skirt with a sheer black silk blouse. Her blond hair was pulled into a carefully arranged ballerina bun, and she was wearing honest-to-God red patent-leather pumps.

"Is there a reason you are putting my assistant in the awkward position of telling you that I don't want to see you?" Ophelia asked, also without looking up from her papers. I supposed this was the newest trend in dismissive office rudeness. "Margaret is a polite soul, you see, and she doesn't like being openly rude to people. I've never had a problem with it."

"Trust me, I've noticed," I told her. "The others appointed me as project leader. The first task in my job description is 'serving as a liaison between the project team and supervisory staff,' which is you. And 'presenting weekly progress reports regarding the project and any obstacles or problems impeding said progress.' And since I have not presented this report in the weeks we've been working, I figured it's time."

Ophelia propped her elbows on her desk and folded her hands under her chin. "Do you have any idea how inappropriate it is to force your way into a meeting with your supervisor?"

I smiled sweetly. "Almost as inappropriate as a supervisor who refuses to meet with her employees because of interpersonal tension rooted outside of the office."

Ophelia's eyes narrowed. I was pretty sure that if there hadn't been witnesses who saw me go into her office, I would have been the first person ever murdered with a Hello Kitty stapler.

A reasonable person with a proportionate sense of self-preservation would have stuck to the tried-and-true methods to avoid digestion by an apex predator: stay still, don't make eye contact, and definitely don't arrange one's face into a big smartass grin.

I never claimed to be reasonable. And my sense of self-preservation was clearly nonexistent. So I just stretched that fake sweet smile into the big smartass grin.

Ophelia's hand twitched toward her stapler, but she managed to wrap her other hand around it and press it to the desk. She took a deep breath, opened her eyes, and said, "Very well. What would you like to report?"

"Aaron and Jordan are turning in quality work and meeting their goals, as am I."

I sighed, crossing my legs and shifting in my chair. I cleared my throat. And I felt like a total bitch for what I was about to do. I didn't want Marty to be fired. He seemed like a nice guy, just a little overwhelmed. But the bottom line was that Marty wasn't pulling his weight. And it would be a lot easier to point out more serious issues with his performance in the future if I pointed out his weak points now. So I took a deep breath and phrased it as carefully as I could. "Marty is having difficulty keeping up. His work has not been up to par, and we're still setting up the most basic functions of the search engine. Not to mention that he just left the office with his computer still logged into the system, which is a problem, security-wise. Aaron, Jordan, and I are going to have to redo all of his work, which will create a slight setback now. But if he doesn't step it up, that slight setback could become a major delay."

"I would suggest that you check his work every day, point out any problems, and retrain him."

"Retrain him? Programming is a basic requirement of his job. That would be like telling someone they have to retrain an accountant in how to do addition. I have to question how he passed the initial interview if he's having problems like this."

"It's not up to you to question the hiring process, Miss Scanlon," she said, quite frostily.

"But it's up to me to retrain employees who got through the lax hiring process?"

"Well, as project leader, you shouldn't have any problems, should you?" She smiled that flat shark's smile. "Thank you. I look forward to your next report. And by next report, I mean the report you present after you have shown enough professional courtesy to schedule an appointment with Margaret."

I nodded. "Ophelia—"

"Thank you."

"Oph—"

"Thankyou!" she exclaimed, not even leaving a pause between the two words. And with that, she turned the pink Hello Kitty–embossed back of her chair to me.

I was pretty sure that between me, the kitties, and the four-hundred-plus-year-old vampire, I was the most mature being in this room. I hoped that with her superhearing, she could hear the way my teeth were grinding.

Had I been right before? Had Ophelia saddled me with a subpar coworker to sabotage the project? Or was she just trying to drive me crazy? It might have seemed like a paranoid, unproductive way of think-ing but not nearly as unproductive as having my work hobbled by a manager who was pissed at me for "stealing her boyfriend."

But that manager also had fangs, and I needed to get out of the office before she put them to use. I was already violating several bullet points from the orienta-tion video. I had pushed up from the chair and gotten about three steps away from Ophelia's desk when I stopped and turned toward her . . .

Screw it, no one lives forever. I kissed vampires in alleyways. I was a badass.

"You know, it's not my fault that Jamie wants to have a real college experience. He's missed out on so much already, being turned before he could graduate from high school. He wants to experience a little bit of the outside world before he settles down, which you know he's going to do with you. I think it would be kind of selfish of you to try to keep him from that. I only helped him with the application process because it can be overwhelming and scary even without all of the vampire issues. And because it was important to him, and I'm his *friend*. That's what friends do for each other."

Ophelia turned back to me, and while her face was a pleasant mask, her eyes could have curdled milk. "Oh, I think I know exactly how close the two of you are," she said. "I hear enough about your friendship every time Jamie and I speak."

"Then you should know that there are no romantic feelings between us."

"But it is amazing how often he comes running whenever you need something or are hosting something or some member of your dysfunctional group has a hangnail and there's an emergency meeting."

I honestly didn't know how to respond to that. It had been such a long time since Iris and I belonged to a family that we just took it for granted that it was normal for us to be so entangled with Jane and the other vampires. Also, we didn't have many friends outside of the circle, so we didn't have a lot of competition for our time and attention. From Ophelia's perspective, I could see how irritating it might be to have your time with your boyfriend split with his big fat geek vampire family, even if Georgie did seem to find us entertaining.

I was sympathizing with Ophelia. This did not compute.

And damned if I was going to tell her about it.

"That seems like something you should discuss with Jamie," I told her.

"I don't think I'll have to," she said, giving me dead shark's eyes that, frankly, freaked me the hell out.

"OK, then." I nodded. "Good night."

Ophelia didn't answer, which was just the cherry on top of her sundae of rudeness.

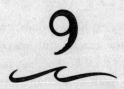

9

Use common sense when dressing for work. Yes, you have the right to wear open-neck blouses that highlight the length and definition of your throat. That doesn't mean you should.

—*The Office After Dark: A Guide to Maintaining a Safe, Productive Vampire Workplace*

A witch, a computer programmer, and a couple of vampires walking into a coffee bar may have sounded like a complicated setup for one of Dick Cheney's inappropriate jokes, but sadly, it was how I was spending my night off.

Nik was working, fielding some last-minute call from Ophelia about a new break-in over in Murphy. When I told Iris that I was planning to spend the evening at Specialty Books, she'd been thrilled, but she'd also called the shop shortly after I'd arrived, either because she questioned my night-driving abilities or she still had doubts about my "going out for coffee with coworkers" excuse for being out so late with Nik. Once again, neither option was great, but I supposed I should be grateful that Cal hadn't attached a GPS locator to my car.

Still, it was nice to have a quiet evening out, even if I was under the careful but intentionally nonchalant supervision of Dick, Andrea, and Jane. I loved Jane's bookshop, with its soothing but whimsical blue and purple color scheme and comfy reading chairs. I loved the old maple and leaded-glass cabinet she used as a sales counter and the tidy, carefully labeled bookshelves that suited her former librarian's sensibilities. It was nice to know some things hadn't changed since I went away to school. Dick still "worked" at the shop, but he mostly stayed in the back because of his tendency to offend some (uptight, humorless) customers. Andrea still ran the espresso machine, because she didn't trust anyone else to keep it from exploding. Jane still made incendiary coffee when Andrea left the shop.

The business had flourished since Jane's shaky opening years before. They'd added on to the coffee menu over the years, and they were now considered one of the best vampire-friendly coffee bars in the state. The shelf stock ran the gamut from mainstream paranormal romances to mystical gardening books, but Jane was best known for her vampire nonfiction, self-help for the fanged set. Internet orders alone were enough to keep the store in the black, something Mr. Wainwright had rarely accomplished.

The nonfiction section, particularly the titles concerning magic and its effects on vampires, was what drew me to Specialty Books that night. Since Nola didn't have a lot of experience with vampire curses and I knew how easy it was to post absolute insanity-babble on the Internet, I was sifting through Jane's shelves to try to find some answers about Nik's state of mind. Jane was eager to help, as she was unaware of vampires' susceptibility to curses and figured if anyone was bound to tick off a witch badly enough to end up hexed, it would be her.

"Thanks for letting me use your research materials, Jane," I said, as Andrea served me a (nonbloody) mocha and a chocolate chess square.

I had all of the related books in the store spread across my little round maple table, including *When Magic Meets the Undead: Spells and Their Effects on Vampires* and *Curses Most Foul: A Guide to Hexing Your Exes*. Even though Ben was a pretty nice guy, it was good to know I had options.

"We'll just tell Iris that you spent the night reading the *Morganville Vampires* books and ridding my computer of viruses, OK?" she said, throwing her long braid of thick brown hair over her shoulder as she wiped down the sales counter.

"I clicked on *one* pop-up ad!" Dick shouted indignantly from the back of the shop.

Jamie, who was sprawled across the cushy purple love seat near the coffee bar, shook his head and raised his hand. He mouthed the words "Multiple pop-up ads." Then he made an explosion noise and spread his fingers wide. I laughed. Even though Jamie wasn't

helping with the actual research, he'd insisted on ac-
companying me to the shop tonight. He claimed he
wanted to spend some quality time with me, now that
I was a grown-up working woman and my nights off
were such a precious commodity. But I suspected he
was just nervous about me walking back and forth to
my car, since that was proving to be such a challenge
of late.

Jane insisted that Jamie wasn't going to help me,
that he was going to read something constructive, so
she'd handed him a copy of *The Jungle* by Upton Sinclair. While I'd had to read that particular title as part
of my senior English class in high school, newly vampirized Jamie had completed his diploma from home
and had missed out on Sinclair's scathing depiction of
the pre-USDA meatpacking industry. The more Jamie
read, the more repulsed his expression, which seemed
to make Jane happy, because at least she knew he was
paying attention.

"If I wasn't already on a liquid diet, this book would
put me off hamburgers for life," Jamie said, making his
patented gag face.

"I was a vegetarian for about six months after reading *The Jungle*," I told him. "I still can't eat hot dogs. But
it's important that you read that now, because you'll be
reading much more disturbing stuff in your freshman
lit class. *Heart of Darkness* will scar you for life."

"I can't tell you how happy it makes me to have you
two sitting around discussing books," Jane said, putting a tall glass of what amounted to vampire choco-

late milk in front of Jamie: bottled blood and Hershey's Special Blood Additive Chocolate Syrup. She actually wiped a pinkish tear from her eye as she ruffled Jamie's hair. He scowled and brushed his hair back into its usual intentionally messy state. But after he drained his little snack, he had a bright red milk mustache on his upper lip, so his indignation was short-lived.

"That is disgusting," I told him.

He winked at me and wiped the errant blood foam away.

"So if you don't want to tell Iris why I'm here tonight, why are you helping me?" I asked Jane.

"Because forbidden love with a hot, mysterious vampire?" she said, gesturing to her paranormal romance section. "I'm not only the president of that club, I'm also a member."

She ignored Jamie's muttered "Gross."

"Besides, you're going to do this whether we help you or not, so it's better that you have some resources and supervision," Jane continued. "And for what it's worth, based on my very quick read of Nik, I don't think he's a bad guy or that he's trying to hurt you. I'm getting a lot of blank spots from him, which backs up his whole amnesia story. Don't get me wrong, Geeg, he has some very warm thoughts that I probably shouldn't share in front of Cal, but none of them are hostile. He honestly doesn't want to hurt you."

I blew out an exasperated breath. "Well, that's disappointing. I was really hoping we would get this magical clue, like 'Gigi emotionally traumatized Nik by reminding him of a hated enemy who attacked him on a Christmas tree farm.' And all I would have to do was prove I was trustworthy around pointy tree stumps or something."

"That's not usually how it works," Jane said, squeezing my arm.

"I just wish I could make Iris see how my situation isn't that different from hers. I know she has a tendency to overreact when I'm in peril, but I thought she'd have adjusted by now. She's still pulling the Mama Capulet routine pretty hard."

"So, since it's upsetting everybody who loves you, maybe you should just walk away from this guy and never ever talk to him again," Jamie suggested brightly.

"I will not take dating advice from the man who knowingly and willingly bloodmated himself to Ophelia Lambert," I told him. "At least Nik's violent episodes are unintentional. Ophelia's violent episodes happen because it's Tuesday or because her hair didn't turn out the way she wanted." Jamie's mouth dropped open, as if he was going to defend his Machiavellian lady love. "But even though I've mocked you mercilessly for dating her, I've never genuinely encouraged you to leave her. Because that's none of my business. I would hope you would do the same for me."

Jamie scowled again. "Oh, sure, bring logic and compassion into the argument. Cheater."

"You and Iris will be fine," Jane assured me, sliding into the chair at my left. "It's not like Jenny and me, where we had to build a relationship from the ground up as adults. You have a strong foundation. This is just a minor bump in the road. And I know this probably doesn't make you feel any better, but her anger and spazzery comes from a place of concern. Trust me, as someone who has been hassled all of her life by someone who means well, it's less annoying than the efforts of someone who is honestly trying to hurt you."

"I will keep that in mind," I promised Jane.

Jane winked at me, giving my shoulders a squeeze. "Good girl. Now, what are you finding?"

I handed Jane my notes, which she read over quickly, making little asterisks on the points she considered important. "You know, until Nola showed up, I wouldn't have believed there was such a thing. I mean, Gabriel told me that witches were real, but until I saw her work her mojo . . . We live in an amazing world, Gigi."

"Well, this amazing magical world has it in for you vampires just as much as us humans, so at least it's equal opportunity." I flipped open her copy of *Hermann's Guide to Supernatural Physiology*. "As you know, vampire energy isn't the same as human energy, because we run on different wavelengths. Basically, witches have to work a little harder to cast on you guys, because your energy is harder to pin down. You would have to have frequent contact with the vampire to cast on him, dose him with the potion, or snatch his hair, blood, et cetera."

"Well, strike amazing, that's just horrible," Jane said, shuddering.

"What's horrible?" Nola asked, strolling into the shop and dropping her purse next to my table. Nola was wearing the blue-and-peach scrubs required for her job at Half-Moon Hollow's free clinic. She looked tired and worn out, which was natural, considering the rigors of being a medical empath who hung around sick people all day, but she was happy.

"The various bits of DNA that witches need for casting," Andrea said, pouring a cup of tea she'd been brewing for Nola, knowing that her chamomile-loving step-great-great-great-great-great-granddaughter was coming for a visit. "It's unseemly."

"And on that note, I'm going to go see what Dick is doing," Jamie said, snapping his book closed. "Gross club memberships and DNA collection are a little much, even for me."

"According to what I'm reading, whoever cursed Nik sees him frequently," I said, showing her the book. "As far as I know, the only people he sees regularly are the other employees at the Council office and me. Since I know that I'm not the one casting on him, I would assume it's another Council employee. But the Council doesn't employ a full-time magical consultant. Also, there's the added complication of Nik not remembering being worked over, spell-wise, so we're dealing with someone pretty powerful, maybe with hypnotic abilities. I don't think someone like that is going to be working as a file clerk. For all her faults, Ophelia is a big believer in taking advantage of her employees' full potential."

"Have you thought about who at the office could be a witch?" Nola asked, sipping her tea. "Someone who might want to harm you, considering that the curse seems to focus on hurting you?"

"Besides Ophelia?" I asked. "Mr. Crown doesn't seem to like me, but I don't think he likes anyone. Margaret, Ophelia's secretary, is pretty snippy with me, but I think it's because I'm borderline rude to her boss, like, all the time. Also, I don't respect her carefully constructed schedule. And there's the lady from accounting whom I caught taking Jordan's yogurt out of our office's fridge. She acted all indignant about being caught, like it was my fault for walking in on her stealing."

Nola nodded. "Either of those last two seems plausible. Witches can be sticklers for time . . . and yogurt."

"So really, there are several people at my office who do not wish me well, and any number of them could be witches. This conversation is not making me feel better."

"You could always quit," Dick called from the back.

"I really can't," I called back. "My postprobationary compensation package of fabulous prizes just kicked in. I'm making more money in a pay period than I made in my entire summer at NetSecure. I've already made a couple of payments on my student loan."

"Money's not always the answer," Dick yelled.

"If the question is how do I establish life as an independent adult who doesn't need to ask her sister for lunch money, then yes, money is the answer," I shot back.

"Also, I don't know if she should pay any mind to the man who slips twenties into my pocket when I hug him!" Nola called.

Dick poked his head out of the storeroom. "We agreed to pretend that doesn't happen!"

Laughing, I shuffled through the stack of books on the table. I couldn't help but feel I was missing something. I was approaching the problem all wrong, but I couldn't figure out why. I stood up from the table and wandered into Jane's magic section. Nola carefully vetted all of Jane's magic texts, for fear of providing the wrong book to an irresponsible practitioner. All of the "dangerous" books were kept in a special storage case, for which Jane had the only key. But those titles were more along the lines of *How to Flay Your Enemy Alive with Your Thoughts* and *Magical Exsanguination for Fun and Profit*. Not exactly the droids I was looking for.

I needed to spend more time around non-nerds.

I tapped my fingers along the spines as I scanned the titles in the magical history section. *Witches of Salem: Fact and Fiction, History's Most Disappointing Magical Politicians, Sorcerers of the Ancient Egyptian Royal Court,* and at the end of the shelf, bottom row, *Magickal Families of the Old World*.

Unlike the slick, soft-covered editions on the shelf, the book was old, battered, and bound in mottled blue linen. The gold lettering was practically worn off the cover. Jane would consider this book gently loved. I opened it and scanned the pages, which listed the most prominent European magical families by country, how they started, and what they were up to at the time of the 1912 printing date. It was sort of funny that this was basically the same thing we were doing for the vampires, just the old, dusty beta version. (I would never ever let Jane hear me say such a thing.) A piece of information floated up to the surface of my brain.

Renart.

According to the Council records, the Renart family started in France, and its members were interesting enough to be on a Council "watch list." I flipped to the index, looking for the Rs. The Renart family was listed on page 326, and it merited several paragraphs:

> *Known for their memory charms and ability to persuade those around them through creative cursework, the Renarts lived quite comfortably in Haute-Normandie for generations. Members of the family were rumored to have dabbled in necromancy toward the end of the eighteenth century, ostracizing them from the magickal community. The family moved to the Louisiana territory under enormous pressure from other magickal families and disappeared into the mundane populations of America.*

Mundane? That was unnecessarily hurtful.

The colorful surroundings of the shop, my friends' voices, everything faded away as I tried to connect all the dots in my head. So the Renarts messed around with necromancy and got booted out of an entire continent. Somehow they were connected to this Linoge character and his violent outbursts. Did messing around with vampires' brains count as necromancy? Violent outbursts, memory issues . . . Nik. This had to be connected to Nik's fugue states. If Marie Renart, the first in the line of Renarts, was Linoge's girlfriend, she could have diddled with his brain so he had violent feeding episodes he couldn't remember. Could one of Renart's descendants have messed with Nik's brain? Had it happened here or while he was traveling? What were the parameters of the curse?

I pulled out my phone and opened the photo I'd taken of the Renart watch list. It ended in 1968 with the birth of a Jennifer Renart in Paris, Illinois, a tiny town only two hours' drive from the Hollow, but there was no date of death listed. Had Jennifer managed to shake her vampire tail and die a peaceful, unobserved death? What had happened to the last Renart?

Jane carefully cleared her throat, peering over the top of the bookshelf at me while she stirred her bloodychino. "There's another option you haven't considered."

"Does it avoid an explanation in which someone is sneaking into Nik's room every night to steal his hair? Because I will jump on it," I told her.

"Cooperation," Jane said gently. "What if Nik isn't as magically manipulated as he seems to be?"

"Why would he do that?"

"I don't know, plausible deniability? He doesn't

want to admit that he's involved, so he uses the 'Oh, I don't remember, baby, I was under an evil curse' excuse. So he gets whatever rewards are involved in doing his master's bidding plus whatever, er, rewards, you might be giving him."

"I refuse to accept that Nik is knowingly involved in all this," I told Jane sternly. "Besides, you were the one who said he doesn't want to hurt me."

"From what I *could see*, he doesn't," she said, throwing her hands up. "But as Miss Worst-Case Scenario, I am pathologically required to put that out there. I just want you to be careful, Geeg, that's all. You're one of the last remaining humans in our little family. I want to do whatever we can to protect you."

"Well, I appreciate it, but cut it out."

Jane nodded. "Duly noted."

"And while we're on the subject of office awkwardness, we found this for you," Andrea said, handing me a paperback with a stark black, white, and red cover.

"*The Office After Dark: A Guide to Maintaining a Safe, Productive Vampire Workplace*," I murmured. Almost every subject in the table of contents pertained to my workplace issues: "Dealing with hostile, fanged supervisors," "How to report issues with human coworkers without looking like a vampire pet wannabe," and "Personal safety at the office." I turned on Jane. "You couldn't have given this to me a few weeks ago?"

"Honestly, we didn't think you'd need it. We thought you would adjust better to the undead work environment," she said, making Andrea snort.

"That's not funny," I told all three women as they laughed at me.

"It's a little funny!" Jamie yelled from the back of the shop.

I arrived home a bit later to find Iris in full preparation for date night. She and Cal were going to try a new vampire-friendly dinner theater in Murphy. They hadn't had an evening alone since I'd moved back home with all of my, well, let's just say issues. I was actually looking forward to having the place to myself for the evening, and not just because I felt so profoundly guilty for intruding on their marriage to the point where they had to schedule time together. I was planning to veg out, eat some of the Ben & Jerry's Phish Food I'd saved for a special occasion, and tend to some much-needed personal grooming that I'd neglected over the past few weeks. There would be plucking, moisturizing, and exfoliating. A lot of exfoliating.

"Gigi," Cal said, his tone far too casual as he stepped into the hallway, struggling with his necktie. "You're home on time."

"Yes, and I was exactly where I said I was, all night. There was no reason for Iris to call the bookshop to check on me," I said, gently batting his hands away so I could fix his tie. And yes, I had no right to be indignant when I had, in fact, lied to him about being with my coworkers when I was with Nik the night before. But I'd worry about that when and if he ever found out about it.

"I wasn't checking up on you. I needed to check

with Jane about . . . business-related things," Iris called from the bathroom, where she was carefully brushing out her coffee-colored curls.

"Smooth, Iris, really smooth," I called back. "Look, I get that you guys are worried. And I know it comes from a place of concern. I love you, and I appreciate that you want me to be safe."

Cal pursed his lips. "I sense a 'but' coming."

"Yes, as in, I'm going to kick your butt if you don't stop treating me like a little girl."

Cal wrapped his arms around my shoulders, resting his chin on top of my head. "I won't apologize. I love you as much as any brother could. I worry for you every time you step out the door. I feel pride every time I hear someone at the office talk about the fantastic work you're doing. And I want to murder every single male who looks in your direction, even if it's an old friend. I know that we've embarrassed you and made things difficult. I don't want to cause you distress. But I will do whatever it takes to keep you safe, even if it makes you temporarily unhappy."

"I know." I sighed. "I know you love me. And I forgive you for the embarrassment and unhappiness."

"Thank you," he murmured into my hair.

"Eventually," I added.

"I knew that was coming." He sighed.

"Is Nik really so bad?" I asked.

"Under normal circumstances, I would say no," Cal said. "But I'm having a hard time looking past the lurking and the lunging."

"So, if we were able to determine why Nik is attacking me and put a stop to it, you would be OK with me dating him?"

There was a long moment of silence above my head, making me look up at my brother-in-law. He was chewing on his lip and had a spacey trying-to-do-long-division-in-his-head expression on his face.

"Cal?"

"I'm trying to find a way to answer that question that won't result in you chasing after a 'cure' for Nik's condition or Iris being upset with me for letting you date a man hundreds of years your senior."

I squirmed guiltily in his arms, because I was already chasing after a cure for Nik, and Iris was going to be upset with Cal any way he answered the question. I felt another pair of arms sliding around my waist and Iris's head settling against my shoulder.

"Oh, good, we're hugging again." She sighed. "I really hate it when we disagree, Gigi. And unlike Cal, I will apologize for making you unhappy. I've just been responsible for you for so long I'm having a hard time adjusting to the idea that you've grown up."

I turned my head and kissed Iris's forehead. "It's OK, Iris. I love you, too." Both vampires squeezed me simultaneously, which was enough to make me wheeze and cough. "Ribs cracking!"

Iris sprang back while Cal raised his arms. I finally got a good look at Iris's apricot-colored sheath dress and her sky-high Iron Fist heels imprinted with little peaches and skulls. It was a far cry from the sensible, stain-proof outfits she'd worn as a human. "Wow, you look hot, Iris! And that's 'hawt' with a 'w,' like the young people are saying these days."

Iris preened while Cal gave a low whistle. "Well, you don't have to sound so surprised."

"I'm not. I'm wondering if I would finally have the coordination and ankle strength required to wear platform heels if I get turned."

"Don't even joke about that, Geeg."

"I'm just saying. My shoe collection could use some perking up."

"I will buy you some wedges," Iris told me. "You could always come with us tonight, you know."

"Because me joining you on your date night isn't pathetic or counterproductive at all. You've had these plans for a week," I told her. "Just go. I am going to take a bath, indulge in total control over the TV, and catch up on some sleep. These night hours are really getting to me."

Iris made a motherly clucking noise, cupping her hands under my chin so she could check for dark circles under my eyes. "Poor thing. Well, enjoy your vegging. I have lip gloss to apply."

She strolled across the slick polished floor with far more grace than I could imagine in my lifetime. Cal, I noticed, was watching her, too, but in a lecherous manner. I slapped his chest. "Dude. That's my sister."

He scoffed. "That's my wife. I get to ogle; it was in the vows."

I shuddered. "Gross."

• • •

I stood at the door and waved as Iris and Cal pulled out of the driveway. The moon shone brightly over the gardens, casting long, eerie shadows through the flowers. My phone beeped from my purse. I locked the door and armed the security system before grabbing it. I had a text notification from a number I didn't recognize. *Hope you have a nice weekend. Big plans?*

The area code was local, but it could have been a wrong number, so I ignored it.

I jogged up the steps to my room and the phone beeped again. *No plans?*

"Let's see, girl home alone, mysterious text messages from an unknown party, there's no way this is the opening setup for a creepy serial-killer movie," I muttered, dropping my phone onto my dresser. "I will not engage in your potentially deadly mind-buggery, sir."

I double-checked the security system, though, just in case. I indulged in a long, hot bath, swirling with essential oils Iris had pressed from her own garden, rosemary and geranium and calendula. I soaked until I was as limp as a noodle, with not one thought of my tragic personal and professional lives. I gave myself a pineapple enzyme facial, pumiced my feet and elbows, and shaved everything worth shaving. By the time I slid into my pajamas, I was smooth and sweet-smelling.

I walked into my bedroom and found another text waiting for me. *Are you there, Gigi?*

So, not a wrong number, then. Who would be texting me from a number I didn't recognize? I was ruthless about updating my contacts. I even had Ophelia saved under "Evil Empress."

Could it be Nik? He'd "confessed" that he had a cell phone, but he'd never given me his number. I would consider that a red flag, trust-wise, but I never needed to call him. He always just popped up whenever I needed him. The texts didn't sound like him. They lacked his flirty wit. But a lot of people didn't sound like themselves in text speak, right?

Cautiously, I picked up the phone and typed in a message that wouldn't be embarrassing, in case it turned out to be a polite catching-up text from Pastor Neely, who was *not* saved in my contact list. *No big plans. You?*

Hoping I hadn't just made an enormous mistake in terms of horror-movie survival, I popped in the latest remake of *The Lone Ranger*. It had nothing to do with the fact that the guy who played the lead looked a lot like Nik, thank you very much. I climbed into bed and formed a nest of pillows for the perfect loafing position. My phone beeped again. *No, but maybe we can change that?*

I smiled. That did sound like Nik. I lay there, snuggled against my pillows, trying to think of a saucy but appropriately hard-to-get reply. But my eyes were so heavy that I was on the verge of falling asleep. It was just after midnight and I was struggling to stay awake. It might have seemed like a sad, lonely way to spend a

Saturday night. But after weeks of being crammed into my office with three other people, plus the joys of being smothered by a large, loud vampire clan, the solitude was almost blissful. And quiet, so very quiet. I was drifting into that twilight haze between sleep and waking.

I started awake at the sound of tapping on glass. I lifted my head from the pillow, blinking rapidly. The rapping sounded again, and I opened the curtains to find Nik sitting on the planter box outside my window. And he had a bunch of sunflowers in his hand, tied with a blue gingham ribbon.

Definitely an upgrade from creepy serial killer.

"What are you doing?" I asked, as he climbed through the window casing and dropped into a dramatic kneel. He presented the flowers with a flourish.

"I figured if we were going to impersonate Romeo and Juliet, we should give it our all."

"Yeah, 'cause their story ended well." I snickered, pressing my face against the waxy petals. Thanks to growing up with Iris, I knew that giving someone sunflowers symbolized adoration and warm feelings, and that knowledge made my heart race.

"I know that you are surrounded by blossoms," he said, gesturing out the window toward Iris's garden. "But I thought you should have flowers of your own, something that bloomed in the sun. And if your sister asks, you received them from a computer-software company that is trying to seduce you into their ranks."

I shivered a little when he said the word "seduce." I

couldn't help it. I dare any card-carrying red-blooded woman to hear Nikolai Dragomirov pronounce the word "seduce" without giggling and blushing. "That's very cute," I told him, as he nuzzled my neck. "I can't believe I just snuck you into my room like a fifteen-year-old. Again. This is becoming a terrible habit."

"Believe it or not, my Gigi, I have never done this for another girl."

"You're right, I don't believe you've never done this before."

"Well, my experience is more related to escaping down a trellis while an unsuspecting husband or father came through the front door," he admitted, gently dropping the flowers to my desk.

My head dropped to his shoulder. "Why do you tell me these things?"

"It never occurred to me not to," he said, sliding his fingertips along the waistband of my pajama pants.

"And that's what frightens me."

He turned me so my back was pressed against his chest, toying with the tie of my pants.

"Why are you here, Nik?"

"I thought I had just made that pretty clear," he said, nipping at my lips. I smacked his shoulder. "I wanted to see you. I have missed you desperately, to the detriment of my dignity. It is shameful. All of the other vampires have been mocking me."

"That's very sweet," I said, kissing him. "And since you were so shamelessly honest about your motives, there is this one really dirty fantasy I've always had."

His tawny eyes went wide and, dare I say it, hopeful. "What is that?"

"Having sex in my own bed," I said, running my lips along the hollow of his throat. "In my own house." I bit his collarbone lightly, barely enough to make a mark on his skin but enough to make him moan and clutch at my back. "Without worrying about being quiet."

He frowned. "In terms of fantasies, that is not terribly dirty."

"Well, you try living on nothing but furtive back-seat gropings and stolen moments in communal dorm rooms. Being as loud as you want on an actual mattress will sound downright decadent."

He laughed but cut it short when the implication of what I'd said landed. "So I take it you have done this before?"

"Do you really want me to answer that?"

There was no way I was going to answer that, because I didn't want my ex-boyfriend dead.

"And as a subquestion, am I asking you questions about the legions of ladies who rolled through your sheets over the years?"

"No, you are not," he acknowledged. "So I suppose it would be petty of me to begrudge you an inexperienced and no doubt inadequate partner." He cleared his throat, glancing at Ben's picture. "It is just the one inexperienced and inadequate partner, right?" He winced as I elbowed him in the stomach and immediately changed his tone to one of cheerful interest. "So how does this fantasy of yours start out?"

"With some white-hot, hard-core . . ." I paused to nip at his chin. "Making out."

"That I can do."

Nik pressed me back on the bed, trailing his fingers down my ribs over my tank top. His mouth skimmed between my breasts and down the line of my bared stomach, leaving a cool, wet line of sensation in its wake. He nibbled a ring around my belly button while tugging down my pajama pants. Then he worked his way back up my body, pausing to trace the inner curve of each breast with his tongue before latching on to my mouth. He kissed me over and over until my lips were swollen and tender, never once letting his fangs scrape my flesh.

"You know, I do not think I have ever simply 'made out' with a human," he whispered, kissing the tip of my nose. "It has always led to more."

"Well, then it will be a night of mind-blowing firsts for both of us."

Waggling his eyebrows, he spread my legs wide, settling between them and wrapping my thighs snugly around his hips. After pulling my tank over my head, he worried the line of my jaw with his blunt teeth. That nagging concern that he would lose control was there, tickling at the corner of my brain. But he was just so damn good with his hands, playing my body like a well-tuned violin, that I was able to willfully ignore that concern.

I unsnapped his jeans and slid them over his hips, pushing them down his thighs with my feet. My eyes went wide at the sight of what had only been hinted at during the previous session on the couch.

Whoa. Ben had been a pretty healthy size, but this—this was a bit more, well, just *more*. Though I belonged to the One Penis Club, I was proud that I knew how to handle the single "member" I'd had contact with. Still, Nik looked as if he might be a bit outside my skill level. What if I couldn't please him? He'd been with more women than I cared to count over the years, women who probably knew *tricks*, and all I knew how to do was—

"We will figure it out," Nik murmured against my neck, as if he could read the apprehensive thoughts bouncing around my head. His hands worked over my body, rubbing and teasing, until I felt like a puddle of melted caramel on the mattress.

Did we have melted caramel in the kitchen? It was an intriguing image.

But all thoughts of dessert-topped vampires were dashed when Nik knelt between my legs, wedging his knees under my tailbone.

"Keep your hands right there," he told me, curling my hands around the spokes of my headboard. "And make as much noise as you want."

I snickered, nuzzling his temple. I could feel Nik between my thighs, testing and stroking, spreading the warm wetness that flowed between us over his length. Then he drove into me, smooth and slick, and even though I was ready, the sensation of being stretched made me cry out. He stopped, eyes focused on my face. I nodded, and he very slowly canted his hips.

I tilted my head back against the pillow, settling into the rhythm and enjoying the opportunity to yip, yell, and moan as loudly as I wanted without fear of being overheard. I clutched at his shoulders, clinging to him as he rose to his knees, settling me against his thighs.

I rolled my hips, keening at the delicious friction of this new angle. His forehead pressed against mine, and he panted along with me, even though he didn't need to breathe. I ran my hands along his long, toned back, my fingertips memorizing every vertebra and scar.

His hand slid up my neck, brushing his thumb across my earring. His eyes went smoky blue, and his mouth moved, as if he was trying to speak, but the words wouldn't come. I clasped his face in my hands, forcing him to look at me. His eyes cleared as I shook his head slightly. "Nik?"

He ducked his head, kissing me and thrusting up, making me shudder. He moved over me, faster and faster, until I could only hold on as he manipulated my hips. And I took full advantage of being able to scream.

I scampered up the stairs in Nik's shirt and my socks, a trail of acrid smoke following me to the second floor.

Nik came running out of my bedroom, yanking on his jeans. "Gigi!" he called over the howl of the smoke alarm as I waved the smoldering bag of microwave popcorn around like a smudge stick. "What are you doing?"

"I don't want Iris and Cal to know you've been in the house!" I said, the last word coming out far too loudly as he disabled the alarm. "So I'm employing a little olfactory camouflage."

"I do not know whether to be afraid or impressed with your level of tactical thinking," he said, pressing one of my shirts over his nose to protect himself from the smoking popcorn stink-bomb in my hand.

"You should be a little of both!" After waving the bag around my room a few rounds, I took it back downstairs and tossed it off the back porch. I found Nik in my room with his head sticking out the open window. "Sorry, it's a little strong."

"That is one of the worst smells in the world," he said, waving his hand in front of his face. "And I lived in an era without indoor plumbing."

"Ew." I shook my head as I flopped into my bed. Nik crawled in next to me, pulling me against his side.

"I hate that we have to go to extremes to hide this from your family," he said, running his thumb along my bottom lip.

"Hey, I almost got Cal to admit that he would be OK with us seeing each other without the threat of you killing me. I consider that progress."

"You, *sladkaya*, have a low standard for progress."

"Speaking of which, what was that earlier?" I asked. "Your eyes glazed over blue, and you looked a little bit like when you go into your zombie state. But you were still you, and you didn't try to bite me, so again, progress. What did you see?"

He stroked a finger over the moonstones at my earlobes. "I remember buying the earrings. After I kissed you—"

"And ran away like a big coward."

"You are going to have to let that go."

I shook my head. "Not anytime soon."

He cleared his throat. "After I kissed you and you left, I circled back to the store and bought them. Because they made you smile, and I wanted to give you something that would make you smile. In all the time I watched you, I did not think you smiled enough. I went to your house and left them on your porch, where you could find them. My only regret was that I would not be able to see you open them—*mmph*."

I cut him off, throwing my arms around his neck and kissing him deeply. He remembered! I was practically climbing the man. He remembered the moment that had meant so much to me. It wasn't just in my head. I wasn't alone in this relationship.

"If I had known you would react this way, I would have fondled your earrings much earlier."

"I thought I was going crazy," I whispered. "I thought my weird brain had made it all up."

"You are not crazy," he promised me. "If either of us is insane, it is the one with the large gaps in his memory."

"Mmm, good point." For a moment, I considered telling him about my research into his curse. But I didn't want to get his hopes up, and I didn't want him to warn me away. I didn't want to hear that I was too young, too inexperienced, too human to find a solution to the problem.

He pulled his shirt on and kissed me. "We will talk soon. But for now, I am going to dive out of your window like an Olympic medalist." When I made another pouty face, he added, "Unless, of course, you would like me to stay, and we can explain this to Iris and Cal."

I bit my bottom lip for a moment before planting a kiss on his. "Try to clear the rosebushes."

10

~

You will be thrown into situations that will shock and unsettle you. It's important to maintain your composure, no matter what you see, hear, or have splattered on your shirt.

—The Office After Dark: A Guide to Maintaining a Safe, Productive Vampire Workplace

I was not as good at office espionage-slash-witch-hunting as I'd hoped.

I searched every Internet database I could think of for Renarts. I even tried a few not quite legal avenues to government records, suffering the indignities of an Internet café/bait shop's so-called free Wi-Fi because I didn't want the search traced back to me. I even tried searching the descendant database to see if Marie Renart had children with Linoge and they might be listed in our information. No dice. The Renarts had disappeared entirely with Jennifer Renart. I found her birth record, evidence of her high school graduation, and then *nothing.* No college enrollment, no marriage certificate, no death certificate, no evidence that she'd legally changed her name. Her paper trail disintegrated into nothing, almost impossible in today's world.

Had she gone into hiding? Had the vampires made her disappear? Why was she hiding?

I was stewing over this series of failures when my desk phone rang, and the Council's front desk staff announced that I had a visitor. I pushed up from my desk, a confused frown firmly in place as I marched up to reception. Who would visit me here? Cal and Iris wouldn't be stopped at the front desk. They had high-clearance credentials that let them sail through whenever they felt like it. Maybe it was one of my other vampire friends?

I poked my head through the reception door to find Nola waiting for me. She was wearing her nurse scrubs and carrying a medical bag labeled "Half-Moon Hollow Clinic." She looked very official, and I was officially confused.

"No—"

Nola launched herself out of the chair and prevented me from uttering anything else. "No, Miss Scanlon, no refusals this time. The doctor *insists* that you get this treatment regularly. And if I have to meet you at work for your convenience, so be it."

Clipping her visitor's pass into place on her shirt, Nola made a very clear "just play along" face and gave Jerry the front-desk clerk the side-eye. I nodded. "Ohhh, I guess, if the doctor insists."

"There's a conference room on your floor that you

can use for privacy, Gigi," Jerry said in a helpful tone. "I hope you feel better."

I made a weird raspberry sound. "It's nothing, really."

"Pernicious anemia is hardly nothing!" Nola exclaimed, as the door shut behind her.

"Pernicious anemia?" I asked.

"It's a real thing," Nola whispered. "And the rumor of your having it will make you very unattractive to any vampires thinking of feeding on you."

I pushed her into the nearest empty conference room. Why did my workplace have so many damn conference rooms? "Thanks, I think," I muttered, making a mental note to text Nik a *not really dangerously anemic* message. "And as much as I appreciate visits in the middle of my workday, what are you doing here?"

She nodded toward one of the chairs. And when I didn't sit fast enough, she pushed me down into a sitting position. Then she rolled up my sleeves and wiped my bicep down with an alcohol wipe.

"I started thinking about what you said at Jane's shop the other night, that your office is full of receptionists and yogurt thieves who want to hurt you," she said, whispering so softly I had a hard time hearing her. "And I thought it would be best to come by and give some of your coworkers a quick scan for magical residue so you can narrow your suspect list."

"Aw, that's so sweet!" I cooed, throwing my arms around her.

With me still attached to her, she pulled a rather large syringe from her bag and uncapped it.

"That is less sweet," I said, pulling away. "What is that?"

"It's a B-twelve shot," she said quietly. "Perfectly harmless. In fact, it might help boost you up, considering your hours, but it's also a plausible treatment for pernicious anemia. Though, technically, you would need injections on a regular basis." With no warning, she jabbed the needle into my arm.

"Ow, sonofabitch, Nola!" I yowled. I hissed, "Why would you actually give me a shot? You could have just put a bandage on my arm and faked it!"

"Oh, don't be such a baby!" she shot back. "And I gave you the shot because you're not an awesome liar, *and* I'm worried about you, keeping such weird hours and working so hard and dating a vampire. The B-twelve can only help. Here, have a lollipop." She waved a big shiny red sucker in my face.

"Don't patronize me," I whined, as she slapped a Monster High bandage on my arm. Nola shrugged and returned the lolly to her medical bag.

"I didn't say I wouldn't take it," I said, snatching it out of the bag. I unwrapped the sucker and shoved it into my mouth. "Now what?"

"Now you pretend not to be able to get me out of the office because the floor layout is just so confusing, while I try to get a read on some of your coworkers."

She took out a tiny brown bottle and unscrewed it to reveal a dropper top. When she squeezed three drops on each palm, the conference room was filled with the sharp, green scent of bay laurel. I wrinkled my nose and waved a hand in front of my face as she massaged the oil into her hands.

"Yeah, I know, it's pungent," she said, waving her hands around to make the oil evaporate faster. "It's a blend to encourage psychic openness, and the main ingredient is bay laurel. The smell will go away in a few minutes, and this will keep me from having to make physical contact with your coworkers to read them."

"You are an evil genius," I said, sticking the sucker into my cheek. "Shall we start with the yogurt thief in accounting?"

We wandered around the office, and I pretended to be unable to find an exit, as Nola scanned the yogurt thief, who was still pissy but showed no "spectral evidence" of casting spells. She scanned the operations department, including poor Joseph McNichol, who spoke with an exaggerated lisp around his missing fangs. She scanned my coworkers in the coding pit of despair; each one of them was pronounced clean as a whistle. This included Marty, who spent most of Nola's visit explaining how he didn't need modern medicine because he stuck to his mother's holistic diet and medicinal plan.

"Nothing," Nola said, as we approached Ophelia's office. "Not a thing. This place is completely free of magic . . . and whimsy . . . and colors besides gray.

I mean, really, how do you not get seasonal affective disorder the moment you walk in the door?"

"I plan on having a nice case of rickets by the end of the summer. Guys dig rickets, right?"

"So clearly, your next injection will be a massive dose of vitamin D." She sighed.

"Miss Scanlon, who is this, and why has she been wandering around this office for the past hour?" Margaret asked, bearing down on us like a hall monitor from hell.

"Margaret, this is Nola Leary. She's a representative from my doctor's office. She was providing me with medical treatment, an exception to the no-visitors policy, which is outlined on page thirty-four of the employee manual. I was just escorting her out."

Margaret's whole face clenched at once. She hated it when people outpolicied her. I had known it would be worth it to peruse the employee manual very carefully. "What sort of treatment? Is your condition contagious?"

"I believe that falls under HIPAA law," Nola said cheerfully.

Margaret gritted her teeth so hard I practically heard them crunching under the enormous pressure of her jaw. "Just get her out of the office, Miss Scanlon. And I will count this time as your lunch break for the day," she sniped.

"It was so nice to meet you," Nola said sweetly. She stretched her hand out to shake Margaret's and let it hang there until it was so socially awkward for Margaret *not* to shake her hand that I felt sorry for Margaret.

And I really didn't like Margaret, so that was saying something.

Margaret finally gripped Nola's hand and shook it, giving the biggest cat-butt face I'd ever seen. Nola's grin ratcheted up to crazy Grinch levels, while Margaret tried to yank her hand free.

Just as she did, Ophelia stepped out of the elevator, barking orders into her cell phone in German. She was wearing a slick black silk power suit and a pink sequined T-shirt. She sounded angry. Then again, everything sounded angry in German; maybe I shouldn't judge. She huffed out a question, rolling her eyes and pulling a small Hello Kitty notebook out of her purse. She spied the pen in the tiny penholder in Nola's scrub sleeves and snapped her fingers at her.

Nola lifted one dark eyebrow. Ophelia rolled her eyes and snapped her fingers again, then pointed at the pen. Nola took the pen out of her sleeve and handed it to Ophelia. In the process, she let her hand brush against Ophelia's wrist. She stared at Ophelia intently. But Ophelia just shot her an annoyed glare and marched into her office.

"Well, we will be moving along," I told Margaret. "Have a nice night."

"Make it a quick exit!" Margaret called grumpily.

As soon as we were out of earshot, I nudged Nola's ribs. "So?"

"Come see me tomorrow morning," she said. "We need to talk."

"Well, that's not cryptic at all," I muttered.

"Just come see me," she said again. "I'll put the kettle on for you."

"Why does my hand smell so weird?" Margaret yelled down the hallway.

I snuck back to my office, where Aaron and Jordan were hard at work. Marty, on the other hand, was pecking away at a "research paper" we'd asked him to do on potential fonts for our part of the projects. Never mind that the regional management had chosen the fonts weeks before. We didn't trust Marty with anything we would have to undo later.

Marty's work had not improved. He resisted all attempts by us to gently guide him through Basic Programming 101. And when gentle guidance failed, we tried blatantly telling him "You need to do *this*," which also failed. He was completely immune to correction.

Aaron and Jordan were pretty unhappy about picking up his slack. Marty was friendly and helpful and always engaged, but he was also slow and didn't meet deadlines. He always had an excuse, of course. There was always a perfectly good reason for him not to have completed something he was assigned. But it was starting to get on everybody's nerves, particularly my own.

And no matter how many times I reported the problems to Ophelia or the HR department, nothing happened. We were all given our benefits packages, including Council-leased, environmentally friendly cars and "grand prize showcase" salaries. And I couldn't help but be irritated on my team's behalf. Jordan, Aaron, and I had earned our perks. Marty, not so much.

Marty was our group's "missing stair"—the problem we all knew about but could do nothing to resolve. I wondered if Marty was related to a vampire or had incriminating pictures of Ophelia or something. It was hard to imagine what sort of act Ophelia would be too embarrassed to reveal publicly, but surely there was something she wouldn't do.

Oblivious to our passive-aggressive pack maneuverings, Marty kept trying to take on new areas of the project. He wanted to prove himself with more responsibilities, but we had to keep routing him back to the things he'd already done. He was unhappy and griped constantly about how he could do more, but we were getting pretty good at changing the subject.

"Hey, y'all, how's it going?" I asked.

"I'm three pages into my research," Marty said, with as little enthusiasm as was humanly or inhumanly possible.

"I hit my benchmark for next week!" Jordan told me with a grin.

"Awesome!" I exclaimed. I jogged over to her desk and gave her an enthusiastic high-five and a gummy candy shark.

"I fixed that issue with the, er, last-name search window," Aaron called over his partition. I nodded, knowing that he was referring to the spreadsheet of surnames Marty had somehow deleted. Aaron had managed to pluck it from the ether with his magical file-retrieving ways.

"I'd say our technical wizardry deserves a caffein-ated reward," Jordan said, her Rainbow Brite hair peeking out from behind her cubicle. She grinned win-somely. "Hint, hint."

I laughed. "OK, OK. Sammy's not at his post, though. So it's Perk-U-Later, my treat."

Aaron's head popped over his cubicle like a ground-hog. "Mocha latte, triple shot, with three sugars and extra whip."

I checked the size of his already-dilated pupils. "It's decaf for you, my friend."

"Nooo!" He fell to his knees and shook his fist at the ceiling in outrage.

"Maybe some nice chamomile tea," I said, shaking my head.

Jordan rolled her eyes. "I'll take a vanilla latte, extra whip. Thanks, Geeg."

"Marty?" I turned around to find Marty standing *right* behind me. I jumped and stepped away. "Yipe!"

"I'll come with you," he said.

"Oh, no, that's OK," I told him. "I don't mind going on my own."

"Nonsense! I could use some fresh air. Besides, I'd hate for you to walk around the block in the dark on your own."

Before I could object more, he exited the office and was halfway down the hall.

"Oh . . . OK." I sighed. Jordan shot me an apologetic look. I drew my thumb across my throat in the interna-tional sign of "Imma cut you!"

Retrieving my purse, I caught up to Marty, who was walking past Margaret's desk. She gave him a thumbs-up and a big grin, which was weird.

We walked out of the building and crossed the Council parking lot. I seriously hoped Nik didn't accost me in the lot, because that would be difficult to explain to Marty. Then again, it was going to be difficult to explain my coffee run with Marty to Nik. So maybe it was better that we didn't see Nik either way.

We managed to order the coffee without incident. I refused to order Aaron's liquid crack, but I did get him decaf and one of the shop's saucer-sized chocolate chip cookies to make up for it. I found myself antsy to grab the coffees and get back to the office. For some reason, being alone with Marty made me uncomfortable, even in the cozy, coffee-scented interior of Perk-U-Later. He wasn't talking. He was just staring at me intently, as if waiting for me to tell him something. I sincerely hoped it wasn't a performance evaluation for the job he'd done so far, because that was not going to end well for him.

Cup carriers in hand, we walked back to the office in awkward silence for a few minutes. "Nice night," I commented, reaching for any topic of conversation. "I hope it cools off soon. It seems the buildup to August is always the worst."

Marty didn't respond, which was, again, weird.

Suddenly, he stopped and grabbed my arm. "I'm glad we had a chance to get out of the office together," he said, his dark eyes shining earnestly by the light of the streetlamp. "I wanted to talk to you."

"Marty, if this is about taking on more responsibility, I just don't think you're ready for anything new—"

"Gladiola, I just wanted you to know that I love you. I've been in love with you for a long time."

Shit. My mouth fell open, and I made a little squeaky noise. I only held on to the coffee carrier through some sort of miracle of muscle memory.

"You're really pretty and funny and smart. And I feel really strongly about you. I think we would make a really great couple. And I was hoping that you might go out for dinner with me or something this weekend? I sent you some texts the other night to try to arrange a date, but you didn't respond."

Double shit. I would so rather give him a performance evaluation.

Suddenly, all of the coffee cups, the Facebook friending, the candy on my desk came together in one horrible puzzle. Marty wasn't a nice, incompetent guy. He was "nice guy-ing" me—a condition that occurred when a guy's definition of friendship was "I'm nice to you because I think there's a chance you'll have sex with me. And when I realize that won't happen, I reserve the right to accuse you of using me." Each of Marty's considerate gestures had a bunch of invisible strings hanging off it, strings meant to pull me in and make me feel obligated to him. After all, Marty was such a nice guy—what sort of horrible girl would refuse to date someone who had made so many thoughtful gestures?

Maybe I could convince him that I was engaged

to someone else or being deported? Any excuse that would let him down gently, because the last thing anybody wants to do is say "I don't find you attractive." I would scramble for any excuse besides that. I didn't understand how the simplest answer was the hardest to give. But I didn't want to give it, either.

"How did you get my cell number?" I asked.

"Oh, Margaret gave it to me. She got it from your employee file."

Margaret really had to stop giving me reasons to be mad at her. In the face of my flabbergasted silence, Marty just kept on going. Oh, my God, did he keep going.

"We could go to the Noodle Palace, if you like. I know how much you like Japanese food, and I'm willing to make an exception to Mother's meal plan just this once. But just so you know, the mercury levels found in sushi are very unhealthy. You're risking serious neurological disorders if you continue to eat this way. I'd be glad to ask Mother to come up with a nutrition plan for you—"

"Actually, Marty, I don't think it's a good idea for us to go out. We're not really allowed to date coworkers, according to the employee handbook."

Never mind the fact that I'd literally played a game of grab-ass with one of our vampire colleagues not long ago. This was definitely a case for careful personal editing.

Marty brightened. "Actually, I checked with Miss Lambert's office, and she said it was fine."

"Oh, that Ophelia." My teeth ground together as I tried to smile my way through this horrific moment. "Wait, did you check with Ophelia or Margaret?"

He gave a stilted laugh, as if I'd caught him at something. "Oh, I've been talking to Margaret about you for a little while. She assured me that we wouldn't be violating the spirit of the office fraternization policy, since we're only here temporarily."

"Well, I'm not comfortable with the 'spirit of the policy,' Marty. I'd rather follow the actual policy. So it's still a no. But thank you."

He gave me a constipated smile and patted my hand. "We'll talk about it later."

Talk about it later? Had I not just given my answer? I'd said no, clear as a bell. Granted, I hadn't given a genuine reason for *why* I was giving him a no, but my answer was still no. It wasn't up for negotiation.

I couldn't speak. I was honestly afraid that if I said anything more to him, a torrent of cursing and shouting like had never been uttered by a human in the Council office would pour out of my mouth and get me fired. Blocking out Marty's steady stream of reasons we should date, I carried the coffee into our office, carefully placed it on Jordan's desk, and swept back out of the room.

I couldn't breathe.

As foolish and silly as I'd felt after my first contact with Nik, at least then I'd known that the only person I'd hurt had been myself. I may not have been super-close to Marty, but I didn't want to hurt his feelings.

But still, what the hell? I bounced between feeling sorry that I might have misled Marty into thinking I liked him and wanting to punch him in the neck. I felt stupid for not seeing the signs. I felt even more stupid for mistaking Marty's "overtures" for sucking up to his boss. I felt bad for letting him down. I felt guilty for actively trying to get him fired when he had a crush on me. I felt angry at Marty for putting me in this position. I was a blender of messed-up emotions, and they were all aimed Marty's way

I needed some fresh air, a walk to clear my head. I had to get out of the office for just a few minutes, even though I basically hadn't spent more than five minutes at my desk that night. I didn't even stop to talk to Nik when I saw him coming out of Ophelia's office.

"Are you all right?" I shook my head and dashed out the door, ignoring him as he yelled, "Gigi!"

I walked blindly around the block, my legs pumping across the concrete, anything to carry me away from the viper pit of embarrassment. The Perk-U-Later door swung open, and I had to duck left to avoid being smacked in the face with the glass.

"Oh!" I yelped, as two strong hands clamped around my shoulders and kept me upright. I gasped, glancing up into warm green puppy-dog eyes. "Ben?"

"Gigi!" My ex-boyfriend, Ben, had one of those sweet, all-American faces that practically screamed "Trust me with your daughter, and she will return to you happy, early, and un-impregnated." He had a cute little upturned nose, high cheekbones, and a wide, smiling mouth—a mouth currently making that awkward Ben face, where he smiled without actually showing any teeth. "Hi!"

The next few moments were a ballet of misinterpreted social cues. He went in for a hug, while I reached out to shake his hand. I raised my outstretched arm for the hug, but by that time, he'd switched over to handshake mode.

Right now, I would give anything for Nik's Swiss-cheese memory. Because I did not want to recall this later.

Despite our promises to stay friends, I'd barely spoken to Ben since we'd parted at winter break. It was difficult to recover from a conversation that started with "Let's get married" from one party and ended with "I think we should break up" from the other.

I'd beaten myself up over my feelings—or lack thereof—for Ben for weeks before his disastrous Christmas Eve proposal, which he saw as a Hail Mary play to save our relationship. I just didn't want to be with him anymore, and that alone made me feel that I was giving girlfriends everywhere a bad name. Ben was a genuinely decent sweetheart of a guy, who did everything right—remembering birthdays, having sacrosanct date nights every weekend, and faithfully Skyping when we were separated by summer internships. He accepted all of the weird supernaturalness in my life without so much as a "Hey, Type O is sort of a weird Christmas dinner."

But he still didn't make my fickle self happy. I loved him, but I wasn't *in* love with him, not in the electric, head-over-heels, launching-a-thousand-ships sort of way I'd seen in Cal and Iris or Jane and Gabriel or even Jamie and Ophelia. But as selfish as it might seem, I wanted that crazy, forever, epic sort of love for myself. When you were surrounded by eternally committed vampire couples, it warped your expectations a little bit.

Maybe it had been a mistake to switch majors so that most of my upper-level classes were also Ben's classes. Maybe we'd spent too much time together. Maybe Ben got tired of seeing me perform so well in an area that was supposed to be *his* thing. Maybe we'd been doomed from the start, when I'd selfishly used him as my cover story as I secretly dated a very dangerous teenage vampire.

Either way, we hadn't spoken, e-mailed, or texted in the six months since. We were still Facebook friends, but we avoided each other's timelines. And none of this mattered now, because Ben was standing right in front of me, with a confused expression on his face.

"How have you been?" he asked, clearing his throat, gesturing for me to follow him back into the coffee shop.

"Great," I told him, shaking my head for reasons I didn't understand. "Great. You?"

"Great," he said. "Are you working in the Hollow this summer?"

"Yeah, I'm doing some programming work for the Council. And you?"

"Oh, uh, I'm just packing some stuff up. I've got a summer internship for Microsoft, in their Atlanta offices," he said, pinching his lips shut and nodding like a bobblehead.

"Great!"

"Yeah, I'm pretty excited about it," he said. "And how do you like working for the Council?"

"It's great," I said, laughing in this awkward breathy fashion that made me sound slightly insane. "The other programmers made me project leader, which should be a nice résumé builder, if I don't screw it up."

Ben's mouth curved up into that familiar fond Ben smile, and he finally resembled the boy I had dated instead of this stiff stranger. "You're not going to screw it up, Geeg. You're going to be great."

If one of us said "great" one more time, I swear, one of our heads would explode.

Ben grinned and rubbed my arm, a gesture I stepped away from immediately. "I'm glad I ran into you. After last time, I had a few things I needed to say to you."

I cringed inside. Honestly, I could only handle so many confessions of true feelings in one night. If he told me he loved me, I was going to jump through the window and run screaming down the street. I was practically twitching as he took a seat at a table near the plate-glass picture window. I remained standing, unwilling to spend more time than was absolutely necessary in this conversation.

He frowned when he saw my tense posture, but he took a deep breath and said, "I lied."

My hands stopped twitching long enough for me to say, "I'm sorry?"

"When I said we could still be friends? I lied," he said. "It was just too hard, and awkward. You seemed so happy every time I saw you, and for some reason, that really pissed me off."

"I had to put on a happy face!" I exclaimed. "What kind of idiot breaks up with someone and then tells that person that she's miserable? It's against the girl code."

"Well, I'm not going to lie, it took me a little while to get over it. I got drunk and cursed your name more than a few times."

"That explains why so many of your friends glared at me all spring," I muttered.

"But I just want you to know, I'm not mad at you anymore. I'm doing fine now. I've actually started seeing someone," he said.

I expected some sort of pang, a twitch of irritation or jealousy. But I was happy for him. I wanted Ben to find someone. He deserved to be happy. And I wouldn't make him happy. I was apparently some sort of romantic train wreck who violated office policies willy-nilly and led nerds to the romantic rocks like some evil cyber-siren.

"She's really nice. She works in my office. Is that weird for you?"

"No, I've started seeing someone, too." I glanced out the window to see Nik standing in the puddle of streetlamp light across the street, a concerned expression on his face. Triple shit.

"It's a vampire, isn't it?"

I turned to Ben and laughed. "Yeah, why?"

He shrugged and sipped his coffee. "I just figured you would end up with a vampire. They say that girls marry guys just like their daddies, and Cal is the closest thing you have."

I shuddered. "For the sake of my romantic future and emotional well-being, please do not finish that thought. If necessary, I will emphasize my point by threatening to smack you."

"You're so violent now! You were such a nice girl before you entered Cal boot camp!" Ben snickered as we stepped back onto the street. "I'm sorry I avoided you, but I would like us to be friends again, Gigi."

"I'd like that, too."

He opened his arms wide to go for a very clearly communicated hug.

I shook my head. "We are the sort of friends who do not hug."

"Fair enough," he said, extending his hand for a shake. I pumped it up and down in a firm, nonmushy manner.

"Go home, Ben," I said. "Say hello to your special lady friend for me."

Ben unlocked his car. "No, no. We're not going to do that. As far as she is concerned, you don't exist. And vice versa. And please do not tell your vampire boyfriend about me."

Ben climbed behind the wheel and drove away, waving to me. I rubbed my hand over my face. "So very awkward."

I felt as if I'd been run through an emotional meat grinder. I'd been angry, frustrated, mortified, hopeful, happy, and sad all in one night. I didn't know how to feel about anything. I wanted to talk to Iris about it, but I didn't know how much help she would be, what with her blind hatred of Nik and her instinctual kill response to anyone who made me the least bit uncomfortable. I scrubbed my hand over my face again, wishing I hadn't left my coffee on my desk. Then again, vodka might be better. Lots of vodka. I wasn't much of a drinker, but tonight I could see the wisdom in blind stinking oblivion.

"Did you have a nice chat?"

I turned around to find Nik standing behind me. His brow was furrowed in concern, but he kept glancing over my shoulder toward the former position of Ben's car. I groaned. "What? What can I do for you?"

"What is this I hear about you being ill?" he asked, cupping my face between his palms. And that's when I realized I'd forgotten to text Nik. Wow, the Council office grapevine worked fast.

"It's nothing." I sighed. "Just something Nola thought would be funny."

"Pernicious anemia is hardly funny!" he exclaimed. "Your friend the nurse finds illness funny?"

"I don't have pernicious anemia. It was just something she made up so she had an excuse to come into the office to see me."

"Why would she need to come see you?"

I shrugged it off, because there was no way I was

going to tell him I had my friend magi-scan my co-workers on his behalf. Guys got weird about that sort of thing. "It's a long story. Now, what brings you to my parking lot?"

"I came to see you, and I found you talking to that *boy*, the boy from the pictures in your room," he said, as if I'd been having a conversation with a leper. A leper who liked dubstep.

"Trust me, *that boy* is no longer my problem or yours. I've got more pressing issues right now."

Nik's vaguely irritated expression changed to one of concern. "Such as?"

"Such as, I seem to have accidentally seduced a co-worker, who wants to work around the spirit of office policy to go on a date I don't want. My ex-boyfriend is hanging out at coffee shops near my office so he can tell me about the new girl he's dating, which has been the bright spot of my evening. My undead boyfriend is cursed, and I'm actually pathetically happy right now that you haven't attacked me in the last five minutes. I am stressed out to my eyeballs."

"I did not understand any of that."

"Of course you didn't." I sighed. "I just can't handle one more upsetting conversation tonight, OK? So if you have a problem with me talking to Ben, we're just going to have to discuss that at another time."

"Do not shut me out, Gigi," he said, sounding genuinely hurt.

"I'm not shutting you out, I'm shutting myself down," I told him. "I just need some peace and quiet, just for a few minutes. I just can't think about anything anymore."

He nodded. "I will walk you to your office."

"Don't bother," I said, walking away from him. "But I would consider it a personal favor if you don't zombie out and chase me down like a cheetah while I'm walking back to the building."

I hung my head the moment the words came out of my mouth. That was bitchy. It wasn't fair that I was sniping at Nik for something he couldn't help, just because I was frustrated and overwrought.

"Nik, I'm sorry. That was rude."

He didn't answer.

I turned around to find an empty sidewalk and a dark street. So we were back to disappearing Nik again. I groaned. "I suck."

11

Office romances are never a good idea, whether you're alive or undead. The walk of shame is still embarrassing, whether it takes place at dawn or at dusk.

—*The Office After Dark: A Guide to Maintaining a Safe, Productive Vampire Workplace*

I hauled myself out of bed early the next morning to visit Nola during prevampire hours. She usually left for work at the clinic around lunchtime, and I didn't want to risk a run-in with Nik when I was still such a basket case. It was bad enough that Iris took one look at me when I walked into the house, all ragged and pale and distressed, and concluded that I'd contracted a horrible stomach virus. She spent the rest of her waking hours fussing over me and plying me with chicken noodle soup, which is exactly what you want to eat at two a.m.

Between the sleepless night and the early-morning doses of high-sodium condensed soup, I looked as if I'd been wrestling with a bear. At least, that's the impression I got from Nola's expression when she opened her front door.

"Wow," she said, blanching and not even bothering to cover it. Instead of her peach-and-blue scrubs, she was wearing a blue tank top and a floaty green-and-white skirt, looking quite the picture of the modern young witch. "Gigi, darlin', have you been drinkin'? I know I said the B-twelve would be a booster, but I didn't mean to go out and test the limits."

"Sadly, I am sober as a judge," I grumbled, shoving my sunglasses on top of my head, into the mess of dark hair I'd piled up. "You offering?"

She crossed her arms over her chest and smirked. "You twenty-one?"

"I thought the Irish didn't really give a damn about that sort of thing. Weren't you weaned on whiskey?" I snorted as she led me into her kitchen.

"Irish-American, you smartass," she scoffed. "And the side of my personality that's interested in holding on to my newly issued Kentucky nursing license has no plans to contribute to the delinquency of an almost minor."

I dropped my bag onto the table and flopped into the kitchen chair. Nola, bless her soul, started a pot of coffee, a concession to Jed's American need for a higher grade of caffeine than English breakfast tea could offer.

"Spoilsport," I muttered into the kitchen tabletop, where I'd planted my face. "I haven't slept. I had a really rough night at the office. And I haven't been able to talk to Iris about it, because I don't want her to march into my place of employment and demand a fifty-foot space bubble between me and a coworker who, as of last night, makes me uncomfortable. It's not that I wouldn't appreciate the buffer, but it doesn't exactly make me look like a professional. So, what were the results of your scans?"

"Nothing." Nola sighed.

"Nothing?"

"Not a single caster in the office," she said. "Even that weird yogurt lady."

"Damn it!" I grunted. "But what was with all that grinning when you were shaking Margaret's hand?"

"Because I could tell it was annoying her," Nola said. "Gigi, this is good news. This means that people who have access to you every day are not trying to make Nik a murderer."

"Well, that's actually reassuring when you put it like that, thank you," I said, nodding. "The problem remains that if my two prime suspects have been eliminated, I'm left with an unknown potential suspect with no discernible motive."

"Look, don't worry. We'll keep researching. If there's anything I've learned with this group, it's that there is no enemy or magic or even force of nature that can't be worked around, once they devote their energy to it."

"Yeah, but people get hurt along the way," I murmured. "I don't want that on my conscience."

"You can't control that, Geeg," she said. "And you'll go mad if you try."

"Yeah, yeah," I said. "So is there any way we can be proactive about this? Because I would love not to be attacked by the man I'm in deep, devoted like with . . . who may not be talking to me because I was sort of mean to him last night."

"You are a very complicated girl, aren't you?"

"Not intentionally. Now, can you answer the question?"

Nola thought about it for a long while, chewing her lip. "Yes."

"Does it involve some sort of spell that ends up making a big red 'A' appear on their forehead? Because that would be helpful."

"Well, magically, there's not a lot I can do without knowing who I'm casting against. And frankly, I don't like the whole threefold return on doing someone wrong, karma-wise. "

"Then I am confused. Also disappointed."

"Have you ever studied the placebo effect?" Nola asked. "People take sugar pills, believing they're taking medications, and thanks to the power of the mind, they actually feel the effects of drugs that aren't even in their system?"

"Yes, but what does that have to do with—ohhhhhh."

Nola's plan was as brilliant as it was devious.

After showering thoroughly and putting on a more respectable outfit, I would go to work, as normal.

Rather than having Nola cast an actual spell, I would stand out in the hallway with my coworkers and very loudly discuss a spell that Nola was planning to cast on the person causing so much trouble for my gentleman companion. Aaron and Jordan were appropriately rapt at my descriptions of the nervous sweats, stomach cramps, and other symptoms that would be inflicted upon said evildoer, living or undead. I didn't know if they believed me or not, but I was their boss, and they were both too polite to call me a liar.

And since Aaron was about as discreet as a full-page newspaper ad, it only took a few hours for the story to make the rounds. As a fun side note, almost everybody in the office now avoided eye contact with me.

Now I just had to sit back and let said evildoer's guilty conscience do my dirty work for me. Of course, doing some actual work, which had been absent from my last few nights at the office, would also be a nice gesture.

It took me a few hours, but I caught up on the tasks I'd abandoned in favor of my own personal telenovela the night before. I checked the search platform Aaron and Jordan built. I started construction on a bridge function that would allow users to track multiple family branches at the same time. And I shredded the research paper Marty had written on fonts before he could mail it to the regional office. Now we just had to come up with another pointless task that would keep him occupied for another week.

I left that particular brainstorm to Jordan and Aaron while I checked off my first major backup task as project leader. Every file that my team had touched since we arrived had been saved to an external drive, which would be placed in a safe, deep within the bowels of the office. I would have to do this once a month all summer to prevent catastrophic loss of our work, just in case every server at the Council's disposal simultaneously crashed. It could happen.

In fact, if Marty figured out how to get around the encryption Aaron had set up to keep him out of the scanned files Jordan had archived, it might happen. For his part, Marty remained unaware of the measures we were forced to employ to protect our work from him thanks to his golden protected-by-Ophelia status. He remained friendly and cheerful. He didn't sulk or give me longing looks from across the room. To me, this said that he definitely had not processed my no to his dinner invitation and he sincerely believed that I would be dating him at some point.

So yes, maybe I was a little enthusiastic about visiting some part of the building where Marty didn't have clearance to breathe. On the long elevator ride to the lower floors of the Council office, I cradled the external drive in my hands as if it was the last egg of a near-extinct species of bird. I had to pass two armed guards and a retinal scanner to get to the safe, where I was blindfolded as the code was entered. And then I verified by signature on a digital pad that the drives had been secured. The various security precautions took a grand total of ten minutes. I was just glad we only backed up like this every month.

Free of my delicate burden, I boarded the elevator, humming absently along with the Muzak version of "Girl from Ipanema." But three floors from my own office level, the elevator jolted to a stop.

"Gah!" I yelled, grabbing the safety bar on the side of the car to keep from face-planting on the floor. A wave of terror fluttered through my belly, making my legs go weak and watery. Was the car going to plummet to the bottom of the elevator shaft? How deep did it go? Why wasn't some sort of alarm going off? I tried to employ all those awesome survival skills Cal had taught me. I didn't want to panic, but damn it, this was how a lot of horror movies started, and I was not prepared for whatever killer virus, zombie horde, or ax murderer might be waiting for me outside the elevator door. I hadn't had nearly enough caffeine for this.

I pressed the red emergency button, but it didn't make a sound. I lifted the red emergency phone, but it didn't have a dial tone. Suddenly and silently, the elevator doors slid open on a well-lit, zombie-free hallway. I stuck my head out of the elevator, and then, remembering that as far as I knew, the car could fall at any moment and decapitate me, I hopped out onto the strange new floor. The doors closed without incident, and I could hear the car ascending to the next floor. No matter how many times I pressed the up button, the car wouldn't come back.

"Weird," I muttered. I scanned the hallway and couldn't see a living or undead soul, just a sign that read "Floor 2B Disposal Rooms." I wasn't sure what the disposal rooms were for, and I was certain I didn't want to find out. Plausible deniability was a good thing.

"Cal, if this is some sort of test, I will tell Iris on you. A lot," I muttered.

Of course, I'd left all of my weapons in my purse in my office. I was going to start wearing pants with bigger pockets. Then again, I was wearing a pencil skirt, so pockets were sort of a moot point. I moved quickly and quietly down the hall, toward the stairs. It was only three floors, right? I could make it up three flights of steps.

Well, I made it up one flight of steps. The door to my floor was locked, and the keypass wouldn't respond to my security badge. No amount of pounding on the door got any attention from my office mates. The door to Floor 1B, however, was wide open, so I entered yet another unoccupied floor, labeled "Holding Cells and Interrogation Rooms."

Just as I passed by the first interrogation room, the door opened, and a pair of arms shot out, dragging me inside the cold, gray cement-block room. I struck out blindly, landing a respectable left hook against the figure's jaw and following through with my elbow.

"Ow!" he yelped.

Nik turned on the interrogation-room light and slammed the door behind us. I slapped at his shoulder. "Stop sneaking up on me!"

"I am sorry," he said. "I was trying to lead you here with the elevator and the malfunctioning doors without being too obvious about it. You are not great with subterfuge."

"Well, I'm sorry about your face. And the bitchiness last night. I was having an awful night, and I took that out on you, and that's not OK," I said, stroking my thumb over the split lip that was already healing.

"No, it is not, but you have also been through higher-than-average stress in the last few weeks. I forget sometimes how young you are and how human. Your nerves are bound to be frayed."

"I'm going to ignore the implications of my youth and humanity as weaknesses and just let you hug me," I said, as he pulled me close. I pressed my forehead into the hollow of his throat.

"Did we just have our first fight?" he asked, trailing his fingers down my spine.

"It was more of a minor disagreement, but sure, we'll count it as a fight."

His golden eyes twinkled in the harsh fluorescent lights as he toyed with the top button of my blouse. "And in a relationship, what generally follows a resolved fight?"

"So this is a relationship?"

He leveled a very serious gaze at me as he backed me against the wide metal interrogation table. "You know it is."

"I don't know that," I told him. "Because I don't know what we are."

"You know what we are, Gigi," he breathed against my lips, sliding his hands under my ass and lifting me onto the table.

"And what are we, Nikolai?" I asked, as he brushed his lips across mine.

"You are mine. And I am yours. As I have never belonged to anyone before, I belong to you," he whispered, before sealing his lips over mine

OK, that still told me nothing, but it sure sounded great, and it was hard to think about vague implications when he was doing that thing with his tongue. My thighs curled around his hips, and I locked my ankles, enjoying the delicious friction this position afforded against his bulging zipper. This was not appropriate workplace behavior.

Nik traced the line of my jaw with the tip of his nose. "Did you know that this is one of the few rooms in the Council office without cameras?"

"Well, you wouldn't want nice people to know what happens in here, would you?" I chuckled, surprised by the dark, husky edge to my voice.

Nik nipped a line across the seam of my lips. When his fangs popped down, I tentatively ran my tongue along the points, making him growl. His hands slid under my skirt, nails severing the sides of my panties. The shreds fluttered to the ground, and from the look on his face, Nik wasn't even sorry.

He yanked my hips closer to the edge of the table, making the shackles attached there clank. I caught him staring at them with a wicked gleam in his eye. Biting the tip of my tongue, I curled my hand around his jaw and shook his head back and forth.

He shrugged. "It is a little much for your first work-place sexual infraction."

"Oh, I love a man who can use big words. Come on, baby, talk nerdy to me."

"Next time," he swore, pushing me back on the table, spanning his fingers over my bare ass. He peppered kisses down my neck, his tongue following his hands as he unbuttoned my shirt.

"Tell me you locked the door," I whispered against his head.

He nodded frantically, snagging the connecting lace between my lilac lace bra cups and snapping it with his fangs.

"I liked that one." I grunted as the bra disintegrated onto the table.

"I will buy you one in every color," he promised, yanking my skirt down my hips and tossing it over his shoulder.

I pressed my palms against the table, balancing my weight so I could rock my hips against him. I grabbed the tail of his shirt, pulling it over his head and mussing his perfect blond hair. His hand wrapped around my throat, pressing me down against the table as he traced a long line from my neck to my breasts, skimming the curve of each with his fangs, just enough to make me shiver. I twined my legs around his rib cage, urging him closer.

His fangs scraped against my belly, leaving a raised

red trail of pleasure-pain against my skin. I heard the faint rasp of a zipper and then felt the hot, smooth weight of him against my thigh. He shimmied his hips, letting his pants fall to his thighs.

I reached between us, palming him, guiding him toward my wet, aching flesh. He thrust inside me with a groan, nibbling along the curve of my jaw. I bit my lip to contain my moan of absolute contented bliss, but then I remembered. Interrogation room. Soundproof walls.

He snapped his hips, and I let loose a throaty howl. He propped his elbows up on the table so he could watch me, clearly pleased that I'd made such a noise, if the bared fangs were any indication. I grinned, snaking my arms around his neck and pulling myself up to press against him.

Nik bucked his hips, nudging against my sweet spot with every roll. He slowly but surely pushed the collar of my blouse aside and let his fangs sink into my throat, just over the jugular. And I barely felt the pain, only the pull of my blood surging up to his mouth. It was as if there was some sort of string connecting the two locations, and it was pleasantly chafing against my clit with every pull.

I curled my hand around his head, clutching him tighter to my neck. His thrusts sent my ass sliding back over the cold metal. The contrast in temperatures gave me gooseflesh, making every movement its own mini-orgasm, leading to one violent spasm that rippled out from my center and curled my toes.

"Mine." Nik threw his head back, lips red and wet, as he fell over the edge with me. He rested his forehead against mine. "Yours."

The door flew open, and I froze, unable to move a muscle, as Marty strolled through the door. Nik moved between the two of us, so Marty wouldn't have a clear shot of me or my bared bits.

"Gigi," Marty said, ever so casually going over papers in a file folder without looking up. "You've been gone for a while. I was looking for you, and I thought I heard you in here—" He looked up.

Nik didn't even have the decency to hike his pants over his exposed ass cheeks. He just smirked over his shoulder at Marty and said, "Is there something we can help you with, Morton?"

"Marty," I squeaked.

"Right. Marky," Nik drawled. "Do you mind?"

"I thought you locked the door," I said, smacking his arm while I buried my hot, red face against his shoulder.

"G-Gigi, what's going on here?" Marty stammered. "How could you—"

I clamped my hands over my face, apparently buying into the theory that if I couldn't see him, he couldn't see me or my destroyed bra hanging over the interrogator's chair.

I heard Nik zip up his pants and the rustle of a shirt settling over his shoulders. "Leave now, Marky."

"It's *Marty*."

I felt my own shirt being gently pressed over my

bare chest. I opened my eyes long enough to see Marty shoot a poisonous look at Nik, then back out of the room and close the door behind him.

"I want the table to open up and swallow me." I thunked my head against the metal. "Is that too much to ask?"

"It was an innocent mistake," Nik told me, helping me slip back into my blouse. "I am sure Mikey will forget about it by tomorrow."

"One, I don't know what sort of office you've been working in, but seeing a coworker spreadeagled on a metal table is one of those things that stays with you for a while. Two, interrogation-table sex is never innocent. And three, oh, my God, I just realized you did that on purpose!" I exclaimed, smacking him.

"I would not say on purpose," he protested, helping me step into my skirt. He turned me around so I rested my palms against the table as he zipped me. "I just did not prevent it from happening."

"I can't believe this." I sighed. And since I couldn't put my bra back on, I was going to be returning to my office with the girls running free. This was why I was not built for clandestine office sex: my lack of foresight and extra undergarments. "That guy—"

"Is infatuated with you and believes that you should be dating him."

My hands stilled over the buttons of my shirt. "How did you know that?"

For the first time since Marty had interrupted us, Nik actually looked embarrassed. "You were so upset after your multiple coffee runs that I might have gone to your office and held your coffee cup to get a read on what happened while you were out. I saw the whole scene with Merle's—"

"Marty's—"

"Heartfelt confession and your horrified reaction. I just thought that if Mel saw that you are with someone else, with his own eyes, he will leave you alone."

"OK, using my coffee cup as a conduit for your psychic abilities so you can spy on me is super-inappropriate," I told him.

He shrugged. "Eh, that is debatable."

"No," I said, shaking my hair loose from its messy ponytail and trying to wrestle it back into submission. "It's really, really not. And second, you didn't just magically cure Marty's crush on me. You just made it worse, because now *you're* the reason I won't go out with him, and you've opened me up to almost daily discussions of your faults and why he is a much better choice for me. Also, he could report me for violating about ten different office policies, which I am guilty of, to an *insane* degree."

"I doubt very much that Ophelia will care, as long as we count this time as your coffee break. Our having sex is the least disturbing thing that has happened in this room in a while. And a lot of people have had sex on that table. Trust me. I touched it."

I took a big step away from the table. "That doesn't make me feel better."

"Well, give me a few minutes to recover, and I will

give it another—ow!" He yelped when I smacked him with what looked like a big canvas purse that had been shoved under the table. "Easy with that!"

"Good night, this thing is heavy!" I exclaimed, as he took the bag from me and checked over its contents. "Are you actually carrying this thing around with you?"

"Yes, Ophelia keeps giving me evidence from the break-in cases to take home. And I do not want to be seen hauling items like *this* around." He plucked a plastic bag from inside the tote, displaying a pewter fairy statue the size of my hand.

"This doesn't look like the kind of thing you'd find in any self-respecting vampire's house," I said, as I slipped into my heels.

Nik chuckled. "That is what I thought, but maybe it is a recently turned vampire."

"The thefts you've been investigating," I said. "Who are the victims?"

He rooted through his man-bag and slid a list across the desk. None of these names looked familiar. And considering that my sister's business served the majority of Half-Moon Hollow's undead, it seemed unlikely that I'd never heard any of these names.

"Come upstairs with me," I said, gathering his list and his fairy statue. I barely paid attention to the stairs or the security doors as I dragged him toward my office. Marty was mysteriously and blessedly absent from his desk.

If Aaron and Jordan were surprised to see me yanking a tall, blond, disheveled vampire behind me like an ill-behaved poodle . . . well, OK, they showed it quite a bit. Jordan's eyebrows disappeared into her purple bangs, and Aaron's mouth dropped open, letting his gum slide out onto the carpet. Charming.

"Guys, this is Nik," I said, closing the office door. "Nik, this is Aaron, and this is Jordan, my coworkers."

Jordan remained stone-still, but Aaron managed to lift his hand and wave it silently.

"We're kind of in a cone of silence right now, if that's OK with you two," I said. "It will just take a few minutes."

"I don't even know what you're talking about," Jordan said, shrugging.

Aaron stared at the ceiling. "What vampire?"

"That girl's hair is all the colors of the rainbow," Nik whispered, as I slid into my desk chair.

"Yes, and she happens to be a very nice girl who is very good at her job, so we're going to avoid making any of the jokes or comments that may be on the tip of your tongue right now in order to prevent hurting her feelings, OK?"

"Aw, that's nice, thank you, Gigi," Jordan said, seeming sincerely pleased by the compliment.

"Cone of silence, Jordan," I reminded her. "You heard nothing. Go back to thinking I undervalue your work, so you should try hard to impress me."

"Too late!" Jordan scoffed. "I haven't tried hard in *weeks*!"

"I was just going to say I would like to know how she dyed it," Nik muttered. "It must have been complicated and time-consuming."

"It was so worth it," Jordan informed him.

Giggling to myself, I fired up my computer and pulled up a list of active local vampires.

Nik watched my fingers dance over the keyboard as multiple windows opened on my screen and mobilized to do my bidding. "Is this something you could get into trouble for?" he asked.

"Meh," I said, jerking my shoulders. "It doesn't fall under my job description, but since I'm technically using Council resources to do Council business, we'll just call this an IT policy gray area." I leaned back and called over my shoulder, "Cone of silence!"

"We see nothing!" Aaron called back.

"We hear nothing!" Jordan added.

"And might I ask why your underlings are so loyal?"

"I may have stumbled upon them making out in the copy room. My discretion was purchased with Red Vines and Starbucks gift cards," I said over the clacking of my keyboard. "Come to think of it, this place is a hotbed of illicit sex and extortion. It's better than HBO on Sunday nights."

"Barely twenty, and you have already mastered the arts of intrigue and bribery. If you had lived during my time, you might have ruled the world," Nik marveled, pulling a small red insulated cooler bag from his manpurse.

I scoffed. "Who says I won't? Also, you forgot the art of parking-lot fisticuffs, which I have also mastered."

Through all of this flattery, I searched through Nik's list of names, but none of them showed up as confirmed

Council constituents. I did some online searching, just to be sure, but as far as I could tell, none of the vampires named actually existed. Meanwhile, he was unpacking his cooler bag. I thought it was a weird time to have lunch, but what did I know about his liquid diet?

"I think the names are fake," I whispered. "They have no credit history, no Council records, no recorded moves, nothing."

"Why would Ophelia ask me to investigate crimes against people who do not exist?" he asked, pulling various artifacts out of his bag and putting them on my desk. The objects were all random home décor items. The fairy statue, a piece of pressed glass in the shape of a crescent moon, a broken photo frame.

"Well, have you seen any actual crime scenes yet, or is she just giving you objects as evidence?"

Nik frowned. "I have seen plenty of pictures of the crime scenes, and surely I . . . I cannot remember seeing any of them personally. That is very strange. Under normal circumstances, I would not investigate any situation without seeing the location with my own eyes. But when I try to remember seeing them this time around, I am just drawing a blank. It seems bizarre that I have not even thought of it before now."

"And the objects Ophelia has had you inspecting? Have you seen anything when you've held them?"

Nik cleared his throat and glanced at Aaron and Jordan, who were studiously ignoring us. "I get a couple of flashes but nothing that would tell me anything about their origin."

I picked up the fairy statue and examined it closely. "I think I recognize this," I told him. "It's from Jane's shop. She's been trying to get rid of them since she opened. She actually gave one to Ophelia last year for her birthday."

"This belonged to Ophelia?" he asked.

"I think so."

I turned around to check if Jordan and Aaron were watching. They swiveled their chairs around, acting as if they weren't.

Nik held the fairy in his hands, and his eyes went all smoky. "Nothing. I am getting nothing."

"Why would Ophelia give you a regift as evidence?"

"This whole investigation has been wrong," he said. "I am making no progress at all. I do not remember making half of these notes. And Ophelia is not riding my ass about my lack of progress. You work for her, you know how she feels about progress."

"Nik, have you ever seen a goose out in the wild?" I asked. "You ever chased it around?"

"You are saying that Ophelia is sending me on a wild-goose chase?"

"No, I just enjoy asking people random questions about their fowl habits," I said, as my stomach suddenly rumbled, loudly enough to get Nik's attention.

"Did you forget to eat again?" he said, nudging me.

"Maybe," I said, wincing. "It's been a busy night."

"Gigi, you have got to take better care of yourself," he chided me gently.

"I know." I sighed.

"Which is why I brought you this," he said, gesturing at the objects he'd pulled from his cooler bag: a small black enamel bento box with cherry blossoms on the top and black enamel chopsticks. "Cal said this was your favorite, before he realized I was interested in you and stopped the flow of all information."

"Aw, you brought me lunch? That's so sweet, but . . ." I cast a longing glance at my computer.

"You are going to take a break," he said, wheeling my chair away from my desk.

"She skips lunch a lot; more often than I would say is healthy," Jordan told Nik. "I think that's why everybody keeps bringing her food. Sammy worries."

"Traitor!" I shouted, but Jordan was positively unashamed. "Slander and lies!"

"Gigi," Nik whispered in mock horror.

"She keeps her own soy sauce in the fridge, in case you forgot it," Jordan added.

"I did forget it, thank you." Nik rose and retrieved my soy sauce from the office fridge. He pulled my rolling chair down to the end of my desk and nudged the food in front of me.

"But . . . information!" I exclaimed, straining toward my computer.

"Not so funny when it's your boyfriend dragging you away, huh?" Jordan crowed.

"Gigi," Nik said, placing his hands on either side of my arms, effectively trapping me in my desk chair.

I smirked. The position had possibilities. I replaced

the smirk with the poutiest, saddest puppy face I could manage.

He groaned. "Not that face."

I ratcheted the bottom lip out just a little bit more.

He rolled his eyes and picked up the chopsticks. "You work, and I will feed you."

"That's so weird and adorable," I told him. He gave a much-put-upon sigh and slid aside the box lid, revealing a Philadelphia roll and a green dragon roll. My mouth dropped open, and I blurted out, "I really love you."

His smile could have lit up the world. "Really?"

I nodded, and he rolled my chair toward him with a sharp jerk that launched me against him. He crushed my mouth against his, swallowing my moans as I slid my fingers over his close-cropped hair. "That is all it takes to get you to confess your feelings? All I had to do was bring you sushi?"

"If you'd remembered the pickled ginger, I'd be giving you a lap dance right now."

He growled and dropped his head. "I was this close!"

"I love you," I told him, kissing his frown away. "I really, really do. Never forget that."

"I would not," he swore. "Never forget that I love you back."

"This is so awkward," Aaron whispered to Jordan.

"Shut up, it's sweet!" Jordan hissed back. "They make such a cute couple."

I kissed him one last time and rolled toward my desk, poising my hands above the keyboard. "Now, feed me."

"Is this what our future will look like?" he asked, dipping a fat pink piece of salmon into some soy sauce. "I will spend my eternity taking a backseat to raw fish and random numbers?"

"Not all the time," I promised him, delicately wrapping the fish between my lips and pulling it into my mouth with my tongue. "Only when I'm on a deadline."

He cleared his throat, watching my mouth. "I think I can live with that."

Two nights passed at work without a tabletop sexual incident. I marked it on my calendar with a smug little emoticon.

Of course, Marty called in sick for those two days, claiming to have the flu, which put off that awkward avoidance of eye contact. But on the bright side, no one came to escort me out of the office for pantsless interrogation-room shenanigans.

With Marty out of the office, Jordan, Aaron, and I held an emergency secret meeting over Sammy's super mocha frappuccinos to determine our progress and try to figure out whether we could do a whole summer's worth of work if he was sick for the rest of the week. (No.) But the good news was that we'd hit all of our checkpoint deadlines for the summer and were on track for the large-scale test in a few weeks.

It was sad that we had to resort to this sort of meeting behind Marty's back, but he was still operating under the bulletproof umbrella of Ophelia's protection. I thought maybe Aaron and Jordan felt guilty about it, because they kept giving each other pointed looks and nudging, as if they had something to tell me and neither wanted to be the one to break the bad news.

Finally, I put my pen down and said, "OK, what's going on?"

Jordan tipped her rainbow hair toward me, only to have Aaron shake his head.

"Kids, use your words!" I cried.

"Knock-knock!"

Aaron's big moment was interrupted by Jamie walking through our office door, holding a grease-stained bag from the Coffee Spot, an old-school diner downtown that served insanely awesome cheese fries.

"Hey!" I hopped up from my seat and threw my arms around him. "How did you get past security?"

"You know that's not how most people greet their friends, right?" Jamie said, as I snatched the bag from his hands and handed it to Jordan. "I come bearing cheese fries."

"How many vampire friends does she have?" Aaron asked Jordan quietly. Jordan shrugged. "And why are they always bringing her food?"

"We need vampire friends to bring us food," Jordan said, chowing down on cheese fries.

"It is at the Council office," I told Jamie. "But seriously, what are you doing here? Are you visiting Ophelia?"

"Yeah, I came to check up on her. She hasn't been feeling well the last few days," he said.

"That's weird," I noted, as Aaron and Jordan spread out Jamie's offering to accompany our sandwiches.

"Well, our office mate Marty is out with the flu," Aaron said. "Maybe it's going around."

"It doesn't really work like that," Jamie explained in a kind bro-to-bro tone. "Vampires don't get sick."

"Also, Marty doesn't actually have the flu," Jordan added under her breath. I stared at her for a long moment, wondering what, exactly, she knew about what had happened earlier that week. She stared right back, but her poker face was much better than mine, and I couldn't get anything out of her.

"At least you know she's not pregnant." I laughed, trying to break the tension. I paused. "She can't possibly be pregnant, right?"

"I am ninety-nine-point-nine percent sure," Jamie scoffed. "But I'm worried about her. She hasn't been herself for weeks."

The small, petty, cynical side of me wondered how closely Ophelia's "illness" was tied to Jamie's looming departure for college. But before I could express this in a way that wouldn't upset Jamie, the vampire herself appeared in our office doorway, mascara running down her cheeks and her hair in disarray. She was wearing baggy acid-washed jeans and a plain black T-shirt with sneakers. She looked as if she'd just done the walk of shame from A. C. Slater's frat party.

Aaron's and Jordan's eyes went wide at Ophelia's disheveled appearance. They immediately turned around and practically leaped into their desk chairs, turning their backs to our bedraggled boss. Apparently, they were taking the "see nothing, hear nothing" approach again.

"I need to talk to you," Ophelia whispered. "Now. Please call Nola and have her meet us here."

With that, she shuffled back down the hallway and out of sight. My mouth gaped as Jamie stared after her.

"What the hell was that?" he demanded.

"Ophelia said 'please,'" I said, pulling my phone from my pocket and dialing Nola's number. "Ophelia never says 'please' to me. This is bad. This is very bad."

"I'm going to go—I don't know what I'm going to do, but that needs to be taken care of." With that, Jamie dashed down the hallway after his broken-down lady love.

Nola made the four-block trip to the office from her clinic in record time. Jamie was actually concerned for Ophelia's health and forced her to curl up on the pink-checked couch in her office with a warmed bottle of donor Type A. Ophelia refused to say anything more, claiming that she only wanted to make her "confession" once.

It took me an embarrassing amount of time to make the connection between Ophelia's symptoms and the rumor we'd spread about Nola's curse on the caster who'd put Nik in his fugue states. In my defense, I'd long since removed Ophelia from my suspect list after Nola cleared her. Well, except for the part where she could kill me with her bare hands. She could still do that.

"What the hell is going on here?" I asked, as Nola bustled into the office. I expected Nola to give Ophelia some sort of examination, but she'd simply perched on the arm of my chair, waiting. It said a lot about either the way she felt about me or how she felt about Ophelia.

Ophelia removed the ice bag that Jamie had so helpfully provided from her head and forced herself into a sitting position. "I hired a witch to put the spell on Nik," she said, her voice trembling pitifully. "You were taking Jamie away from me. He was going to college, with you, away from me. I was just so angry, and there you were, smiling and happy all the damn time, because you were going to have him all to yourself at that stupid school. And I snapped. As a courtesy, Nik notified me when he came into town over Christmas to visit Cal. I trumped up the robbery cases to have an excuse for him to come back to town. I hired the witch, and she cast the spell. I didn't mean it. It all happened so fast."

"I imagine that sort of deal took at least a few e-mails to iron out details," Nola deadpanned. "It couldn't have happened that fast. What exactly did the witch do?"

Ophelia sighed. "After Iris was hospitalized, you developed a habit of donating blood to the blood bank near your college campus every three months."

A horrible sinking sensation took hold of my stomach. "Oh, no."

"I arranged for one of your donations to be 'misdirected' and sent here. If it makes you feel any better, it took quite a bit of bribery and coercion to persuade the phlebotomist to hand over your pint of blood. The witch used it to put Nik on your trail, so to speak.

Without knowing why or remembering how, he would attack you and continue to attack you until you were dead. But unbeknownst to us, he was already on your trail. He knew you, had feelings for you, and that complicated the spell. The witch had to improvise, and little by little, we've lost control of the situation. Magic is a living, breathing thing, and it has mutated beyond what we expected. The original intent of the spell is there; Nik will keep on attacking you. But he's fighting it. The more he remembers about your first encounters, his first blush of feelings toward you, the more the spell tries to reestablish itself, and the more violent the attacks become."

Jamie's face had gone bone-white as Ophelia described putting a magical hit on me without any remorse or regret. My stomach churned but not for myself—for Nik and what they must have done to him to put him in this state. The edges of my vision went red and hazy, and it was all I could do not to lunge at Ophelia.

"Was it a Renart?" I asked.

Ophelia shot me an incredulous look and then nodded.

I glared at her. "I traced the family to this area. With the genealogical information that you knew I would be handling this summer. Honestly, it's like you wanted to be caught."

"It was a Renart," she said, eyeing me carefully. "We've tracked the family for years, in case they decided to return to their old tricks. We have to protect our interests."

Suddenly, Jamie sprang up from his seat and threw his chair against the wall, shattering the chair and making a considerable dent in the wall, not to mention making Ophelia flinch. His fangs were fully extended, and for the first time since he was turned, he looked ready to rip out throats.

He placed his hand on my arm and squeezed gently. "I'm so sorry, Gigi," he whispered. "I don't know what to say. I'll find a way to help you make this right, I promise."

Ophelia's voice wavered. "Jamie."

"Don't," Jamie growled. "Don't talk to me."

He swept from the room in the most vampirelike state I'd ever seen him in. Ophelia seemed to shrink in her chair, looking very young and sad and vulnerable. And I just couldn't find it within me to give a damn.

"Why Nik?" I asked, through gritted teeth.

Ophelia practically whispered, "I knew that his gift involves him going into a sort of hypnotic state to receive information from the objects he touches, which made him more open to suggestion without completely scrambling his brain. He didn't enter into the curse willingly, if it makes you feel any better. The witch stepped in while he was reading an object with a particularly complicated history and cast while he was out of it."

"What did you give him?" Nola asked.

"The Hope Diamond."

"I thought that was in the Smithsonian?"

"That's a copy," Ophelia said. "Council officials took possession of the actual stone more than fifty years ago to protect humans from it."

Nola frowned. "Because anyone who owns it dies?"

"Common misconception. The diamond just makes the owner more susceptible to magical energy. And with its multiple owners and tragic history, Nik was under long enough for the witch to cast."

"OK, so what do we do to break the curse? True love's kiss? Magic fleece? Killing the witch who cast the spell? Killing the vampire who hired the witch who cast the spell?" I asked, giving Ophelia the death glare.

"Killing the target fulfills the requirements of the curse," Ophelia said. "And if that doesn't work, there's a sort of back-door solution for this kind of spell. An act of loving sacrifice from either party usually nullifies the magical agreement."

"What does that mean?"

"I don't know. It's open for interpretation. I told you, I made a hasty decision to start this process. It's not like it came with an owner's manual!" she cried.

"So who is the Renart witch who cursed him? I'd like to talk to her. Or at least have Nola talk to her. Is it Margaret?" I asked. "It's Margaret, isn't it? She's awfully witchy."

"The witch isn't important," Ophelia said.

"The hell she isn't!" I yelled.

"She isn't! I can't tell you about her anyway. I signed a nondisclosure agreement."

"There are magical nondisclosure agreements?" I asked.

"The spell is cast." Nola shrugged. "There's no magical undo key, Gigi. We've talked about this. Our best option is to try to break it or fulfill it. Or you and Nik could separate. If he went to another continent, put enough distance between you, it might reduce the pull."

"Blood magic is powerful." Ophelia shook her head. "It will only get worse. If Nik doesn't complete his task, fulfill the curse, he will slowly go insane. He will lose bits of his memory, until he no longer remembers you or his past or even his own name."

I refused to cry in front of Ophelia. That was the only thing that kept me from breaking down right there. This was a fairy tale from hell, complete with cursed princes and witches and insanity. What was I going to do? What would Cal do in this situation? What would Iris do?

I closed my eyes and listened to Ophelia chatter about Nik's slow descent into madness. Iris would find a solution. Iris would stop wallowing and figure it out. So that's what I would do. She would also find a way to get back at Ophelia, even if it cost her a limb.

"Why are you telling us all of this now, Ophelia?" Nola asked. "You've sat back and watched for months as Nik and Gigi struggled with this. Why come forward now?"

"It's the curse you put on whoever did Gigi harm. I've never felt so ill before." Ophelia groaned. "Even when I was human, I've never felt such pain in my belly or tightness in my chest. My head is pounding, and everything aches. Even though I know it's not possible, I feel like I could die. Please remove whatever spell you've placed on me. I've told you everything you need to know. Or at least, everything I can tell you. That should count for something."

Nola stared at her but said nothing.

"Well?" Ophelia cried.

Nola shrugged. "That's not how it works. You just have to suffer through it until the curse on Nik is broken, however that happens."

Ophelia's face crumpled just a bit before she managed to get it back under control. "I understand."

"Good luck with that, Ophelia. I'll see you tomorrow, dark and early," I said, pushing up from my chair and striding from the room with my middle finger in the air.

Nola followed close on my heels. "Are we going to tell her there's no spell on her?" she asked quietly as we walked toward the elevator. "And that the symptoms are all in her head?"

I shook my head, pursing my lips. "Nope."

12

Know the difference between an acceptable loss and a hemorrhage.

—*The Office After Dark: A Guide to Maintaining a Safe, Productive Vampire Workplace*

I left Jamie to figure out what to do with his insane girlfriend. I didn't know whether telling her it was all in her head would make her feel any better, and frankly, I didn't care.

I did, however, file a complaint with Mr. Crown about Ophelia's behavior. And for once, he actually sounded cheerful, as if my report of Ophelia's trying to maim me and then refusing to name the witch responsible was the best news he'd heard in centuries.

Armed with information, I raced across town to tell Nik what I'd learned. The drive gave me much-needed time to think. What did Ophelia mean by a "loving sacrifice"? Did that mean one of us had to die? Did it mean we had to give something up, like a prized possession? It could be interpreted so many different ways, but I seriously hoped it didn't mean the death thing, because that would suck.

Surely we could find a way around it. I would deploy the full resources of the Jameson-Cheney-Calix Collective, and we would find some super-clever solution to this problem that didn't involve death or insanity. Now I just had to explain to Nik that my blood had been used to make him Ophelia's supernatural bitch. That was going to be an awkward conversation.

I pulled into the Victorian's driveway. Nik's car was there, but I saw that Jed's truck was gone, and the lights were out on their side of the house. I jogged across the lawn and was surprised to find the door unlocked.

"Nik!" I called, dropping my bag by the door and stepping out of my shoes. "I have news!"

Silence.

"Big curse news, Nik! This was not the reaction I was expecting!" I yelled, walking into the parlor, only to find Nik sprawled across his couch, fast asleep. "Aw."

As cute as he was, all vulnerable and sleep-tousled, it was weird to see a vampire take a nap. In general, they didn't want to waste a minute of their evening, when they could be out being all badass and bite-y. Was Nik ill? Maybe switching back and forth between fugue states was draining his energy? Was there such a thing as Flintstones chewables for vampires?

I thought about waking him up, but the expression on his face was just so cute. He looked innocent and young, like a regular human boyfriend my parents would be downright tickled if I brought home. I couldn't bear to wake him. So I settled for retrieving my phone from my bag and taking some pictures, because I'm all class.

Iris was wrong. I'd watched her relationship closely enough that I knew what I would be giving up if I attempted a relationship with Nik. I could be losing the chance to have children, grow old, live a violence-free life. It was a chance I was willing to take.

With my brand-new screen background in place and my phone secured in my bag (where I could do no more damage to my reputation as a non-creep), I crawled onto the couch next to Nik and snuggled my head against his chest. "If you don't wake up, I'm going to take advantage of you while you sleep. Meaning I will take more pictures, only they will involve putting funny hats and fake mustaches on you."

No response.

"Dude!" I exclaimed, laughing. "We're not supposed to get to the sleeping-through-date-night portion of our relationship for a couple of years."

Still snoozing like a little vampire baby.

I threw my leg over his hips and straddled him, crossing my arms over his chest and resting my chin on my hands. "Niiiik. Wakey wakey! Or I'm going to go upstairs and start without you."

Nothing.

Rolling my eyes, I leaned forward and kissed his mouth. Finally, he stirred, rolling his hips under mine and sliding his hands up my arms. I broke away, grinning down at him. "Hey, there, Sleeping Beauty."

Nik's eyes opened, a hazy and faded blue.

Shit.

"Nik?" I whispered, as his lips pulled back in a snarl. "Damn it!" I yelled, springing back from the couch and over the coffee table. He jumped to his feet in a predatory crouch. I was trapped. I couldn't duck around him to get to the kitchen or the front door. And I couldn't exactly bolt for the window Bruce Willis style. Even if I did manage to get out of the house, I couldn't outrun him down the dark country road back to town. I had to have my keys, which were in my bag, by the door, which I couldn't get to. With my phone. And all my weapons.

This was the worst date night ever.

I sighed. "Damn it, Nik, I really don't want to have to do this again."

Growling, he lunged at me, and I sidestepped around him. He looped his arm around my neck, dragging me backward. I dropped all of my weight and yanked down on his arm, turning him on my hip and throwing him to the floor. Unfortunately, he managed to grab me around the waist and drag me down with him.

"Ow, Nik!" I griped as he snapped at my neck. I grunted, shoving the bony edge of my forearm against his throat, keeping him outside biting distance. I wrapped my leg around his, thrust my hips up, and rolled us so I ended up straddling him.

"This is not how I wanted us to end up in this position," I told him.

Nik struggled, but I was able to keep him pinned by some miracle of cursed vampire uncoordination. It gave me a precious few seconds to consider my next move. A loving sacrifice. Could that mean that instead of resisting him, I should submit to the attack? Let him bite me? Would he snap out of it before he drank too much? Would he hurt me beyond healing? His teeth looked so sharp, flashing even in the low light of his parlor.

Would my arm count? Would having Nik's teeth wrapped around my wrist like a bracelet be painful enough to be considered a sacrifice? I wiggled my arm up his neck and across his mouth, while keeping him pinned. But Nik resisted, working his chin around my wrist to snap up at me.

My arm wasn't sacrificial enough, it seemed. I took a few quick, deep breaths and leaned forward, my face screwed up as his bared fangs loomed closer and closer to my throat. Squealing, I closed the gap, pressing my neck against his mouth. He sat up, crushing me to his chest. His fangs sank deep, and the pain took my breath away. My fists beat blindly against his shoulders as I tried to jerk away, but Nik's arms had me trapped.

Of all the stupid things I'd ever done, this was by far the stupidest. But there was no turning back now. And if I started having regrets, maybe the magic wouldn't work, and I would have to do this all over again.

I would have to have a long talk with myself later about my subconscious's passive-aggressive death wish.

Nik's mouth worked at my neck, pulling my blood in huge mouthfuls that left me feeling cold and dizzy. I panicked, panting and blinking away hot tears, but I refused to think about how quickly I'd lost control of the situation or how close I could be to death. I focused my thoughts on my feelings for Nik, the love and affection I had for him, and how badly I wanted to help him. I pictured a life together free of fear, a real life that allowed us to be open with Cal and Iris.

And pretty soon that picture started to fade, because I was losing too much blood.

Struggling against him, I worked my arm free of his iron grip. I reached back to slap at him or jam my thumb into his eye, but a little voice in my head stopped me in mid-swing. *Trust.* I had to trust that he wouldn't drain me dry. This was the sacrifice.

I slumped against him, my arm falling slack to my side. I was so tired, too tired to keep my arm up. Hell, I was too tired to balance on my knees over Nik. My weight dropped bonelessly against him, and my knee fell forward, hitting him square in the crotch.

The pressure at my neck disappeared as Nik cried, "Oof!"

He flopped back against the couch, dragging me down with him. I landed face-first against his chest but managed to prop myself up on my elbows. It was amazing how *not* having your life's blood sucked from your jugular improved your upper-body strength.

"Ow," Nik grumbled. His eyes slowly cleared, and he seemed completely confused about why I was on top of him. "Gigi? Who kicked me?"

"Now you come out of it?" I mumbled. "Now?"

"Why do I taste . . ." He paused to smack his lips. "You?" He glanced down at the wound on my neck, and if it was possible, he seemed to go even paler. "No, oh, no, what did I do, Gigi?"

"I let you bite me," I told him, as he tore a strip off his shirt and pressed it against my neck wound. He stood, dragging me with him, sweeping me up. "I made a sacrifice . . ."

"Damn it, Gigi." He grunted, sprinting to the kitchen and grabbing me a full-sugared Coke. "How much did I take?"

"I'd say I'm short a few pints," I said, giggling weakly as he propped me up and held the soda can to my lips. "Do I get orange juice and a cookie?"

"That is not funny," he told me sternly, carrying me out to his car.

"I disagree."

"Keep pressure on it," he said, placing his hand over mine as he pulled out of the driveway. "I am taking you to the hospital for a transfusion. And maybe some psychotherapy. Why the hell would you *let* me bite you?"

"I don't think I need the hospital," I protested. "I just need some fluids. And a cookie. I let you bite me because I wanted to break the curse. Do you think it worked?"

"I am sure it did," he assured me.

"Good," I said, closing my eyes and leaning my head back against the seat rest. "I need you whammy-free, so Cal and Iris will relax and let us date."

"Whammy-free?"

I nodded. "I wanna walk through a parking lot unscathed, just once."

"That sounds reasonable. Stay awake for me."

"OK."

I didn't stay awake.

I woke up in a cold, institutional room with an IV hooked up to my arm. I tried to move to my left side but realized I had to amend that to "arms." One IV was pumping blood into my right arm, while another pumped saline into the left. And there was a little plate on my nightstand with a chocolate chip cookie.

Damn it, Nik had taken me to the hospital. Though, from what I remember, Half-Moon Hollow Hospital didn't have pale gray walls. The hospital rooms were painted light blue. And this smelled wrong. Rather than the strong scent of disinfectant, I smelled freshly brewed coffee and new carpet. It was an aroma I'd become used to over the last few months, the smell of the Council office.

This was bad.

"Hello?"

No response.

"Hello?" I yelled, sitting up in the bed and examining the IV port. "How the hell do I get this thing out of my arm?"

Mr. Crown walked in, and I actually recoiled in my bed, IV forgotten. He smirked and dropped an outdated copy of *People* onto my sheets.

"Miss Scanlon, erudite as always. How are you feeling?" he asked.

"I feel uncomfortable with the fact that I've been unconscious within arm's reach of Ophelia."

Mr. Crown's smile went frosty. "Ophelia has been relieved of her duties until an investigation into her actions is complete . . . or until she provides the name of the witch who cursed Mr. Dragomirov. For now, she is under house arrest. You do not have to worry about her 'visiting' you. Mr. Dragomirov did the right thing bringing you here. I can't have one of my vampire investigators draining an intern, no matter how confused their sexual entanglement," he said, a vague expression of annoyance crinkling the corners of his mouth. "It's unseemly."

"Where is Nik?" I asked.

"Gigi?" I heard a voice call through the infirmary door.

"Tell me you didn't call Iris."

"Gigi?" Iris burst through the door at vampire speed, stopping just short of toppling onto my hospital bed.

I groaned. "You called Iris."

"Gigi!" she exclaimed, checking me over as if I was a newborn baby—fingers, toes, eyes, and nose. "Are you all right?"

"It's OK, Iris," I croaked. "I'm fine."

She took a deep breath and made a visible effort to lower her voice. "You're not fine, Gigi. I can't believe you *let* a vampire drain you. Have you learned *anything* from my life?"

"They've got me all topped off."

"Don't you dare make jokes right now," she said.

"Well, I'll leave you to your dramatics," Mr. Crown said with a sigh. "When you get out of here, Miss Scanlon, you will have a lot of paperwork to complete." And then he strolled from the room like an undead Tim Gunn.

"You need to calm down," I told Iris. "You are verging on a Mom moment. Remember that time she came screaming up to the school in her bathrobe because the school secretary told her you'd tripped coming off the bus? And everybody saw her running across the lawn in her floral-printed nightgown, flapping in the breeze, and you stopped talking to her for three weeks?"

I closed my eyes and slipped my hand over my eyes, ignoring the painful tug of my IVs.

"They actually have forms to fill out when one employee exsanguinates another?"

"Yes, they do." I felt the mattress dip under Iris's weight as she climbed into bed with me. I kept my eyes closed, even as she rested her chin on my shoulder. I just couldn't stand to see the "I told you so" face. "So Cal says, please don't date that vampire. And you think the reasonable response is to immediately date that vampire."

"Yes."

"So, do you have any questions for me?" Iris asked. "Dating a vampire can be confusing. There are differences in your schedule and diet and attitudes toward sex."

"Iris."

"You may have noticed, the biting, it can be really uncomfortable," she said. "We do that a lot. I mean, every time we have sex. There is a lot of biting. It's expected."

"You are not going to scare me off of dating a vampire. Jerk."

She tipped her head carefully against my shoulder. "This isn't what I wanted for you. But I shouldn't have tried to push a normal life on you, Gigi."

"I'll be OK, Iris. Really."

Rising onto her side, she cradled my cheek in her hand. "I just need to know, why are you risking so much to be with someone who could hurt you? Who *has* hurt you?"

"Why did you risk so much to be with Cal? You could have lost custody of me. You could have been rejected by the few living people in the Hollow we had ties to. Because you loved him—overwhelming, crazy, stupid love, completely free of logic and occasionally pants. I used to watch you guys and think, I want that. I want the kind of love that makes you forget what's good for you or what makes sense. With Ben, I liked him a lot, and he made sense, and he was good for me, but there was no . . . spark, you know? And I know that rational people say the spark is a myth, and you shouldn't base important decisions on gut feelings that could be hormones and/or intestinal distress. But I believe in it, because *you* have it. So basically, you have no one to blame . . . because I learned it from watching you."

"Don't use logic and precedent against me." Iris sighed. "It's just unfair."

I was released from the "hospital" into Iris and Cal's care. Nearly losing all of my blood had merited me three days' sick leave, most of which I spent sleeping in a chaise longue in the backyard to soak up some sun. I didn't want to compound my already bizarre health problems with a case of rickets. I kept track of my team's work through e-mail, but I wasn't allowed to come near the office until I was cleared by Nola.

A strange sense of quiet hung over the house, as almost every vampire man in my life seemed to be avoiding me. Cal had a pretty hard time speaking to me, but it had more to do with his own guilt about bringing Nik into my life than with being angry with me. Likewise, Jamie was avoiding my calls. Jane said that he was having trouble processing what Ophelia had done and his role in it. She assured me that he'd be back to annoying me as soon as he "pulled his head out of his butt."

And Nik was on complete radio silence. He didn't call. He didn't visit. He didn't even send a note. It was as if he'd never existed. Every time I spoke his name, everybody clammed up and avoided eye contact.

When I was really low, the old fear that maybe I'd imagined the whole thing came back. I wondered if my "hospitalization" had actually been a trip to a mental-health facility. I was sitting on my front porch after sunset, drinking orange juice and trying to figure out how exactly one asked one's sister, "Hey, you would tell me if I'd hallucinated a vampire boyfriend, right?" when Nik stepped out of the shadows of our yard and walked up our front steps.

For a hallucination, he looked . . . well, he looked like hell. Pale and haggard and about as well groomed as walk-of-shame Ophelia. I stared at him. He stared right back, but his eyes were their normal color, so I wasn't worried about a second round of draining. I had so many things I wanted to ask him. Where had he been? Why hadn't he come to see me before now? What the hell was he thinking? But instead, what came out of my mouth was "Are you still cursed?"

He seemed caught off-guard by the query and nodded. "I had Nola look me over. She says the signature is still there."

My heart sank. All of that blood down the drain for nothing. My experiment had failed.

"I am leaving," he said. "After I meet with Council representatives, I am leaving the Hollow, and you will not hear from me again."

My mouth fell open, and I really hated making such a stupid face at a moment like this. "What are you talking about? Ophelia says that if you do that, you'll go crazy. You'll forget about me, you'll forget everything, until you aren't you anymore."

"It is for your own safety, Gigi."

"Don't—don't you do that. Don't try to tell me what's for my own good. Or that you're trying to protect me or any bullshit like that. You don't get to make decisions like this for me. You don't get to just decide to walk away."

"Well, you do not get to decide that we are in a relationship."

"Is this because of the sacrifice thing?" I asked. "You think if you give me up, that will break the curse?"

"It does not matter," he said. "Either way, you will be safe, and that is all that matters."

"How can you say that? How can you say it doesn't matter? Can't you pick another sacrifice? How about a virgin? We can sacrifice a virgin. But maybe Jane can find some really clever way to go about it, and we can just use olive oil. Extra virgin."

"No."

I gritted my teeth and tried to control the vertigo making my head spin. He was leaving me. He sounded pretty determined about it, too. This didn't sound like a decision he wanted me to talk him out of. This wasn't a test to prove how much I cared about him. He was leaving me, and all I would have left would be a few shreds of dignity. So I took a deep breath and nodded. "OK. I'm not going to go on some crazy, depressive, self-destructive bent because you've decided to give up. Screw you and your masochistic, self-sacrificing, tragic-hero bullshit. If you want to leave, go. I won't try to stop you."

He cleared his throat. "Well, I am glad you are handling this so well, and with such maturity."

"I'm handling it a lot better than the five-hundred-year-old vampire, so I think I'm ahead of the game," I sniped, standing up from the porch swing. I stuck out my hand to shake his.

Nik nodded and pulled me into a searing kiss, twice as devastating as the one he'd given me that first night by the jewelry store. I locked my knees to keep them from buckling under me. I kept my arms stick-straight at my side. He pulled away and kissed me on the forehead.

"Good luck to you." I said, with the best stiff upper lip I could manage. Collin would have been very proud.

He kissed both of my cheeks. "Good-bye, Gigi."

"Good-bye, Nik." I closed my eyes, squeezing them tight, knowing that when I opened them, he'd be gone.

I hated being right.

13

If you did not bring the blood that's in the office fridge, do not touch the blood that's in the office fridge.
—*The Office After Dark: A Guide to Maintaining a Safe, Productive Vampire Workplace*

The summer was coming to a close, and not quickly enough.

I refused to mope. I would not miss work, or meals, or sleep, even if it meant hitting myself over the head with a tack hammer to knock myself unconscious. I put the moonstone earrings into a box and gave them to Cal for safekeeping. I didn't trust myself not to throw them into the Ohio River. I reported to work every afternoon. I did my usual exemplary programming. I ignored the rumors about Ophelia and what had led to her suspension. (The most popular theory was that she was accused of draining an entire pet store full of puppies.) I ignored Marty, who was back to leaving candy on my desk and asking me out on dates that wouldn't happen.

It sucked beyond the telling of it. I felt nothing.

Food didn't taste the way it should. I woke up feeling as if I hadn't gotten any sleep. Nothing made me laugh. Everything just felt beige.

Taking this internship had been the worst decision I'd made since fringe bangs. My heart was broken. My relationship with my sister felt as if it was on shaky ground. It didn't look as if anyone who worked under Ophelia would be hired long-term. And Peter Crown's interim management was even less warm and cuddly than Ophelia's had been, if that could be believed. Gaunt and grumpy, Mr. Crown was far too comfortable setting up his own totalitarian regime, telling us that any and all complaints and concerns should be directed to the Department of Shut Up and Do Your Job. Margaret actually wept as she watched the cleaning crew haul Ophelia's Hello Kitty desk accessories into banker's boxes. But fortunately for our department, Mr. Crown understood next to nothing about computers, so he basically left us alone. Also, he told Margaret to stop crying with such authority that she would follow him anywhere.

I just wanted to go back to school, where I could trust most of the people around me, where I understood how things worked, where a potential mugging was my chief concern while walking across parking lots.

We were wrapping up the final phase of coding and planned to send our last batch to the regional branch for the big test that Friday. Because of Mr. Crown's lack of experience, this meant a lot of phone calls between myself and the project leader in the Chicago office. The chief advantage there was that it prevented a lot of awkward conversation with Marty.

I was unraveling emotionally. My temper seemed to be dangling on a weak string, and the slightest nudge would make it snap. I was shaky and angry and snappish with just about everybody but Iris, Cal, Aaron, and Jordan. My stomach felt as if it was roiling all day and night, and my hands trembled over the keyboard. I'd resorted to taking frequent bathroom breaks just to collect myself and maintain my composure.

On one such break, I was in the ladies' room, washing my hands, when Margaret came up behind me at the sink. She was staring at me. Hard. Clearly, she blamed me for her boss getting the heave-ho, since I had the nerve to provoke Ophelia into trying to put a magical mob hit on me and all.

Still, I smiled pleasantly, because even if I was about to engage in a bathroom catfight, I was a lady. "What can I do for you, Margaret?"

"For a start, you can stop stringing Marty along," Margaret said. "Just say yes when he asks you out. He's such a nice guy. You should give him a chance."

"And I don't see how that's any of your business," I told her sharply.

Margaret grabbed my arm before I could step away. She scoffed, tucking her graying hair behind her ear. "You think you're a hot commodity because you got a vampire to pay a little attention to you? Trust me. You have a reputation around here, Gigi, and it's not good."

"Oh, I'm sure I do. But since we're talking about damage, what did you do to Nik?" I demanded.

Margaret scowled at me. "What the hell are you talking about? Listen to what I'm telling you. You're damaged goods. No vampire is going to want you now. You're lucky that Marty wants anything to do with you."

I really, really wanted to hurt her. Hitting vampires was like hitting practice dummies. It was hard to hurt them, and they instantly recovered from any damage you did. Margaret, on the other hand, was human. I could injure her pretty seriously. And I found that I wanted to. Something angry and savage inside me relished the idea of breaking her bones, making her bleed. The ease with which my hands curled over hers frightened me. But still, my lips pulled back from my teeth in a snarl, and I was fully prepared to wrench her arm behind her back, when Jordan came sauntering out of the stall. She shook her purple bangs out of her face and rearranged them in the mirror, as if her co-workers weren't locked in a death grip just beside her.

"Really, ambushing a girl in the ladies' room?" she said, rolling her eyes. "That's so cliché."

"Gigi and I were just having a personal conversation," Margaret said in a pleasant tone. "So why don't you toddle along and try to find a hair color that occurs in nature?"

"Nah, I'm good here. I kind of want to see how this plays out." Jordan crossed her arms over her Van Gogh's TARDIS T-shirt and leaned against the gray vanity. Margaret narrowed her eyes at her but didn't move. I tried to figure out how I could maneuver from an arm grip to a double arm pin, followed by shoving Margaret's head into the toilet, swirly-style.

But I could feel Margaret's hold on my arm loosening, as if she was losing her resolve. Jordan was making it too uncomfortable for her. It was as if Margaret had just enough nerve to confront me but not quite enough to go after two people simultaneously. Clearly, I had underestimated Jordan, who was some sort of social-engineering genius.

Finally, Margaret tossed my arm aside, huffing in disgust. "Remember what I said, Gigi."

"Oh, I'll remember," I snarked, as Margaret walked out of the restroom. "Thank you, Jordan, I appreciate it."

"No problem, boss lady. I was 'nice guy-ed' once at my school's mock UN. The representative for fake Cambodia wouldn't take no for an answer. He sent his friends after me in the ladies' room, too. Fake Switzerland was anything but neutral about the matter. She guilt-tripped the hell out of me about how I should at least 'give him a chance,' despite the fact that I had no interest in him. Never would, but I guess that didn't matter. Have you thought about reporting Marty for harassment?"

I thought of Ms. Gibson and the multitude of insane problems she had to deal with every day, including co-workers who pulled stakes on each other and drained each other's blood. Somehow, I didn't think she would see my situation as a priority. I shook my head. "Making sad-puppy faces at me and making passive-aggressive overtures through coworkers don't violate office policy. I checked."

"Well, if you hit the angry stage, I am in for ironic Lifetime-movie, woman-done-wrong retribution."

"Thank you," I told her solemnly. "I will keep that in mind."

Jordan winked at me. "It's as close as I get to handing you a friendship bracelet."

Jordan and I returned to work, ignoring Margaret as she scowled at us from her desk. I buried myself in conference calls for the next few hours, ironing out some compatibility issues between our format and the design department's specs. I hung up, hopeful that we would be able to test this thing without glitches in the coming week so I could walk away with a clear conscience. I felt a presence over my left shoulder and rolled my eyes skyward, praying it wasn't Marty.

"Aaron and Jordan were talking about getting something to eat after work, Gladiola. Do you want to join us?"

Dang it.

I swiveled my chair around and found Marty standing just a little too close to my desk. I leaned left and spotted Aaron, who was silently waving his arms and shaking his head no.

"Oh, that's sweet of you to invite me, Marty, but I have plans with my family," I said, with the fakest smile I had ever produced. "You know, overprotective vampire siblings, they're all about the quality time."

That's right, overprotective vampire siblings; think about that for a second, Marty.

"That's too bad," Marty said, his eyes glittering balefully. "Maybe next time."

I smiled. "Sure. You guys go ahead, though." Marty turned back toward Aaron and Jordan. I mouthed "Thank you!" to them both. "You've worked hard this week; take off early. You've earned it. I just need to stick around and finish up a few calls."

"Oh, we shouldn't," Marty protested, as Jordan and Aaron gathered up their bags.

"Good night!" Aaron called.

Jordan lingered and mouthed "Are you OK?" behind Marty's back. I nodded and waved her off. "Good night, Jordan."

Jordan sent a sharp look toward Marty's back. "Good night."

"Gigi." Marty sighed, sitting on the corner of my desk. "I know you've had a rough time lately. I can't say I didn't see it coming. Vampires aren't exactly known for their attention span in relationships."

"You're treading close to some territory that is none of your business, Marty."

Marty's dark brown eyes were all pity and condescension as he laid a hand on my shoulder. "I know you. I know what you want and what you need. No one is going to make you happier than I would."

If he didn't move that hand, he was going to lose it. What was the office policy on using choke holds on coworkers?

"Look, I know you think you're in love with this vampire, but you're too good for him, too sweet. He doesn't understand you. Vampires never do. What are you going to have in common? Even if he does take you back, what's going to happen? He's going to bite you and leave you. And then where will you be? Maybe you should stop chasing after something that's never going to happen. Maybe the guy you're looking for is right in front of you."

The violent reaction inside my head frightened me. I wanted to hit Marty until my hands bled. I wanted to scream and shout every curse word I knew at him. My office phone cord could be put to horrifying and creative use. But none of that would change Marty's mind about his feelings for me or how well he "understood" my relationship with Nik. Nothing would convince him that I was being honest with him or myself. Nonreaction was the best reaction. I just had to communicate that to my tensed muscles.

"Have a good night, Marty." My phone rang. I gave Marty an absolutely mirthless smile and picked up the receiver, turning my back to him.

I kept myself busy with minutiae for a while. I caught up on paperwork and backed up files. I wrote a progress report for the regional manager, including glowing praise for Aaron and Jordan. I also wrote a less luminary evaluation for Marty, but I was proud that I kept my comments limited to his incompetence and inability to finish his work. At one point, I came back from the bathroom, and my usual peppermint mocha was waiting for me on my desk. Sammy must have taken pity on me on his last round through the office.

I appreciated his thoughtfulness, but it was a bit muggy for coffee, so I neglected it in favor of finishing up more paperwork. I took a few more calls from the West Coast offices about formatting issues. I was basically a model employee for almost an hour, eliminating errors wherever I could find them.

Sipping my now lukewarm coffee, I used the beta program to search Cal's name, and my name popped up as a living relative, with a footnote stating that I was also related to Iris. I entered Nola's name, and she popped up as a relative of Dick Cheney's. I tried to think of a potential negative result to prove the effectiveness. Linoge. At this point, I really had nothing to lose, even if the search came back to me. If I was going to be fired for hoarding files, I was pretty sure it would have happened by now. And I only had a few weeks left at the Council. Screw it.

I entered the name "Linoge." And the results window came back positive.

"Sweet mother of dragons." I gasped.

The entire Renart line showed up in the results window. Marie Renart had indeed been Pierre Linoge's eighteenth-century love bunny, and she bore him two children before he'd been turned. I guess he didn't make a very good undead boyfriend, and her alternative to breaking up with him was to send him on a memory-addled feeding rampage.

Jennifer Renart was the last living descendant of Pierre Linoge. Her last-known address was listed in Half-Moon Hollow in 1991.

Renart was local. I could find her. Why this hadn't shown up in any of the other Council records, I had no idea. And it sort of sucked that while I was trying to track down Linoge's relatives, one of my coworkers had apparently found the file in the giant pile of folders and entered the information in the archive. But now I could go to the library or the county clerk's office or the property valuator's department, and I could track this woman down. Hell, maybe Jane could use one of her not-quite-legal subscriptions to library databases to help me. It wasn't her fault the library management hadn't changed the passwords since she'd been fired.

I packed up my bag, grabbed my coffee, and drained it on the way out the door. A strange, bitter aftertaste had me wincing as I tossed the cup into a hallway wastebasket. That didn't taste like Sammy's usual yummy creation. Maybe the milk had gone bad while I let it sit on my desk?

Well, at least it would keep me awake on the drive home. I slung my bag over my shoulder and checked my phone as I motored down the hallway. I would be glad later that I looked so busy and important when I ran into Nik. Well, plowed into him, was more like it, and nearly knocked him into the employee exit door.

"Gigi," he breathed, his hands closing around my arms to keep me steady on my feet.

"I thought you didn't want to see me," I said, sounding very cold as I stepped away from him. Because even if I was eager to find information to help him become uncursed, I was still a little pissed at him.

"I am signing some final statements with the Council, trying to piece together exactly what Ophelia did," he said, rubbing his hand on the back of his neck. "How have you been?"

"I'm well, thank you."

That's right, I was cold as ice. In the movie version of this conversation, I would be played by a really young Cate Blanchett.

"Gigi—"

"I really have to be going," I said. The "to have a nervous breakdown behind the wheel of my car" was silent.

"Well, let me walk you to your car."

"There's no need," I said breezily. "With you inside, I probably stand a much better chance in the parking lot."

"Gigi, please."

And he just looked so damned sad that I sighed and said, "Fine."

He nodded toward the door and held it open for me. I made every effort not to come within two feet of touching him, much less making eye contact. He moved silently at my left, staring through me as if I had the secret meaning of life tattooed on my neck.

I finally found my car, clicked the keyless entry, and tossed my purse onto the passenger seat. I held on to the door for a long moment, thinking very carefully about how I wanted the next few minutes to play out. I could get into my car and drive away. I would never see him again. And I would know that I'd at least had my dignity when he left me. He hadn't seen me cry over him or whine and beg. But I couldn't let him leave without asking, "Do you think your sacrifice broke the curse?"

"Gigi. I am sorry."

"Yes or no, Nik?"

"No," he whispered. "Nola says it is still there."

"So even though this plan of yours hasn't worked, you're going to leave me anyway?"

"Maybe if it is more final, maybe if I actually lose you, the requirements of the curse will be met, and you will be safe."

"OK, fine. That's just fine." I blinked back tears, staring down at the pavement so he wouldn't see them. I wanted to tell him that I missed him, that I was being a jerk, that I shouldn't have pretended I could get through this without being hurt. But the lump in my throat kept me from saying anything. I couldn't seem to take a breath deep enough. I sank back against the car behind me, shaking off the waves of cold and dizziness that radiated through my head.

"Gigi?"

"Nik," I began, swallowing and trying to dislodge the pressure. But it stayed there, like a stone wedged in my windpipe. I coughed, clutching my neck. "I don't feel very well."

I wheezed, forcing myself to inhale deeply, just so I

felt that I was getting some oxygen into my lungs. This wasn't just a lump in my throat. I couldn't breathe. I couldn't draw enough air to produce more words. My eyes went wide, and I looked up to Nik. He cradled my elbows in his hands and let me down gently to the ground.

I opened my mouth and tried to force air into my lungs, but I just couldn't seem to take it in. My lips started to tingle, and I felt so tired I just sank back onto the asphalt, boneless and weak. What was happening to me? The worst possibilities spun through my brain. A heart attack? A stroke? I was too young for either, but that didn't stop my chest from feeling as if I was wedged under a Mack truck tire.

A crippling wave of nausea rolled up from my belly to my throat, threatening to spill everything I'd eaten for the last two days onto the pavement. Could I have food poisoning? The milk in my coffee had tasted off, but I didn't think a little spoiled cream would hit me this fast. None of this rational, linear thinking seemed to matter much, as a cloudy white haze of pain spread over my brain, making me howl.

"Gigi? What is happening?"

"Can't breathe," I wheezed, clutching at his arm. My panicked, shaking fingers ripped at my collar, anything to help pull air down my throat.

Nik pulled out his cell phone, dialed, and began speaking in a rapid-fire language I didn't understand. He dropped the phone to the ground and pulled me into his lap. "Gigi," he said, eyes wide and looking more frightened than I had ever seen him. "We have discussed this before. But now, I ask you again. Do you want to be turned? Or would you rather die before becoming a vampire?"

I tried to say yes, but the sound wouldn't come. I wanted to nod, but I couldn't seem to make my head move. My lips moved silently, begging him, *Please, help me, please! Anything but dying like this!*

Nik nodded, his fangs dropped, and he snapped them down onto my neck like a striking snake. I would have screamed if I could from the pain of his fangs tearing through my skin. He drew huge mouthfuls of blood, even though he recoiled from the taste and spat it out. He bit my wrists, leaving gashes, letting my blood flow onto the ground.

I couldn't even cry out from this new slashing pain. I was so cold. I was so tired. He pulled and pulled at the wounds on my neck, seeming to gag with every mouthful. He bit at his own wrist, leaving his own blood running down his arm. He held it over my mouth. I turned my head away so it wouldn't drip on my face, but he turned my head, forcing it against his torn skin.

"Gigi, you have to drink." I parted my lips, licking them tentatively as the blood dropped into my mouth. It was sweet, like melted bittersweet chocolate, flowing over my lips and into my throat. I wanted to pull the arm close to snuggle against him and curl around him like a cat while I drank from him. But I was just so exhausted I couldn't move. Even the act of opening my mouth to swallow his blood seemed like an insane effort.

Nik bit into his free arm and switched, pushing this new free-bleeding wound against my lips. It was too much, too fast, and I turned my head away, coughing, fighting to draw breath

"More, my Gigi, you have to drink more for it to work. Come on, *sladkaya*, please," he begged, cradling me against his chest.

I opened my mouth, tried to drink more. But I was just so scared, so tired. I couldn't think. Everything around me seemed to be spinning, and I couldn't help but think this would be the last time I would see any of it. I was drowning, dying, choking on the air I couldn't pull into my lungs. My heart stuttered and sped, like a broken-down horse lunging for the finish line.

Nik's face swam in front of my eyes. "Drink," he whispered, nudging the wound against my mouth, but I shook my head.

This was it. With a strange clarity, I finally grasped that this was the end of my life. No more Christmases. No more birthdays. No more snow or rain or starlit nights. No more breakfasts with Cal ruffling my hair and making me late for work. No more movie nights with Iris curled up on the couch.

Iris.

Oh, God, Iris. I knew that Cal would take care of her, help her not feel so guilty, but I hated that I was leaving her alone. She'd been right, of course. I should have left the world of vampires alone. If I'd just taken some office job at a human company, I wouldn't be dying in a parking lot. I'd be bored as hell, but at least I'd still be alive.

With all of the will I had left, I forced my arm to move, reaching up to touch Nik's face. My fingertips left bloody trails across his skin. I drew enough breath to whisper, "Love you." I smiled.

"Drink," he commanded, forcing his wrist against my mouth.

I gagged as he forced more blood down my throat. I felt tears, hot and bitter, running down my cheeks and soaking into Nik's jeans.

"This part is always difficult," he told me. "But when you wake up, you will be like me."

My heart sped up, beating like a wild, trapped animal against my ribs. And then it didn't beat at all.

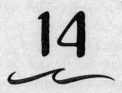

14

Working with an undead office staff requires adaptability.
You will learn to think on your feet, or you will fail on the
flat of your back.

—*The Office After Dark: A Guide to Maintaining a
Safe, Productive Vampire Workplace*

Jasmine.

My room smelled of night-blooming jasmine, heady
and sweet.

Why did my room smell of jasmine?

I sniffed, rubbing at my eyes. "Iris?" I croaked. My
mouth felt sore, raw, and dry as the desert, as if I'd just
had my wisdom teeth yanked out without anesthesia.
My puffy unicorn slippers were waiting at the end of
my bed as usual. I could feel the weight of the moonstone flower earrings at my lobes. I was dressed in my
favorite Soft Kitty pajamas, which I did not remember
putting on. For that matter, I didn't remember going
to bed the night before. And I was thirsty as all hell.
I smacked my lips. Not just cotton-mouth thirsty but

bone-deep, just-crossed-the-Sahara thirst that threatened to close off my throat at any second.

Had I been sick? Considering the fuzzy head and dry mouth, drunk seemed more likely. I didn't remember going out the night before. And I definitely wouldn't get fall-down drunk with Cal and Iris at home. Why couldn't I remember anything from the night before?

I slowly sat up and shook my head. I felt strange, and not just hungover strange. It felt as if I was forgetting something really important, and when I realized what it was, I would feel really stupid.

Almost every surface in my room was covered in vases containing arrangements of jasmine. "Iris? What's with the funeral sprays?" I called.

I squinted around the room, blinking. Everything was in perfect twenty-twenty focus—better than twenty-twenty, really. I could see everything. The bit of dust I'd missed the last time I'd cleaned my desk. My friends' cramped handwriting on cards hanging on my pinboard. I could count Ben's eyelashes in our prom photo. That couldn't be right. I squinched my eyes shut. Without visual stimuli, a multitude of noises came roaring through my ears. I could hear the clinking of glasses against the kitchen counter. I could hear muffled voices—Iris and Jane, no, Andrea saying something about a Friends and Family of the Undead meeting. I could hear the engines of cars driving down the highway five miles from our house.

I waited for my heart to race or my breath to quicken.

That's when I realized what I'd forgotten. Breathing. I'd forgotten to breathe this whole time. And of all the things I could hear, my heart was as silent and still as the grave.

Oh, holy crap on a cracker, I was a vampire.

"Iris!" I yelled, standing too quickly and bolting across the room on my unsteady baby-vampire legs. I could move so quickly now, so easily. It was as if I'd spent all of my human years covered in some weird jelly film, and now I was free. I hopped up onto my bed, landing flatfooted like a surfer on a board. Grinning madly, I leaped to the ceiling, clinging to the plaster by some miracle of gravity avoidance and crawling along like Spider-Man.

"Whatcha doin'?" Iris asked from the doorway.

"I believe she is enjoying her first moments as a vampire," Nik said, appearing behind her shoulders. "Are you going to come down, Gigi?"

"Not anytime soon!" I giggled, rolling in a somersault over the ceiling fan, around the doorjamb, and into the hallway. I slid down the bannister on both feet and sprang back up to the ceiling, where I moonwalked into the parlor.

"Very mature, Gigi!" Iris called down the stairs.

"I'm permanently twenty. That means I don't have to mature!" I yelled back.

"I did that on my first night," Jane said, sighing with vampiric nostalgia.

"Yeah, but you accused me of slipping you drugs,"

Gabriel said, snorting, as I dropped to the floor in the full Batman crouch. Nik followed, jumping over the bannister and joining the gathered vampires as they watched my theatrics. I launched myself at them and wrapped one arm around Jamie's neck and the other around Nik's. Cal chuckled, ruffling my hair, while Iris caught up to me and kissed my cheek. Vampire group hugs were the best.

"I am so sorry," Nik whispered as my family withdrew from the hug. "I am so sorry I hurt you. I am sorry you had to be turned. I am sorry I made you think I did not want you. I am willing to be less of a, what did you call it, Jane?"

"Emotional jerkwad," Jane supplied.

"I refuse to say it, but yes, that," he said. "I want to be with you, Gigi. Even if it makes Cal very uncomfortable. Even if it makes me uncomfortable. I am willing to change. I even bought a laptop."

"Wow!" I gasped.

"He bought a computer? That's how he shows he's changed?" Gabriel whispered.

"I'll explain later," Cal murmured.

"Thank you," I told Nik. "Thank you for being there when I needed you. I love you."

"Never forget that I love you, too, *sladkaya*," he whispered.

I wiped at my eyes, shaking off the emotional moment I was experiencing in front of *every* person I loved.

"OK, so we've established that Nik is part of the

pack now. So am I hot?" I asked, turning toward the mirror over the mantel. "I bet I'm super-hot, because I was at least a seven before."

Iris buried her face in her hands. "And so modest, too."

I stared into the mirror. I *was* hot. Well, not just hot—dangerous and beautiful, a predator who attracted and pacified her prey with bright colors and smooth textures. My skin shone with that porcelain perfection only the undead could manage, making my cornflower eyes seem even larger and more electric blue. My hair was a richer chicory color with coppery highlights and a more lustrous sheen. I smiled, showing teeth so white it almost hurt to look at them.

My fangs dropped, razor-sharp, nicking my bottom lip. I winced and raised my fingers to my bee-stung lips, where a ruby drop of blood welled against the soft pink cushion. Nik caught my hand, eyeing my mouth hungrily, and ducked his head to rake his tongue over the wound as it closed, healing now that my vampire cells were revved up and ready to realign.

The parts of my brain that were still somewhat human rebelled at the very idea, but the rest of me, the primal, predatory creature I'd become, delighted in sharing my blood with the man I loved. I welcomed a kiss from my sire, winding my arms around his neck and practically purring as he drew at the wound.

"I can't look," Cal muttered. "Tell me when it's over."

"I heard that." Laughing, I broke away from Nik, who groaned softly and dropped his head to my shoulder. "I can hear everything. I can see everything. I can smell everything . . . Gross, Jamie, is that how you always smell?"

"Under normal circumstances, no. I did this special for you," he said, raising his arms and advancing on me. "I haven't bathed in three days, and I may have rolled around with Fitz for good measure. You made me worry, Gigi. Armpit vengeance is mine."

"Remember when I was little and I used to beg Mom and Dad for a baby brother?" I asked Iris. "I was wrong."

"This isn't what I wanted for you," Iris said, brushing my hair back from my face.

"But it's what I wanted." I glanced at Nik. "It's what I asked for."

"I'm slowly coming to accept that. I'm just sad. You were the last of our line," Iris said, sniffing. "I was kind of counting on you to carry on the family name."

"Who's to say I was going to have kids in the first place?" I laughed. "I would be a terrible parent. My hours are weird, and I can barely remember to feed myself, much less another person. Besides, it's not like there aren't thousands of Scanlons out there to carry on the family name. It's not that unique."

"You know, I said the same thing to my mom, and she got really quiet, then drank a whole bottle of cooking sherry," Jane said. "So far, your conversation is going better."

As Jane said the word "drank," my mouth seemed that much drier, Dust Bowl dry, and I could feel my fangs stretching through my gums. Weird. I touched my fingertip to them and winced, watching a droplet of blood well from the tiny wound. The wound disappeared almost immediately.

I felt as if I could drink the contents of a whole Igloo cooler and come back for more. A scent wafted through my bedroom door like fresh-baked chocolate chip cookies and roast beef and curly fries and all of my favorite foods all in one. My mouth watered, and I could actually feel the drool spilling over my lips.

Classy.

"What is that?" I asked Nik, wiping discreetly at my mouth.

"I heated something up for your first feeding," Dick said, coming through the door to offer me a steaming mug of deep red liquid. "It's donor blood, AB negative, which is super-rare. We wanted you to have something special."

"Unless you wanted to try a live feeding first," Iris said. "Which is probably better for you, to get used to the process. We could call a surrogate service right now and have one here within the hour. "

"Don't hover, sweetheart," Cal chided gently.

"I don't think I could wait," I said. "Also, I don't think I'm ready for the whole biting experience yet. So I'll just take what's in that cup."

I took it from Dick's hands, even though my own shook with a hunger so fierce it made my belly tremble. He winked at me and wrapped his fingers around mine to steady me. "Over the lips and past the gums, look out, tummy, here it comes."

"Please don't nursery-rhyme me right now," I said, shaking my head. I raised the mug to my lips and blew instinctively on the liquid, even though I knew it wouldn't be hotter than ninety-eight point six. I looked up and realized that all of the older vampires were watching me.

"Could you guys turn around or something? You're making me nervous."

There was a collective chuckle, but they all turned around to give me some privacy. Nik's expression was faintly wounded. "Even me?"

"Nah, I need someone to tell me if I have a blood mustache." I licked my lips over the blood, inhaling the dark, delicious fragrance and letting it roll into my mouth.

Blood was fan-effing-tastic. Nothing had ever tasted so good, so sweet, so savory. The Japanese had a word for it—*umami*—a flavor that hit all five basic tastes at once. Which reminded me, damn it, that I was never going to have sushi again. But as I took another sip of donor blood, I thought I could live with that.

I drained the last of the mug and was relieved to find that my throat didn't feel as if I'd been gargling barbed wire anymore.

"OK?" I asked Nik, who brushed his thumb over my top lip. He winked at me and gave me a long, smacking kiss.

"Stop that!" Cal groaned.

"Can we turn around now?" Jamie asked.

Nik's lips pulled away from mine, and I shut my

eyes tight as images flooded into my brain. Nik hovering over me as I struggled to breathe. Nik draining me, even though my blood seemed to burn his mouth. The sensation of his blood flowing down my throat. His whispering that I would be OK, that when I woke up, I would be like him.

"Why am I remembering all of this?" I hissed, twisting Nik's shirt in my fists. "It's like going through it all over again. It hurts."

"It happens sometimes, when you make first contact with your sire," Jane said, rubbing a hand over my back. "It will be over in a minute."

And suddenly, I made the connection between the poison in my system and the way Nik spat out my blood and the pale, waxy pallor to his cheeks that I was just now noticing. Nik had been poisoned, too, trying to save me. Whatever was in my system could have killed me.

"You could have died, you jerk!" I cried, hitting his arm.

"Ow!" he yelped, rubbing at his arm. "It actually hurts when you hit now. Stop it. And yes, I could have died, but since you *were* dying, that means you took precedence."

"You do not get to make decisions like that without talking to me first!" I exclaimed, poking him in the chest. "Wall colors and DVDs for movie nights and ill-advised haircuts, those are all judgment calls you can make without discussion. But making the choice to sacrifice yourself to save me without so much as a

Post-it note? That's not . . . And suddenly, I'm realizing that I basically did the same thing when I let you bite me and almost drain me, so my righteous indignation is sort of over the top. Sorry about the poking."

Nik was laughing so hard by this point that bloody pink tears were rolling down his cheeks.

"Oh, and I found some information on the witch who probably cursed you. I'm going to need a little more to track her down, but I think if we do and we threaten her enough, we might be able to get her to remove the curse."

"We will get to that," Nik said. "For now, just drink."

I decided to be a good girl and drain the cup, but only because I was *starving*.

"OK, so what happened?" I asked, wiping at my lip to avoid a blood mustache. "What happened to me?"

Iris sighed. "You're going to need another mug of that blood."

Jane, Gabriel, Andrea, Dick, and Jamie were circled around the parlor like some sort of war council. It seemed that they all had their own theories about how and why I was poisoned, and none of them jived with the "household accident" explanation that the Council was circulating among my coworkers. Of course, this explanation mentioned neither my poisoning nor my being turned into a vampire, just that I was hospitalized in unstable condition, which demonstrated the underhanded and unreliable nature of the Council's public relations office.

"OK, Gigi, we've heard the Council's version of what happened to you, but clearly, that was . . ." Cal paused for the right word.

"Bullshit," Dick supplied.

Cal nodded. "From what Nik tells us, you were poisoned with something strong enough that it made your blood almost undrinkable, but we don't know how. I'd like you to walk us through that night, everything that you can remember. I checked with the office security personnel, and there are no cameras pointed at your door. So we don't know who might have slipped you the poison. So, please, did you accept food or drink from anyone?" Cal asked. "Did anything you ate or drank taste funny? Did you touch a package or some sort of testing sample that you weren't supposed to?"

"You mean, did I pick up the envelope labeled 'ricin' and lick it? No. And no, I made my own breakfast and lunch from the same groceries I've used for the last few days. I brown-bagged my dinner, also made from those groceries."

"Did you leave it in the office fridge?" Cal asked.

I nodded. "But it tasted fine to me. I didn't have any symptoms for hours after eating. And other than my coffee order, I didn't eat or drink anything else that day." I frowned. "My coffee order . . ."

"What about your coffee order?"

I thought back to that cold cup of coffee I had glugged down before I left the office. And I could not believe that was the last human food I'd eaten. I felt so cheated. Iris, at least, got to choose a last meal. When

Cal turned her, she was chewing on a limited-edition Godiva truffle.

"I sent the other programmers home early because I had some calls I needed to make. I went to the restroom around one a.m., and when I came back, my usual, a peppermint mocha, was waiting for me on the desk."

"Was that normal?" Gabriel asked.

I shrugged. "Sammy, the coffee guy, leaves around one. Sometimes, if he has time, he'll drop something off, because he worries about us driving home for the night uncaffeinated. If we're not sitting at our desks, he'll just leave it for us."

"When did you drink it?"

"I was distracted while I was working, so I let it go cold. I drank it all in one swoop as I was leaving work," I said. "Come to think of it, the coffee did taste funny. I thought maybe the milk had gone off, since I'd left it alone all night."

"Does Sammy have any reason to hold a grudge against you?"

"I don't think so," I said. "It would be more likely that someone tampered with my coffee after Sammy dropped it off."

Jane frowned. "So the question is, who do you know who wants you dead?"

"Besides Ophelia?"

"Besides Ophelia." Iris nodded.

"Have you checked with Ophelia?" I asked. "Because this has her fingerprints all over it."

Jamie rolled his eyes. "Ophelia and I have had several long, long, loooooooong talks since she confessed to outsourcing the curse for you. She swears that she didn't have anything to do with it. Sophie scanned her and says she's telling the truth. So who, besides Ophelia, would want you dead?"

I shuddered at the thought of being scanned by enigmatic, elegant, "first name only" Sophie, a vampire bureaucrat and undead lie detector who literally ripped the truth from one's lips using her scary vampire talent.

"Besides Ophelia?" I checked again.

"Besides Ophelia!" the others chorused.

"There's Marty, but if he was going to drug me, I'm pretty sure I would wake up chained up in a holding cell in his basement." I thought about it for a long moment. "Again, I'm going to have to go with Margaret. Even though she passed the first magic test, she's never really warmed to me. In fact, she used the term 'damaged goods' to describe me. And Ophelia's facing censure because of me; Margaret'll want to get revenge. She worships Ophelia. Besides that, for a while there, I thought maybe she was the one who cursed Nik, so I may have been a little hostile toward her."

"Did you stab her in the thigh with a silver stake, too?" Gabriel asked. When Dick slapped the back of his head, Gabriel grumped. "What? I've learned not to underestimate Gigi's hostilities!"

"Would Margaret have had the opportunity to dose your drink?"

"I left my desk unattended a few times to run to the fax machine down the hall, visit the ladies' room, that sort of thing. She could have dropped it into my coffee while I was out. And don't lecture me about safety, Cal. I know not to leave my drink unchaperoned at a bar, but I thought I would be safe at my office."

"I wasn't going to say anything," Cal said, holding up his hands. Iris smirked at him. "I was going to say a little bit."

"Any idea what the anonymous poisoner gave me?" I asked, making Iris clear her throat. Clearly, we had reached her portion of the "presentation."

"Boy, are you lucky that you have a sister who's an expert in this crap. I recognized the signs of night-shade poisoning in Nik that I saw in Cal that first day I tripped over him in his kitchen," Iris said. Cal cleared his throat. She rolled her eyes. "I mean, when Cal heroically rescued me from walking in a straight line on my own two feet."

She flipped open her now-familiar copy of *The Natural versus the Supernatural*. She showed me an illustration of a plant with flat, broad, tobacco-like leaves and weird brownish-purple flowers. "This is deadly nightshade, *atropa belladonna*. Nightshade produces a bitter alkaloid poison called atropine, which, in small doses, is used in medications to slow heart rates and sometimes counteract nerve agents. In humans, nightshade poisoning causes dry mouth, dizziness, confusion, nausea, and a whole host of unpleasantness. In large doses, it can cause death within minutes."

"What happens to vampires who ingest deadly nightshade?" I asked, giving Nik a pointed look.

Iris pulled out her own small press book, *Bitten Botanicals: Rare Plants and Their Effects on the Undead*. She opened to the first chapter, in which she described Cal's tangle with bittersweet nightshade, deadly nightshade's bitchy cousin.

"Let's just say very bad and potentially immortality-ending things, so don't yell at Nik anymore, OK?" Iris said.

"Oh, *now* you're protective of Nik," I muttered.

"No, you're just really loud, and I have sensitive ears," Iris said, shrugging. "We found you two in the parking lot. You were already, uh, you were out." She cleared her throat and blinked a few times. "Um, Nik was fading fast. We brought you both home."

"OK, so why didn't the nightshade make me sick all over again when I drank Nik's blood?" I asked.

"He poured it into you so quickly it hadn't had time to enter his bloodstream yet. And afterward, we all took turns feeding both of you to help flush out your systems."

"All of you?"

"We activated the vampire emergency phone tree. Me and Cal, Jane, Gabriel, Dick, Collin, Andrea, even Sam. Jamie insisted on feeding you every chance he got. We figured the more vampire blood you had running through your system, the better."

I blinked away the tears that were gathering at the corners of my eyes. When I was dying, these people had stepped up to help me. I had their blood flowing in my veins. They were really my family now.

"Aw, honey, don't cry," Dick said. "I'm a sympathetic crier, and an ugly one at that. You don't want to see that."

"It's true," Gabriel assured me. "He looks like a weeping pug. Jamie put the footage of Dick watching *Titanic* on YouTube. It's up to half a million hits."

"I just really love you guys." I sighed, wiping at my wet cheeks. My hand was stained pink. I'd forgotten that vampire tears contained small traces of blood. "Gross."

"It takes some getting used to," Andrea assured me. "You'll be fine."

Nik rubbed my back reassuringly as he tucked me against his side. Cal made a disapproving noise, which we both ignored. We could not, however, ignore the knock at the door, which Jamie jumped to answer. In fact, he didn't seem surprised at all that we would get a visitor at this time of night.

"Jamie," I said suspiciously. "Who's at the door?"

"Ophelia wanted to stop by and see how you were doing. She promised me she'd apologize."

"No, Jamie, don't—gah!" I grunted as Jamie dashed to the door at vampire speed and admitted his evil girlfriend. While she was wearing a gorgeous red sundress and heels, Ophelia seemed deflated somehow, smaller and younger, but less tragic than she'd looked in the walk-of-shame ensemble.

"Ophelia, what are you doing here? Are you here to intimidate me as one of your newest constituents?"

"You're not my constituent. At least, not for now."

I smiled, because I very much enjoyed reminding her of her status as exiled from the Council. "Oh, right, because you tried to arrange for my cold-blooded murder."

"No, because I falsified expense reports while I tried to arrange for your cold-blooded murder. I should have known better than to use Council funds to pay the witch who cursed Nik," she said, even as Nik growled, low and deadly.

"So that means that you have no real authority over me?" I said, an evil, Grinch-ish grin spreading across my face. "You can't really punish me?"

"No, but I can still—" Ophelia didn't even manage to finish the sentence before I swung my fist in an upward arc and punched her nose hard enough to make it spurt blood. Jamie watched impassively as Ophelia collapsed to the floor.

She wiped at her nose, glaring at me. "I was *saying* that I can still fight back if you challenge me. I'll consider that challenge issued."

I scoffed. "Bring it. I'm just as strong as you are, and you haven't had to fight in years."

Jane dragged me away from Ophelia, while Gabriel and Dick held her arms. I looked to Jamie, feeling a bit guilty for punching his bloodmate right in front of him.

He shrugged. "She kind of had that coming."

"I disagree." Ophelia sniffed, wiping at the blood trailing from her nose.

Iris smiled sweetly as she helped Ophelia up from the floor. "For now, why don't you remove your bony ass from my house, before I show you where she learned that right hook?"

Ophelia tried to pull the imperious "Who do you think you're talking to?" eyebrow arch. Iris shook her head. "You tried to kill my sister, wench. Polite and respectful treatment stopped a couple of minutes ago. You're lucky there are so many witnesses around."

"I just wanted to stop by and see how you're faring," Ophelia said. "And as usual, you have Jamie's attention, so you must be fine."

"Ophelia," Jamie growled.

"Oh, don't start that again," I cried. "Jamie and I are not interested in each other! I have a . . . special gentleman vampire friend . . ." I turned to Nik. "I'm sorry, I still don't know what to call you. You're too old to be my boyfriend." I turned back to Ophelia. "Nik. I have a Nik. I don't want Jamie. Jamie, do you want me?"

Jamie wrinkled up his face, as if I'd just offered him olive loaf with a lovely side of persimmon jelly. "Ugh, no."

"This is the most uncomfortable conversation I have ever witnessed. And that includes all of Jane's," Dick whispered to Gabriel. "I don't know where to look."

Without warning, I threw my arms around Jamie's neck and pulled him in for a kiss. It was the most awkward connection of lips ever experienced by man or vampire. His lips were cold and dry. Our teeth clacked together. And he nearly gouged me in the eye with the tip of his nose. I could hear Nik growling again behind me and Andrea whispering, "Easy now."

Gripping Jamie's collar, I pushed him away, and we both wiped at our mouths with the backs of our hands. Ophelia's eyes were wide and as blank as saucers. Jamie's expression had gone from "persimmon jelly" to "roadkill." I felt Nik's hand closing over my arms and dragging me away.

"Warn me when you're going to do that!" Jamie exclaimed, wiping at his mouth. "No, scratch that, never do that again!"

"I literally feel like I just made out with my brother," I said, gagging slightly. "What have you been eating?"

"Sometimes I like to stir my blood with a Slim Jim," Jamie muttered. "Gives it flavor."

"Gah," I said, shuddering. "Good God. OK, Ophelia, do you see?" I waved a hand between me and Jamie. "This. Will. Never. Happen. We have no chemistry, no desire to be together in any way besides friendship. Ever. And if you have a problem with how much time Jamie spends with me and my family, you two need to sit down and talk that out. Jamie, I would also suggest you stop being obtuse and spend more time with your girlfriend, if that's what she's asking you to do. And if she's not asking for it directly, you should do it anyway, because women are terrifying creatures who sometimes expect the men around us to read our minds."

Ophelia nodded slowly. "I see that I have made a terrible error in judgment. And for that, I owe you an apology."

"Yes, you do," I said. "Just so you know, that doesn't count as an actual apology. Now, you and Jamie, you go . . . wherever, to talk." I grabbed Nik's sleeve. "And you, you're with me."

Snagging a bottle of blood from the coffee table, I dragged Nik by the hand, out the front door and through the yard. He cleared his throat. "Well, that was, er, decisive."

I glugged blood from the bottle to try to rid myself of the Slim Jim aftertaste. "I hate that I had to do that to prove a point. And I'm sorry if it made you uncomfortable. I just get so sick of her bullshit."

"No, it was quick thinking, and at least it settled any doubts I had about your relationship with Jamie."

"Should I go find Ben and kiss him in front of you for good measure?" I asked.

"No," Nik said, stopping me and pulling me into his arms. He kissed me, long and sweet. His lips, which had always felt cool to me, were just as warm as my own.

I threaded my fingers through his hair and pulled him closer. I laughed against his mouth, then sighed. "That was better than Slim Jims," I assured him.

"Why, thank you."

I tilted my head up, staring at the millions of tiny pinpricks of light in the velvety black night sky. I could see every crevice and bump in the moon's surface, count every leaf on every tree branch. "Is this what you see, all the time?" I marveled.

He grinned, kissing my forehead. "And you will, too."

"This is my life now." I sighed. "Weird."

"You will not be alone in this life. I will be with you."

"Well, how nice of you to make that decision without any input from me," I deadpanned. "Again."

"Are you going to hit me in the nose, too?" he asked, covering said facial feature with his hand.

"Thinking about it."

He sighed, clutching my hand to his chest, where his silent heart rested. "Gladiola Grace Scanlon—"

"Easy."

"I throw myself on your mercy," he said, dropping to his knees. "I was very, very wrong to have left you to try to protect you. I can see now that I cannot live without you. And I will spend the rest of my life trying to show you that you might feel the same way about me. I will grovel, if that is what you want."

"This doesn't count as groveling?" I asked, raising an eyebrow.

"Oh, no," he said, shaking his head. "Groveling is sadder and involves more crying and promises of one-sided sexual favors."

Despite my desire to double over laughing, I asked, "And what about the next time you go all cursed and bite-y? Will you panic and leave me again?"

"I am not going to go all cursed and bite-y, because I am no longer cursed."

"Really?"

"I went to Nola while you were under your three-day sleep. She said all traces of magic are gone. Apparently, my being willing to drink so much of your blood to turn you, even though it meant I could die, was enough of a loving sacrifice to undo the spell. I am no longer cursed, thanks to you."

"Thanks to *you*," I said, wrapping my arms around him. "Good for you."

"You are still going to require the groveling, right?" he whispered into my hair.

"How could I not, with all those promises of one-sided sexual favors?" I murmured into his chest. He laughed, and I gave him a vampire-strength squeeze. "What am I going to do about college?"

"Iris made some calls. If you want to wait until you have your bloodthirst under control and finish up your coursework at UK, your professors would be willing to adjust your schedule. If not, there are plenty of vampire-friendly schools where you could finish your degree bloodbath-free. I will help you find one, and live in an off-campus apartment that is tasteful, but not so ostentatious as to make your classmates uncomfortable . . . when they visit you . . . because you will be living there with me."

"I hope you're prepared to hide your stuff when Iris and Cal come to visit," I told him. "Because they will not approve of me living in sin."

He grinned. "I spoke with Peter Crown, who is heading the local Council until the upheaval settles out. He is prepared to offer you a permanent position and a promotion as a result of your work this summer. And as one of their undead constituents, you qualify for an even better benefits package."

"What?" I exclaimed, insulted. "That's not fair! I mean, yay for me and all. But I'm extremely offended on behalf of my human coworkers. Not to mention, I'm sort of a terrible employee. I break into offices that aren't mine to do illicit computer searches. I have sex on interrogation-room tables. I accept bribes to look away when I catch coworkers in compromising positions in the copy room. I got poisoned by one of my coworkers and died in the parking lot. If anything, they should fire me."

"It is something you are going to have to get used to. While your methods are, let us say, unorthodox, your team still met their deadline. And that was with one employee who was not pulling his weight. Imagine what you could do with fully functioning underlings. And as for the additional benefits, the Council looks out for its own."

"Well, maybe I don't want to be one of the Council's own," I muttered.

Nik smirked, pulling a piece of paper from his pocket. "Mr. Crown thought you might want to know what the benefits package entailed."

I scanned the piece of paper, marveling again at the clarity of my night vision, as I absorbed exactly how badly Mr. Crown wanted to retain my services.

"And her lovely eyes bug out of her head . . . now."

"I am totally OK with being one of the Council's own," I said, folding the paper and tucking it into my pocket. "Do you think I could negotiate similar treatment for Jordan and Aaron?"

"I do not see why not. But before you head back to the office, there is something you need to think about," he said, kissing me thoroughly and leading me into the woods. "The Council is telling whoever will listen that you suffered an accident that landed you in the hospital. They do not want their human employees to panic in paranoia over what their undead coworkers might do to them. And Ophelia's management is under review, meaning she has not been allowed anywhere near her office. For once, the Council office gossip is contained, meaning that whoever poisoned you does not know they killed you. They do not know you are a vampire now."

15

Whether your annoying coworker is living or undead, it's important to handle office conflicts with patience and finesse.

—*The Office After Dark: A Guide to Maintaining a Safe, Productive Vampire Workplace*

I'd never worked undercover before.

There was a good reason. I seemed to suck at it. I was way too twitchy to lie still in my hospital bed in my fake hospital room. Nik managed to persuade what was left of the Council authority to check me in under an accidental-poisoning diagnosis and "multiple organ failure," and my admission was postdated to line up with my attempted murder. They just fudged my room assignment to make it look as if I'd been in intensive care (no visitors) while I was in my death sleep.

"Stop twitching," Dick muttered from the doorway, where he and Sam were standing. They were wearing lab coats and stethoscopes and pretending to compare notes from the clipboards they were carrying. They'd been chosen for this assignment because they were the only vampires in our circle who rarely spent time at the Council office. (Dick actively avoided the place whenever possible.) Cal, Iris, and Nik were waiting in a room across the hall, handling the long-range recording equipment needed to capture what I hoped would be a stunning confession, so the Council could do whatever horrible, secret things they did to people who messed with Council property.

(Meaning me.)

"You're supposed to be poisoned. Act all pathetic and listless," Dick said at a volume only vampires could hear.

"But I don't feel pathetic and listless. I feel like I want to pop the poisoner's head off like a Pez dispenser," I mumbled.

"It's a solid instinct," Sam whispered.

"We are in a hospital," I whispered. "There would be lots of medical personnel present."

"There will be no decapitations!" Dick hissed. "I promised Crown this would be handled with little to no bloodshed. I will not take the fall for you!"

I snickered, making Sam laugh.

Dick groaned, "At least close your eyes!"

I stubbornly kept my eyes open and counted the number of pinholes in the ceiling tiles. The truth was, I needed a distraction. My spanking-new supersenses were a little overwhelming in normal situations, but the sounds and smells of the hospital had me on overdrive. I could hear every cough, every beep, every argument between dysfunctional family members. And the smells. Forget silver spray. If humans could bottle the essence of hospitals and shoot it into vampires' faces, we would never bite a living soul. Pinhole counting was my only defense against one prolonged gag.

When I was done with the pinholes, I closed my eyes and tried to work on some of the relaxation exercises that Cal recommended for controlling my bloodthirst. I made a little room in my head and committed every single detail of this hospital room to memory. The sickly beige of the tile, the whispery hum of the machines, and the multiple layers of olfactory offenses. I wanted to create a "sense memory" of how this hospital floor smelled. And whenever I thought about biting an innocent person, I would think of that smell, and I would never be hungry again.

"Heads up," Sam whispered. "Creepy little guy with flowers at twelve o'clock."

"Wait, what?" I whispered.

"He's heading for your door, Geeg," Dick whispered.

In the tiniest sliver of light between my closed eyelids, I could make out the shape of Marty walking into my room. Dick and Sam both scowled at Marty's back but made no move to stop him as he closed my hospital room door. Marty was carrying a big, showy arrangement of calla lilies. Death flowers. Also poisonous.

Prick.

Marty had poisoned me? I could accept that Margaret did it, because it was always the quiet, middle-aged women who ended up on the news after poisoning their entire church congregation's coffee, being described as "so sweet she wouldn't hurt a fly." For some reason, the idea that someone I'd spent the better part of three months working with in a very small room had tried to murder me really hurt my feelings.

"Gladiola, can you hear me?" he whispered, stepping closer to my bed. I could *feel* him crossing the room, as if I could sense his energy intruding on mine. The scent of frustrated anger, thick and yellow, like burned hair, rolled toward my nostrils, which did not help the whole "prolonged gag" situation. I felt his cold, clammy fingers brush across my cheek, and it was all I could do not to sink my fangs into his hand.

Maybe he was just visiting me because of his weird crush on me.

"Gladiola, I didn't want it to end like this, but you gave me no choice."

Probably not.

I forced my face to relax into a "coma" face, dead calm, motionless, completely absent of the "Imma kill you!" energy I felt boiling under the surface of my skin. But under the hospital blanket, I was clutching the sheets so hard my fingernails were ripping through them.

Marty had killed me. He'd put plans into motion that resulted in my death. I couldn't believe I'd been afraid to hurt this guy's feelings. I let him push me around with his *feelings* and his stupid ego. And now I was dead. I understood now how easy it was for vampires to lose their grip on their bloodthirst. I was so angry I could taste it on the back of my tongue, like the sulfur of a struck match. In the coils of my new predator brain, I knew that the only thing that would chase that acrid taste away would be the sweet, warm gush of blood from Marty's throat over my tongue.

Just a few inches, a sly, cold voice whispered inside my head. *He would never see it coming. He thinks you're weak. He doesn't think you're strong enough to hurt him. Show him how wrong he is. Take your payment for the pain he's caused you!*

My predator brain seemed to be a little bit nuts. I felt my fangs growing, long and sharp, against the insides of my lips. I resisted the urge to stretch my jaws and let them pop free. The snake voice did make one good point. Marty thought I was weak, that I was just a harmless girl he'd pushed around. Well, Marty was in for one very nasty surprise. I wasn't going to settle for a confession. Marty was going to learn what it felt like to be afraid.

I let my eyelids flutter open dramatically, like something out of *Grey's Anatomy*. My eyes went wide, as if I just couldn't believe I'd woken up in the hospital, and oh, heavens, I was just so disoriented, there was no way poor confused human me could possibly be thinking about ripping out Marty's spleen through his ear with my superstrength.

"Where am I?" My husky voice had just enough disorientation to it to make Marty sink against the side of my bed and stroke my hair. Honestly, if I ever got tired of computers, I was going to look into acting. Because if I could make this tool think I wanted him to touch me, I deserved a damn Oscar.

"I'm so sorry," he said, his pale cheeks pinched and so pale they were almost gray. "I didn't mean for this to happen."

"Marty? What's happening?" I whispered.

"I loved you. I loved you so much," he said. "But you only have yourself to blame. If you'd just done what I told you, if you'd listened, I wouldn't have had to act out like this. I get a little crazy when it comes to you, Gladiola."

OK, we were apparently taking the direct route to psycho town, no detours.

"What do you mean?" I asked.

"You know, I wasn't even sure I wanted the job at the Council at first. My mother was the one who circled the ad in my college newspaper. I think she just wanted me out of the house for the summer. She didn't want me to be stuck in my room playing video games. She came with me for my interview. She just wanted to make sure it went well."

I was confused about why Marty was telling me all this. Was he trying to make me feel sorry for him? I could sympathize with having helicopter relatives, but frankly, having a mother who wouldn't let you breathe without coaching was no justification for poisoning people.

Marty was still rambling. "And she started talking to Ophelia about her work, her spells and hexes. Mother has always had a steady hand with hexes. Ophelia was interested, of course. All she had to do was guarantee my employment, no matter what I did."

"Is your mother Jennifer Renart?" I asked.

He nodded. "Jennifer Renart McCullough, but she changed her name to Serena back in the 1970s. Isn't that weird? I thought it was such a good sign, that you showed an interest in my family. I found that file about my vampire ancestor in your desk drawer, and I knew. I knew that you were just as interested in me as I was in you. How did it all go so wrong?"

"You looked through my desk?" I exclaimed, just a bit too loud.

"Well, you can be such a closed book sometimes. How else was I supposed to get to know you better?" he asked, before assuring me, "I didn't know about Mother's assignment. Mother always keeps the strictest confidence for her clients. If I'd known it was you, Gladiola . . . well, I don't know if I would have stopped her, because you turned out to be such a disappointment."

He sniffled, and I could hear his hand swipe across the wet skin of his cheek. Seriously? Was he crying over my hospital bed while whining about his mommy and me not loving him? Wow.

"I knew I loved you from the moment we met. Do you remember? You were wearing that beige pantsuit, and you looked so grown-up and polished and professional. You were mature, like me, Gladiola. And you would understand me like the other girls couldn't, like my mom understands. And I knew I would love you.

Only someone I really loved could hurt me the way you did. And even after what you did to me, I couldn't attack you directly," Marty said, brushing my hair back from my face. "Not with your vampire family members lurking around watching you all the time like a bunch of guard dogs. I mean, honestly, they're a little spooky. They don't care anything about your privacy. They're always there, in your face, refusing to leave you alone. Even though you were cruel to me, I felt sorry for you. I had to find a way to help you. I broke into your employee file and memorized your background information, including your . . . less savory hobbies. I mean, honestly, what kind of girl takes knifework classes? I wouldn't give you the chance to hurt me physically as much as you'd hurt me emotionally."

Seriously, I was willing to stake myself if he would just shut up.

"But martial arts and blades can't stop poison, can they?"

"Marty," I wheezed. "What did you do?"

"I told you. I told you that you had to give up on that stupid vampire and open your eyes to what was right in front of you. But you wouldn't listen!"

"Did you give me something?" I asked, hoping to lead him away from his indignant bitching and into confession territory.

"Yes!" he cried. "I gave you code! Special code that had spells locked inside the binary that were supposed to make you see that your relationship with the vampire was dangerous and doomed. I don't know why it didn't work!"

His crap coding was deliberate? Well, that explained a lot. And I hadn't been the first to see Marty's cursed program. Aaron was the one who had pulled Marty's coding off the server for me. Maybe his seeing it first undid the magic? And since Aaron wasn't into dating vampires, it hadn't really affected him. Handy information to have but not really what we were looking for.

"No, Marty," I whispered. "Did you give me something to make me sick?"

"Nightshade. My mother grows it in her garden. I put it in your soy sauce. You ate so much sushi it was the best way to make sure you got a consistent dose. Getting it once or twice a week over time would have made you sick. I would have been there to help you, to take you to the hospital in time."

Suddenly, the rolling stomach and shaking hands, the emotional roller coaster I'd experienced just before I was turned, made sense. With the nightshade in my system, I'd been getting sicker by degrees but ignored the symptoms, thinking that I was just upset over Nik's departure. I'd been dying for weeks and didn't even know it.

"We got it," I heard Dick whisper outside. "That's enough to charge him."

But Marty was still expounding on the awesomeness of his plan. I hated to interrupt him while he was giving me so many reasons to punch him in the throat.

"I would have been your knight in shining armor, and you would finally see me. You'd finally return my feelings and love me the way I deserved to be loved."

"But you couldn't know that you'd be there when I got really sick," I said, sounding a bit too healthy. And testy.

"Easy there," Sam said, loudly enough for me to hear but not Marty.

"Well, you didn't use enough!" Marty huffed. "I had to up the ante. I doubled the dosage and put it in your coffee order. I waited all night in that parking lot for you to come out, so I could catch you while you were getting sick. But again, your stupid vampire interfered. It's your fault, your fault that I had to hurt you. It's your fault that I'm hurting you now."

"What are you going to do now?" I asked, as Marty pulled a syringe out of his pocket and tapped the port on my IV bag.

"You don't deserve to live, not after what you did to me." He gave me an evil smile. "Wasn't that one of your criticisms on my progress reports? 'Marty doesn't finish his work'?"

I nodded. "I'm so sorry, Marty. I didn't mean it." The asshole actually laughed at me as I weakly "fumbled" for his hand. Meanwhile he meddled with the IV bag that wasn't actually connected to my hand.

"Marty," I whispered. "I put something else on your progress report."

He paused before injecting what I assumed was more nightshade into my IV bag. "What's that?"

"I wrote, 'Marty misjudges situations and attempts to step in where he doesn't belong.'" I grabbed his wrist and twisted it so hard that I heard something snap. "You've really stepped in it this time, Marty."

I sprang out of bed, standing over him while he howled and dropped to the floor. He clutched his hand to his chest, whimpering like a wounded dog. I slid into my unicorn slippers and robe, completely calm, as if I woke up every morning to a man cowering on my hospital-room floor.

"Gladiola, what are you doing?" he yelled, scrambling across the floor like an injured crab.

"I'm going to tell you one last time," I growled, crouching over him and baring my fangs. "The name. Is. Gigi."

Marty shrieked, practically crawling under my bed to get away from me.

I grinned nastily, and he recoiled from me. "So you're a nice guy, right? A nice guy who deserves my time and attention. I'm obligated to be in a relationship with you because you showed me some basic kindness. A cup of coffee means I'm bound to you for life?"

I lined up Marty's head with my leg as if I was prepping for a field goal and kicked for distance. My foot connected with his nose with a satisfying crunch, and Marty flopped onto his back. My only regret was the little spatter of blood on my unicorn slippers.

"Well, guess what, douchebag?" I spat, grabbing him by the hair and dragging him up so we were at eye level.

"V-v-vampire," he spluttered around the blood pouring from his nose.

"That's right. You poisoned me. You killed me. You put me through a needless and painful death. So you're going to get a lot of my attention from now on. Meaning that every few years, when the vampires let you out of a dark hole at the bottom of nowhere to decide if they should set you free or shove you back into that hole to let time, old age, and despair finish you off, I'm going to be there. And every time, I'm going to root for shoving you back into the pit. Because that's what you deserve."

I dropped him back to the floor. Sam and Dick walked into the room just in time to see his head smack against the tile.

"Gigi," Dick chastised me. "We said no bloodshed."

"He slipped," I said, pushing past them to grab my purse from the patient closet. I was done with Marty. He was the Council's problem now.

"Arrest her," Marty whined through lips that were swollen and bloody. "She assaulted me. I wanna press charges."

"Other people might question it, but I'd say you had it coming," Dick said. "And I think you should be more concerned with the charges the Council will be leveling against you."

"You're lucky she didn't follow through on the Pez plan, dumbass. Now, get up," Sam said, pulling Marty to his feet.

Marty's legs instantly buckled under him, and he smacked his head against the floor again.

"That one's on you!" I called over my shoulder, leaving the room.

"Yeah, yeah," Sam grumbled, and I could hear him say, "Martin McCullough, I am taking you into the custody of the Half-Moon Hollow Regional Branch of the World Council for the Equal Treatment of the Undead. You have the right to refuse questioning. You have the right to contact the human authorities when we make means of communication available to you. These are your only rights, and the Council can waive them at any time, because we're vampires, and the federal government offers us very little supervision. Also, just for your information, I think you're a douchebag."

I stepped into the open elevator at the end of the hall, snickering at Sam's little improvisation. Vampire hearing had its advantages.

16

The key to maintaining any relationship, whether it's business or personal, is flexibility. You have to know how to adapt and find the bright side, no matter what life throws at you.

—The Office After Dark: A Guide to Maintaining a Safe, Productive Vampire Workplace

To say that vampire life required an adjustment was an insult to the word "understatement."

Without the distraction of sweet, sweet revenge, I had to adjust to living with every sense turned up to eleven. All of the emotions I'd held in check under the shock of waking up a vampire came rushing out as panic and agoraphobia. Human pulses sounded like hammers pounding in my ears. Picking up smells coming from trash cans or cheap scented candles felt like being punched in the face. I retreated to the house for almost two weeks, because I didn't trust myself out in the world just yet.

Iris assured me that this was perfectly normal, that when she'd first been turned, she hid out in her tub with a bottle of dessert blood and a Harlequin novel for the first few days. And while her presence was a comfort, it was Nik who got me through the rough patches. He was with me every minute of every night, talking to me, telling me stories, poking fun at me when I needed to laugh at myself. And when the bloodthirst got really bad or I realized how much I was going to miss sushi, he distracted me with other tactics that required seclusion—and sometimes props.

I had to fill the hours (and hours and hours) somehow.

Since I was poisoned in the office, I had technically been injured "on the job" and was therefore entitled to a heck of a workers' compensation package. (All vampire fine print is scary fine print.) The Council was very graciously hanging on to my job until I could tolerate being close enough to humans to come back to the office. Until then, I was working from home on a very secure Council-issued laptop and building up my tolerance to human smells through careful feeding and spending time with Nola and Zeb while under watchful vampire supervision.

Aaron and Jordan tried to visit, stopping by with a big "get well" basket of bottled blood and all of the *Walking Dead* seasons on DVD, which was touching and yet slightly insensitive. But I was too nervous to let them past the front porch. Nola and Zeb knew the risks of vampire social training. My coworkers did not. So we settled for Skype chatting, keeping me updated on the (successful!) testing phase and the office scuttlebutt. My being turned was the office gossip of the year, being chewed over either as evidence of the ridiculous dangers of including humans in the vampire work environment or as the most romantic story this side of young adult novels.

Immediately after the hospital sting, Jordan and Aaron saw a handcuffed Marty being dragged through the office to the detention centers in the lower levels. And he had not been seen since. Margaret came to our office to tell Aaron and Jordan that Marty would not be returning to work, but she blatantly ignored all other attempted questions.

Iris's issues with Nik were slowly but surely easing. She still had a problem with the age difference and the fact that Nik had drawn me into the deep, dark world of vampires. But she shut up pretty quickly when I pointed out that Cal had done the same for her, and I didn't remember her asking my opinion about it.

The bright side was that we now had all the time in the world to spend together. We didn't have to worry about me getting hurt or sick or old. I would be able to annoy Iris until the end of time. It was every little sister's dream come true. And with vampire strength, it was a lot easier to kick Cal and Nik out of the house so we could watch movies and drink dessert blood. They protested mightily, but I suspected they enjoyed their boys' nights as much as we did. They were just too smart to tip their hands. Wily, wily vampires.

One particular night in my second week postvampire, we were enjoying Tommy Night (Tom Hiddleston movies plus shirtless Tom Hardy movies plus bloody Tom Collinses). Since I would technically never reach twenty-one anyway, Iris had waived her usual "no corrupting the minors" policy. Iris kept fiddling with her phone, her text chime sounding repeatedly.

"Hey, you're neglecting Tom Hardy's naked abs." I threw a couch cushion at her as she checked her text messages. "I'm pretty sure that's a felony in some states. No business tonight, Iris. You promised."

Iris shook her head. "It's not Beeline. It's Jane. She says she and Dick need to meet with us this evening. Something about official Council business."

"What would Dick and Jane have to do with official Council business?"

"Yeah, the Council is not in the habit of explaining their motives to me." Iris shrugged, reaching for her glass. "Welcome to the world of vampire politics: nothing makes sense. They should be here in a few minutes."

"We should probably be sober for this," I told her.

We stared at each other for a long, silent moment, and then chugged the rest of our drinks. Nik and Cal arrived home, still arguing over whether Gabriel or Zeb would have won the hand of poker they'd been forced to abandon after Jane's text. Nik insisted Zeb would have folded under Gabriel's threatening glare, but Cal claimed that Zeb was so accustomed to the threat of vampire blustering that he would have blithely bluffed on.

"You don't seem to be very upset about your evening being disrupted," Iris said.

"We were losing," Nik said. "I am not used to losing card games to humans. It is unsettling."

"I told you not to underestimate Zeb," Cal said, flopping onto the couch next to my sister. "He survived being Jane's friend during her clumsy human phase. Also, he's married to a beautiful, vicious werewolf and has managed to negotiate her pack's violent in-law dynamics without significant injury. I've said for years that his goofy puppy-dog charm is a carefully constructed ruse meant to put us at ease so he can work us like a puppet master."

"I miss Jolene, and the twins." I sighed.

"Whenever you're ready, Zeb and Jolene are ready to bring the kids to see you," Iris said. "You're already doing so well, Geeg. I don't think you're going to have any trouble controlling yourself."

The knock at our door made me spring to my feet.

Dick and Jane were standing on our front porch looking completely miserable, like unwilling door-to-door evangelists. Jane was wearing a pantsuit, though it was certainly more stylish than my own. And poor Dick was in a white dress shirt and plain blue tie, absolutely no writing or funny pictures or anything. He pulled at his collar as if it was out to strangle him.

"Why are you guys just standing out there?" I asked. "Are you going to try to recruit us to a really boring cult?"

"We're here on official Council business," Jane said, sighing.

"You keep saying that, and it doesn't make any sense," Iris said.

"I do not think this word means what you think it means," I said with a snort. When no one laughed, I huffed. "You people should all be ashamed of yourselves. We are going to watch *The Princess Bride* again this weekend."

"Can we come in, please?" Dick asked, still tugging at his collar. "I'd hate for anyone to see me dressed like this."

"Sure, sorry," Iris said, and ushered them in. "What's going on?"

Jane peeled off her suit jacket and flopped onto our couch in her slacks and camisole. "God, I hate business casual," she said. "The pantsuit is a lie."

I nodded. "Right?"

Dick immediately stripped out of his button-up and tie, revealing a T-shirt that read "Female Body Inspector."

"You are all class, my friend," Iris said.

"Yeah, he went old-school offensive." Jane sighed. "He needed to know he was wearing something inappropriate to survive our 'induction.'"

"Induction?" I growled. "Would you please stop being vague and get to the point?"

Dick tossed his tie into our fireplace. "The Council is 'displeased' with Ophelia. And by that, I mean she's lucky she's not getting the Trial."

"Wow," I murmured, dropping down to the couch

as my legs folded under me. I felt a little bit sorry for Ophelia. I mean, sure, she tried to have me killed, but she did something desperate and stupid for love, which I sort of understood. I would find a way to punch her in the throat, though. It might take me a really long time and some emergency personnel, but I would find a way.

"For now, they've stripped her of her place on the local Council," Jane said. "And she will be placed under the mentorship of a local vampire with an exemplary discipline record, who can teach her to behave in a proper, non-murder-y manner. And you know that ban on turning that she was issued when she turned her sister about four hundred years ago? It got extended for another three hundred years."

"Do we *have* any local vampires with an exemplary discipline record?" I asked.

"They're still looking," Jane admitted. "And given the amount of 'unorthodox' vampire activity in the area, the national-level Council officials aren't willing to leave that spot open for any amount of time, especially with the spot already left open by Mr. Marchand's demise."

"I told them that it was going to bite them in the ass, not filling Waco's spot for so long," Cal said.

"Well, with Sophie requesting 'retirement,' the national Council was not willing to leave the local branch solely in Peter's hands. So they made two emergency appointments."

My mouth fell open, and I clapped my hand over it. "No!" I exclaimed. "As in 'See Dick and Jane legislate'?"

"More like 'See Dick and Jane make decisions for a shadowy para-government organization that makes them uncomfortable,'" Jane muttered.

Dick leaned his head against the couch. "You're speaking to the newest representatives of the local Council for the Equal Treatment of the Undead."

"We are now part of the leadership for all of the vampires in this region. And they gave Dick Cheney authority," Jane said, as if she still couldn't believe it had happened. "They trusted *Dick* with making decisions that affect the local vampire population."

"I don't see how me having authority is more frightening than you having authority," Dick shot back.

"Between the two of us, I'm the one with a clean arrest record," she retorted.

"No, you aren't," he said, shaking his head.

"That was one time!" she exclaimed. "As opposed to your multitude of times!"

"This is getting us nowhere." Iris sighed.

"Why didn't they pick Gabriel? No offense, Dick."

Dick shrugged. "No, I asked them that myself."

"According to Peter Crown, who nominated us, he wanted some form of entertainment at the meeting, and he thought that Dick and I would be able to provide that somehow," Jane said. "I think they did it to try to bring the crime rate down, putting Dick out of commission with legitimacy."

Dick cleared his throat and with great pomposity said, "Well, my first official act as supreme ruler—"

"I am ninety percent sure that was not the title they gave us," Jane interjected.

"We requested that Ophelia be allowed to enroll in the college of her choice. She's never obtained a full undergraduate degree. I think it's time." Dick was clearly very pleased with himself and preened more than a little bit.

"And I wonder if the college of her choice will be UK," Iris said with a smirk. "Maybe that will keep her from trying to kill you again."

"Maybe. What about Georgie?"

"Georgia has requested permission to live on her own, with some supervision. I think it would be good for both girls to have some space."

"Well, at least Ophelia will stop being angry with me," I said. "Wait, that means Ophelia will be roaming around my college campus next year? Dang it, Jane!"

"That was a consequence I did not see coming," she said, chewing her lip.

"I thought you were a psychic!" I hissed.

"Not that kind of psychic," she said, pouting.

"You will be fine," Nik promised. "I will be close by, and I think Ophelia is so embarrassed by being caught that she will have a hard time making eye contact with me, much less have time to intimidate you."

"It's the annoyance factor, not intimidation," I protested. "I punched her in the face. You take away a great deal of personal power when you punch someone in the face."

"To punching Ophelia in the face!" Iris exclaimed, raising her glass. But when she realized that no one else in the room had a drink, she hopped up from the couch. "Oh, sorry, I'll get some drinks, and we can toast Ophelia's facial beat-down properly."

"Ooh, do you still have that Godiva blood liqueur?" Jane asked, following her into the kitchen. "I loved that the last time we were here."

"I'm mixing my own," Cal told me. "Your sister's had a few too many 'battered Tom Collinses.'"

"It's Tommy Night; you never know what's going to happen!" I called after him.

Dick whipped his unbuttoned dress shirt off, nearly ripping one of the sleeves. "I'm going to throw this away. I can't stand it. It's like being strangled by cotton."

"That is going to make all of those Council events where you're supposed to dress like a grown-up a painful experience for you," I told him.

Dick closed his eyes, and if his rapidly moving but silent lips were any indication, he appeared to be praying. He bolted into the bathroom and slammed his shirt into the wastebasket.

Nik stared after him, his lips pursed.

"So this is my family," I told him. "Welcome to the madness."

"I think I can handle it," he told me. "At least they are entertaining."

"That they are." I laughed. "Now, what would you

say to taking advantage of this sudden solitude and sneaking upstairs?"

"He would say no!" Cal yelled from the kitchen. "And I would remind him that I have superhearing and no reservations about sharing some very damning details of a weekend in the Swiss Alps in 1892!"

"Really?" I grinned at Nik. "Damning details?"

"It was not that bad," he assured me. Nik cast a speculative glance at the staircase and whispered, "I will bet we can reach the top of the stairs before Cal can exit the kitchen."

I stood up and pulled him from the couch. "You're on."

Nik swept me off my feet and sprang for the stairs, clearing the bannister before I could tuck my face into his neck. He sped up the steps, his feet barely brushing the wood as he moved.

"Gigi," Cal called. "What are you doing?"

"Nothing!" I yelled down the hall, as I landed on my feet just outside my bedroom door.

"Keep one foot on the floor!" Iris yelled. "That was Mom's rule!"

"Don't encourage her!" I heard Cal exclaim.

We slammed the door behind us, and I jumped onto my bed, enjoying the bounce from Nik's landing beside me. I kicked off Nik's shoes and threw my leg over his hips, straddling him. He cupped my jaw in his hands and kissed my forehead.

"You're stuck with me now," I told him. "Forever. I hope you're prepared for that."

"I am."

"It's not because you're afraid of Cal, is it?"

"No, I am afraid of you. You are terrifying," he said, yelping when I dug my knuckle into his ribs. He brushed my hair behind my ears and nuzzled his forehead against mine. "Never forget."

"Never forget I love you," I answered, kissing his mouth.

With my family's conversation drifting up from the kitchen and the love of my unlife wrapped in my arms, I was more content than any person deserved to be. I wasn't afraid of the future. I wasn't afraid of being hurt. I was strong. I was loved. I had an unusual number of Tasers.

Whatever came next, I would be ready.

Keep reading to see how it all began for Iris and
Gigi in Molly Harper's Half-Moon Hollow romance

The Care and Feeding of
Stray Vampires

And don't miss the next Half-Moon Hollow
adventure, coming fall 2015 from Pocket Books!

1

The thing to remember about a "stray" vampire is that there is probably a good reason he is friendless, alone, and wounded. Approach with caution.

—*The Care and Feeding of Stray Vampires*

How did an internal debate regarding flavored sexual aids become part of my workday?

I was a good person. I went to church on the "big days." I was a college graduate. Nice, God-fearing people with bachelor's degrees in botany should not end up standing in the pharmacy aisle at Walmart debating which variety of flavored lube is best.

"Ugh, forget it, I'm going with Sensual Strawberry." I sighed, throwing the obscenely pink box into the basket.

Diandra Starr—a poorly thought-out pole name if I'd ever heard one—had managed to snag the world's only codependent vampire. My client, Mr. Rychek. When she made her quarterly visits to Half-Moon Hollow, I was turned into some bizarre hybrid of Cinderella and the Fairy Godmother, waking up at dawn to find voice mails and e-mails detailing the numerous needs that must be attended to *at once*. Mr. Rychek seemed convinced that Diandra would flounce away on her designer platform heels unless her every whim was anticipated. No demand for custom-blended bath salts was considered too extravagant. No organic, free-trade food requirement was too extreme. And the lady liked her sexual aids to taste of summer fruits.

I surveyed the contents of the cart against the list. Iron supplements? Check. Organic almond milk? Check. Flavored lube? Check.

I did not pretend to understand the dynamics of human-vampire relationships.

Shopping in the "special dietary needs" aisle was always an adventure. An unexpected side effect of the Great Coming Out in 1999 was the emergence of all-night industries, special products, and cottage businesses, like mine, that catered to the needs of "undead Americans." Companies were tripping over one another to come up with products for a spanking-new marketing demographic: synthetic blood, protein additives, dental-care accessories, lifelike bronzers. The problem was that those companies still hadn't figured out packaging for the undead and tended to jump on bizarre trending bandwagons, the most recent being a brand of plasma concentrate that came pouring out of what looked like a Kewpie doll. You had to flip back the head to open it.

It's even more creepy than it sounds.

Between that and the sporty, aggressively neon tubes of Razor Wire Floss, the clear bubble-shaped pots of Solar Shield SPF-500 sunblock, and the black Gothic boxes of Forever Smooth moisturizing serum, the vampire aisle was ground zero for visual overstimulation.

I stopped in my tracks, pulling the cart to an abrupt halt in the middle of the pharmacy section as I recalled that Rychek's girlfriend was a vegan. I started to review the label to determine whether the flavored lube was an animal by-product. But I found that I honestly didn't care. It was 4:20, which meant that I had an hour to drop this stuff by Mr. Rychek's house, drop the service contracts by a new client's house in Deer Haven, and then get to Half-Moon Hollow High for the volleyball booster meeting. Such was the exotic and glamorous life of the Hollow's only daytime vampire concierge.

My company, Beeline, was part special-event co-ordinator, part concierge service, part personal organizer. In addition to wedding planning, I took care of all the little details vampires didn't have time for or just didn't want to deal with themselves. Although it was appropriate, I tried to avoid the term "daywalker" unless I was dealing with established clients. It turns out that if you put an ad for a daywalker service in the Yellow Pages, you get a lot of calls from people who expect you to scoop Fluffy's sidewalk leavings. And I was allergic to dogs—and their leavings.

On my sprint to the checkout, I cast a longing glance at the candy aisle and its many forbidden sugary pleasures. With my compulsive sweet tooth, I did not discriminate against chocolate, gummies, taffy, lollipops, or even those weird so-sour-the-citric-acid-burns-off-your-tastebuds torture candies. But between my sister Gigi's worries about the potential for adult-onset diabetes in our gene pool and my tendency toward what I prefer to call "curviness," I only broke into the various candy caches I had stashed around the house under great personal stress. Or if it was a weekday.

Placating myself with a piece of sugarless gum, I whizzed through the express lane and loaded Mr. Rychek's weekend supplies into what Gigi, in all her seventeen-year-old sarcastic glory, called the Dork-mobile. I agreed that an enormous yellow minivan was not exactly a sexy car. But until she could suggest another way to haul cases of synthetic blood, Gothic-themed wedding cakes, and, once, a pet crate large enough for a Bengal tiger, I'd told Gigi she had to suck it up and ride shotgun in the Dorkmobile. The next fall, she'd used her earnings from the Half-Moon Hollow Country Club and Catfish Farm snack bar to buy a secondhand VW Bug. Never underestimate a teenager's work ethic if the end result is averted embarrassment.

I used my security pass to get past the gate into Deer Haven, a private, secure subdivision inhabited entirely by vampires and their human pets. It was always a little spooky driving through this perfectly maintained, cookie-cutter ghost suburb during the day. The streets and driveways were empty. The windows were shuttered tight against the sunlight. Sometimes I expected tumbleweeds to come bouncing past my car. Then again, I'd never seen the neighborhood awake and hopping after dark. I made it a policy to be well out of my clients' homes before the sun set. With the exception of the clients whose newly legal weddings I helped plan,

I rarely saw any of them face-to-face. (I allowed my wedding clients a little more leeway, because they were generally too distracted by their own issues to bother nibbling on me. And still, I only met with them in public places with a lot of witnesses present.)

Although it had been more than ten years since the Great Coming Out and vampire-human relations were vastly improved since the early pitchfork-and-torch days, some vampires were still a bit touchy about humans' efforts to wipe out their species. They refused to let any human they hadn't met in person near their homes while they were sleeping and vulnerable.

After years of working with them, I had no remaining romantic notions about vampires. They had the same capacity for good and evil that humans do. And despite what most TV evangelists preached, I believed they had souls. The problem was that the cruelest tendencies can emerge when a person is no longer restricted to the "no biting, no using people as food" rules that humans insist on. If you were a jerk in your original life, you're probably going to be a bigger undead jerk. If you were a decent person, you're probably not going to change much beyond your diet and skin-care regimen.

With vampires, you had to be able to operate from a distance, whether that distance was physical or emotional. My business was built on guarded, but optimistic, trust. And a can of vampire pepper spray that I kept in my purse.

I opened the back of my van and hitched the crate of supplies against my hip. I had pretty impressive upper-body strength for a petite gal, but it was at times like these, struggling to schlep the crate up Mr. Rychek's front walk, that I wondered why I'd never hired an assistant.

Oh, right, because I couldn't afford one.

Until my little business, Beeline, started showing a profit margin just above "lemonade stand," I would have to continue toting my own barge and lifting my own bale. I looked forward to the day when heavy lifting wouldn't determine my wardrobe or hairstyle. On days like this, I tended toward sensible flats, twin sets, and pencil skirts in dark, smudge-proof colors. I liked to throw in a pretty blouse every once in a while, but it depended on whether I could wash synthetic blood out of it. (No matter how careful you are, sometimes there are mishaps.)

And the hair. It was difficult for human companions, blood-bank staff, and storekeepers to take me seriously when I walked around with a crazy cloud of dark curls framing my head. Having Diana Ross's 'do didn't exactly inspire confidence, so I twisted my hair into a thick coil at the nape of my neck. Gigi called it my "sexy schoolmarm" look, having little sympathy for me and my frizz. But since we shared the same unpredictable follicles, I was biding my time until she got her first serious job and realized how difficult it was to be considered a professional when your hair was practically sentient.

I used another keyless-entry code to let myself into Mr. Rychek's tidy little town house. Some American vampires lived in groups of threes and fours in what vampire behaviorists called "nesting," but most of my clients, like Mr. Rychek, were loners. They had little habits and quirks that would annoy anyone, human or immortal, after a few centuries. So they lived alone and relied on people like me to bring the outside world to them.

I put the almond milk in the fridge and discreetly tucked the other items into a kitchen cabinet. I checked the memo board for further requests and was relieved to find none. I only hoped I could get through Diandra's visit without being called and ordered to find a twenty four-hour emergency vet service for her hypoallergenic cat, Ginger. That stupid furball had some sort of weird fascination with prying open remote controls and swallowing the batteries. And somehow Diandra was always shocked when it happened.

As an afterthought, I moved Mr. Rychek's remote from the coffee table to the top of the TV.

One more stop before I could put in my time at the booster meeting, go home, and bury myself in the romance novel I'd squirreled away inside the dust jacket for *The Adventures of Sherlock Holmes*. If Gigi saw the bare-chested gladiator on the cover, the mockery would be inventive and, most likely, public.

My new client's house was conveniently located in the newer section of Deer Haven, at the end of a long row of matching beige condos. As usual, I had to count the house numbers three times before I was sure I was at the right door, and I wondered how wrong it would be to mark my clients' doors with big fluorescent-yellow bumblebees. And yes, I knew it seemed inconsistent to name a company that dealt with vampires after a sunny, summer-loving insect. But bees were so efficient, zip-ping from one place to another, never forgetting the task at hand. That was the image I wanted to convey. Besides, way too many vampire-oriented businesses went with a Goth theme. My cheerful yellow logo stood out in the "undead services" section of the phone book.

Entering the security code provided on his new-client application, I popped the door open, carrying my usual "Thank you for supporting Beeline" floral arrangement inside. Most vampires enjoyed waking up to fresh flowers. The sight and smell reminded them of their human days, when they could wander around in the daylight unscathed. And they didn't have to know that I'd harvested the artfully arranged roses, irises, and freesias from my own garden. The appearance of an expensive gift was more important than the actual cost of said gift.

Mr. C. Calix certainly hadn't wasted any money on redecorating, I mused as I walked into the bare beige foyer and set the vase on the generic maple end table. The place was dark, which was to be expected, given the sunproof metal shades clamped over the windows. But there was little furniture in the living room, no dining-room table, no art or pictures on the clean taupe walls. The place looked barely lived in, even for a dead guy's house.

Scraping past a few cardboard packing boxes, I walked into the kitchen, where I'd agreed to leave the contracts. My foot caught on a soft weight on the floor. "Mother of fudge!" I yelped, then fell flat on my face.

Have I mentioned that I haven't cursed properly in about five years? With an impressionable kid around the house, I'd taken to using the "safe for network TV" versions of curse words. Although that impressionable kid was now seventeen, I couldn't seem to break the habit. Even with my face smashed against cold tile.

"Frak-frakity-frak." I moaned, rubbing my bruised mouth as I righted myself from the floor. I ran my tongue over my teeth to make sure I hadn't broken any of them. Because, honestly, I wasn't sure I could afford dental intervention at this point. My skinned knees—and my pride—stung viciously as I counted my teeth again for good measure.

What had I tripped over? I pushed myself to my feet, stumbled over to the fridge, and yanked the door open. The interior light clicked on, illuminating the body stretched across the floor.

Shrieking, I scrambled back against the fridge, my dress shoes skittering uselessly against the tile. I couldn't seem to swallow the lump of panic hardening in my throat, keeping me from drawing a breath.

His shirtless torso was well built, long limbs strung with thick cords of muscle. Dark waves of hair sprang over his forehead in inky profusion. The face would have been beautiful if it hadn't been covered in dried blood. A straight nose, high cheekbones, and full, generous lips that bowed slightly. He had that whole Michelangelo's *David* thing going—if David had been an upsetting religious figurine that wept blood.

A half-empty donor packet of O positive lay splattered against the floor, which explained the rusty-looking dried splotches on his face. Had he been drinking it when he . . . passed out?

Vampires didn't pass out. And most of them could sense when to get somewhere safe well before the sun rose. They didn't get caught off guard and collapse wherever they were at dawn. What the hell was going on here?

I eyed my shoulder bag, flung across the room when I'd fallen on my face. Breathing steadily, I resolved that I'd call Ophelia at the local World Council for the Equal Treatment of the Undead office and leave her a message. She would know what to do. And I could get the hell out of there before the hungry, ill vampire rose for the night and made me his breakfast.

I reached over him, aiming my arm away from his mouth. A strong hand clamped around my wrist. I am ashamed to say that I screamed like a little girl. I heard the telltale snick of fangs descending and panicked, yanking and struggling against a relentless vise grip. A tug-of-war ensued for control of the arm that he was pulling toward his chapped, bloodied lips. He tried to lunge for me, but the effort cost him, and his head thunked back to the floor with a heavy thud.

With my hand hovering precariously over his gaping, hungry mouth, I did the only thing I could think of—I poked him in the eye.

"Ow," he said, dully registering pain as I jabbed my index finger against his eyelid. The other eye popped open, the long, sooty lashes fluttering. It was a deep, rich coffee color, the iris ringed in black.

"Ow!" he repeated indignantly, as if the sensation of the eye-poke was just breaking through his stupor.

With him distracted, I gave one final yank and broke free, holding my hand to my chest as I retreated against the fridge. I took another donor packet from the shelf. I popped it open and held it carefully to his lips, figuring that he wouldn't care that it wasn't heated to body temperature. He shook his head faintly, wheezing. "Bad blood."

I checked the expiration date and offered it to him again. "No, it's fine."

His dry lips nearly cracked as they formed the words, "Poisoned . . . stupid."

"OK . . jerk," I shot back.

The faintest flicker of amusement passed over his even features. "Need clean supply," he whispered.

"Well, I'm not giving you mine," I said, shrinking away from him. "I don't do that."

"Just wait to die, then," he muttered.

I had to bite my lips to keep from snickering or giggling hysterically. I was sure that crouching over him, laughing, while he was vulnerable and agitated wouldn't improve the situation.

Shouting for him to hold on, I scurried out to my car, carefully shutting the door behind me so that sunlight didn't spill into the kitchen. I had a case of Faux Type O in the back, destined for Ms. Wexler's house the next day. I grabbed three bottles from the package and ran back into the house. Sadly, it only occurred to me *after* I'd run back into the house that I should have just grabbed my purse, jumped into my van, and gunned it all the way home.

But no, I had to take care of vampires with figurative broken wings, because of my stupid Good Samaritan complex.

Kneeling beside the fallen vampire, I twisted the top off the first bottle and offered it to him. "I'm sure this is clean. I just bought it. The tamper-proof seal's intact."

He gave the bottle a doubtful, guarded look but took it from my hand. He greedily gulped his way through the first bottle, grimacing at the cold offering. Meanwhile, I popped the other two bottles into the microwave. I even dropped a penny into each one after heating them to give them a more authentic coppery taste.

"Thank you," he murmured, forcing himself into a sitting position, although the effort clearly exhausted him. He slumped against the pine cabinets. Like all of the Deer Haven homes, the kitchen was done in pastel earth tones—buffs, beiges, and creams. Mr. Calix looked like a wax figure sagging against the pale wood. "Who are you, and what are you doing in my house?"

"I'm Iris Scanlon, from Beeline. The concierge service? Ophelia Lambert arranged your service contract before you arrived in the Hollow. I came by to drop off the paperwork."

He nodded his magnificent dark head slowly. "She mentioned something about a daywalker, said I could trust you."

I snorted. Ophelia only said that because I hadn't asked questions that time she put heavy-duty trash bags, lime, and a shovel on her shopping list. The teenage leader of the local World Council for the Equal Treatment of the Undead office might have looked sweet sixteen, but at more than four hundred years old, Ophelia, I'm pretty sure, had committed felonies in every hemisphere.

Scary felonies.

"Well, you seem to be feeling a bit better. I'll leave these papers here and be on my way," I said, inching around him.

"Stop," he commanded me, his voice losing its raspy quality as he pushed himself to his feet. I froze, looking up at him through lowered lashes. His face was fuller somehow, less haggard. He seemed to be growing a little stronger with every sip of blood. "I need your help."

"How could *I* help you?"

"You already have helped." As he spoke, I picked up the faint trace of an accent, a sort of caress of the tongue against each finishing syllable. It sounded . . . old, which was a decidedly unhelpful concept when dealing with a vampire. And since most vamps didn't like talking about their backstories, I ignored the sexy lilt and its effects on my pulse rate. "And now I need you to take me home with you."

"Why would I take an unstable, hungry vampire home with me? Do I look particularly stupid to you?"

He snorted. "No, which is *why* you should take me home with you. I already know where you live. While you were running to your car, I looked in your purse and memorized your driver's license. Imagine how irritated I would be, how motivated I would be to find you and repay your *kindness,* after I am well again."

I gasped, clutching my bag closer to my chest. "Don't you threaten me! There seem to be a lot of handy, breakable wooden objects in this room. I'm not above living out my fonder Buffy fantasies."

His expression was annoyed but contrite. Mostly annoyed. He cleared his throat. "I'm sorry. That was out of line. But I need to find a safe shelter before dark falls. I have a feeling someone may be coming by to finish me off. No sane person would attack me while I was at full strength."

I believed it, but it didn't stop me from thinking that Mr. Calix was a bit full of himself. "How do I know that you won't drain me as soon as you stabilize?"

"I don't do that," he said, echoing my earlier pronouncement while he swept my bag from my hands. I tried snatching it back, but he held it just out of my grasp, like some elementary-school bully with a My Little Pony backpack.

Scowling at him, I crossed my arms over my chest. "Considering you just vaguely threatened me, I have a hard time believing that."

"Check my wallet, on the counter."

I flipped open the expensive-looking leather folio and found what looked like a shiny gold policeman's badge. "You're a 'consultant' for the Council? In terms of credibility, that means nothing to me. I've met Ophelia."

His lips twitched at my reference to the cunning but unpredictable teen vampire.

"Why can't you just call her?" I asked. "She's your Council rep. This should be reported to her anyway."

"I can't call her. The Council supplied me with that blood. Left here in a gift basket before I arrived," he said, giving a significant look to the discarded packet on the floor. "Therefore, I can't trust the Council. I can't check into a hotel or seek help from friends without being tracked."

"I have a little sister who lives with me. I don't care how you ended up on the floor. We don't need to be a part of it." I grunted, making a grab for my bag as his tired arms drooped. "I am not running a stop on the vampire underground railroad."

"I can pay you an obscene amount of money."

I'm ashamed to say that this stilled my hand. If anything would make me consider this bizarre scheme, it was money. My parents had died nearly five years ago, leaving me to raise my little sister without much in the way of life insurance or savings. I needed money for Gigi's ever-looming college tuition. I needed money to keep up the house, to pay off the home-equity loan I'd taken out for Beeline's start-up capital. I needed money to keep us in the food that Gigi insisted on eating. And despite the fact that the business was finally becoming somewhat successful, I always seemed to just cover our expenses, with a tiny bit left over to throw at my own rabid student-loan officers. Something always seemed to pop up and eat away at our extra cash—car repair, school trip, explosive air-conditioning failure.

An obscene amount of money would provide enough of a cushion that I might be able to sleep for more than a handful of hours per night. Mr. Calix slid to the floor, apparently drained by the effort of playing purse keep-away.

"How obscene?" I asked, coughing suddenly to chase the meek note from my voice.

"Ten thousand dollars for a week."

I quickly calculated the estimate to replace the aging pipes in my house, plus Gigi's first-semester tuition and the loan payment due next month, against what the Council paid even the lowliest of its underlings. I shook my head and made a counteroffer. "Twenty-five thousand."

"Fifteen thousand."

I pursed my lips. "I'm still saying twenty-five thousand."

"Which means you never quite learned how negotiating works."

It was a struggle, tensing my lips enough to avoid smirking. "How badly do you want to get off that floor, Mr. Calix?"

He grumbled. "Done."

"One week," I said as I knelt in front of him, my voice firmer than I would have thought possible under the circumstances. "That means seven nights. Not seven days and eight nights. Not seven and a half nights. *Seven nights.*"

"Done."

"Excellent." I gave him my sunniest "professional" smile and offered my hand for a shake.

"Don't push it," he muttered, closing his eyes.

I sighed, pulling my cell phone out of my bag to call Gigi. I wasn't going to make that booster meeting, after all.